A CURSE OF TOOTH AND CLAW

THE OZERO CURSE

NICOLETTE ELZIE

NIGHTSHADE PRESS

CONTENTS

*For Audrey and Kevin Jr. May you fight relentlessly
for one another as Kiki does.*

AUTHOR'S NOTE

A Curse of Tooth and Claw is a dark fantasy romance.
It is a fractured fairy tale of the Mexican folktale, The Bear Prince: not a retelling.

A Curse of Tooth and Claw contains mature and graphic content not suitable for all audiences. Dark romance isn't black and white. What some readers may consider "light" may be "dark" for others.
I HIGHLY prefer for you to go in blind, but if you would like a detailed

trigger warning list, you can find it at
https://nicoletteelzie.com/content-warnings/

CHAPTER ONE

WELCOME TO THE SHOW

KIKI

There were three things Quirera Xochicale hated most in life. The first was the sound of her real name. It was her mother's name and one she didn't want to be reminded of daily. She preferred Kiki, though the Commander of her regiment seemed to relish in Kiki's discomfort and used her real name anyway.

The second thing Kiki hated was Solana Ramirez, the very Commander responsible for

Kiki's assignment on the Wall tonight despite it being her ninth night on Watch in a row.

Kiki stood along the ramparts of the single most treacherous stretch of Wall closest to the Cicatrix, a strip of darkness that stretched the length of Ozero and split it in half, north to south. The third thing Kiki hated was the monsters that crept from the shadowy depths of the Cicatrix.

As an Attendant in the Demon Corps, it was Kiki's job to kill whatever traipsed out of the Cicatrix. Her hatred of the wraiths that occasionally ventured out of the depths of hell shouldn't have come as a surprise to anyone. Kiki, however, had a burning hatred for the divide that had ripped across the kingdom fifteen years ago. She'd lost her parents to the divide and the rest of her family with them at the tender age of five. To make it worse, it wasn't like her family was simply on the other side of the darkness and all Kiki had to do was pay a couple of hundred pieces of gold to charter a boat through the southern sea to go around the Cicatrix. In any case, such a sum would be nearly impossible for someone like her to scrounge. Still, at the very least, the task would be somewhat possible, if not probable. No. The problem was that the day the land was torn apart by the darkness, it took her entire family with it.

"You're doing it again," said a voice nearby.

Kiki glanced at her best friend. Yarixa's cheeks were already pink from the cold and she wore her brown hair plaited into twin braids that ran the length of her spine and ended at the weapons belt slung low over her hips. Across her chest, Yarixa wore a bandolier of small obsidian tlazons. Each throwing lance was the length of Kiki's palm with an arrow-pointed tip. Like Kiki, Yarixa wore the black leathers of an Attendant in the Demon Corps. Attendants were Slayers-in-training and were required to patrol the Wall along with the rest of the full-fledged Slayers.

Kiki ran a finger along the rows of tlazons strapped across her own chest, the act providing some much-needed comfort while being this close to the Cicatrix. When thrown with precision, the tlazons were lethal and could stop a demon in its tracks. Still, Kiki preferred close-quarter combat when given a chance. She checked that her machete was clear in its sheath as the moonlight glinted across the obsidian blade.

"If you mean that I'm brooding again, then yes, I am," Kiki replied as she rubbed her tired eyes. "If it weren't for Solana, I'd be in the barracks with a meal in my stomach and a book in my hands."

Yarixa rolled her eyes as she thumbed the pendant that hung from a leather string around her neck. "I think you mean if it weren't for your little prank with the eggs this morning, you wouldn't be on Watch for the next three nights."

Kiki bit back a smile. "It's not my fault she was born with a stick up her ass."

Yarixa stifled her own laugh. "No. It's your fault that you got caught, though."

At that, Kiki did laugh, if only a little bit, and the sound came out as more of a choked whisper. It wasn't wise to make loud noises this close to the Cicatrix.

Yarixa jabbed Kiki in the ribs with a sharp fingernail and raised her eyebrows in a glare. Kiki scoffed and cupped her hand over her mouth to stifle her laughter.

Kiki stared out at the black horizon in front of her. The Cicatrix. As far as her eye could see, darkness stretched across the skyline. If Kiki stared hard enough, she swore she could see glowing blue eyes staring back at her, but when she blinked again, they disappeared. Kiki wasn't sure if there had been anything lurking to begin with or if it had been a trick of the shrouded moonlight in combination with her own fatigue.

Kiki wiped a bead of sweat from her brow. "Tell me a story," she whispered.

"Why can't you ever be quiet?" Yarixa said in hushed tones.

"I'm bored, and I know you are too." Kiki grinned when she saw the look on her friend's face. "Just one, and I promise I'll be quiet for the rest of the watch."

Yarixa gave her a knowing look. "After fifteen years of friendship, I know better than to believe you."

Kiki made her eyes go wide and pulled her hands into a prayer. "Please!" she begged.

"You're pathetic," Yarixa grinned. Still, she tucked her obsidian machete back into her belt and leaned against the Wall in preparation. "If I get caught doing this, I'm blaming you."

"Deal," Kiki said, fighting to keep her voice low.

Yarixa knelt down and began drawing a scene in the grime against the stone. "Some say the Cicatrix is a punishment for the people's sins." Yarixa's finger tore a slash through the dirt. "But those that know better say that the Cicatrix is a curse laid on the land by a scorned man."

Kiki perked up at that. "This is a new one," she said, leaning closer to the drawings.

Yarixa continued to draw as if the story took on its own life. Kiki imagined the figure of a man standing over the crouching shapes of those who'd betrayed him. She could almost see the mists of power that flowed from his fingers until they spiraled out of control and pooled into a cloud of endless darkness.

"They say there is only one way to lift the man's curse," Yarixa continued, her voice a sepulchral melody in the way that only good stories are told. "A sacrifice must be made."

Kiki interrupted then. "No, I don't like that. Change it."

Yarixa huffed and stopped drawing. "Do you want to do this instead?"

Kiki crossed her arms over her chest. "I'm just tired of those ones, that's all."

"Fine," Yarixa said as she swiped her hand through the dust and began drawing again. "The only way to break the curse is to find the man and restore his heart." With that, she drew a figure and the shape of a heart next to it. "Better?"

Kiki nodded. "I like your love stories best. You always kill my favorite characters in the scary ones."

Yarixa chuffed at that and started to draw again. Just then, the sound of a breaking branch ripped through the silence of the night. Yarixa's finger stilled above the dirt, and her eyes grew wide with fear as she exchanged a look with Kiki.

With slow movements, Kiki turned her body towards the source of the sound. It had come from the direction of the Cicatrix.

Leaves crunched in the distance, and the subtle shift in the shadows revealed that something was indeed there.

In a low whisper and with her eyes trained on the shifting shadows, Kiki said out of the side of her mouth, "Light the beacon."

Yarixa remained frozen in a crouch. "Maybe it's just a deer." Her eyes darted from Kiki to the blackness ahead of them. "Or a coati. Wasn't it a coati that got Luna kicked off the Watch?"

"Hush," Kiki ordered before adding. "It was a tapir, and she woke the whole fortress over it."

A rumbling growl snaked through the air. Kiki dared to lean over the railing as she strained her eyes to see what had slithered from the bowels of hell this time. Light from the shrouded moon draped a pair of horns in silver light. A flash of white revealed a set of razor-sharp teeth.

Kiki sucked in a breath. "That's no deer." She pulled a pair of tlazons from their sheaths in preparation. "Yari. Go."

Yarixa stood with aching slowness as if her body had turned to lead. Her shallow breaths sent white puffs of vapor circling overhead.

Kiki snapped her gaze to Yarixa. "The alarm," she hissed between her teeth. "Now!"

Yarixa took a hesitant step back before turning towards the nearest ladder and scrambling down.

Kiki released a breath of relief. She loved Yarixa dearly, but she was a lousy Attendant at best and a liability at worst. Kiki had a better shot of killing this thing on her own without having to worry about Yarixa.

The demon skittered across the no-zone; its claws clattered against stone and scraped against the wood of fallen trees. Kiki rolled her shoulders in anticipation. Her fingers itched to release a tlazon toward the creature, but she knew better than to waste her first shot. After all, she was no longer a green Attendant with zero kills under her belt. She stole a glance at the rows of black stars inked along the insides of her wrists. One for each kill. The reminder steadied her breath and eased the tension in her shoulders.

Kiki raised her hand, tlazon poised to strike. The demon was twenty feet from the Wall now. Enough distance to deliver a killing blow if Kiki put enough force behind her throw and hit the monster squarely in the heart. For most Slayers, such a thing was unlikely, and most couldn't send a tlazon that far with the power of their arm alone. But most Slayers weren't Kiki Xochicale.

A grin spread across her face as she braced for the attack.

"Welcome to the show, assholes," she snarled.

CHAPTER TWO

TROUBLE

KIKI

K iki spun and sent twin tlazons flying. The lances, each inlaid with jade and sharpened to a razor's edge, sliced through the air. Time slowed as the first set of tlazons, impossibly graceful, landed solidly in their target. The demon shrieked as its body burst into a cloud of dust.

Moonlight glinted off of a pair of silver horns as another demon stepped out of the shadows of the trees. Kiki scanned the open field, adrenaline coursing through her veins, and saw another pair of demons jump over a log and sprint into the no-go zone.

Kiki pulled her bow from her back and drew out a jade-tipped arrow, placing it on the bowstring. She crouched behind the parapet and drew back the arrow, focusing her aim on the horned demon only a few yards away. The fletching brushed her cheek as she released the string, and the jade tip sang a sinister melody as it arched through the air.

Where is Yarixa? Kiki thought to herself as she watched the arrow sink into the demon's neck. Kiki cursed and notched another arrow.

A horn blared behind her, and Kiki watched as the warning beacons flared to life, scattering the darkness with lances of orange light. She closed her eyes in relief at knowing that Yari had safely retreated into the safety behind the Wall. Now, all she had to do was hold off whatever crawled from the Cicatrix until backup arrived.

The demon roared as it yanked the arrow from its neck and tossed it to the ground. The ground shuddered as more demons rushed from somewhere deep in the woods. The trees shook, and their remaining leaves fell from their branches.

Kiki took a deep breath as she notched another arrow and pulled back her bowstring. She waited for the horned demon to enter her sight. When it did, she released the arrow, which sank into the pulsing green heart at the center of its chest, and exploded into a gale of oozing black ichor.

Kiki swung her bow back over her shoulder as she turned to face a demon that had made it to the Wall and was now scaling up its length. She reached down, grabbed a fistful of obsidian stones the size of pebbles, and hurled them down at full force. The stones burst into a spray of jade needles, hitting the demon's chest like hail and slowing its ascent. But it kept coming.

Kiki threw a handful of tlazons at the demon, anything to make it easier to kill. As the demon drew closer, she pulled her machete from its sheath and tightened her grip on the hilt.

The demon's abdomen sagged like melting wax as it lumbered over the stone railing. It was at least three feet tall with a bony, hairless body. Its skin was sickly brown, and its chest heaved as it panted, exposing rotting gums and yellow teeth. Even from a few feet away, Kiki could smell the stench of rotten meat and feces. Its yellowed eyes narrowed as it moved toward her and opened its decomposing mouth with a low growl. The smell wafted over her, and Kiki gagged.

"We really have to stop meeting like this," Kiki growled as she thrust her machete forward and impaled the demon's throat. A gush of black blood splattered her face, and the demon fell to the ground with a thud as Kiki pulled her machete out in a wide arc. The demon's head toppled off its shoulders and landed in a puddle of inky ichor.

A headless demon was still a dead demon.

A snarl from the right had Kiki spinning on her heel to face the demon that had breached the Wall. Yellow orbs burned with an inhuman rage as the demon leaped toward her. She turned her body in the same instant and met its attack, wielding her machete with both hands like a staff.

She passed the blade smoothly to her left hand as she swung and extended for a follow-through blow. The demon snarled as the obsidian blade slashed through its skin, revealing a crimson rip from its shoulder to the hip.

Inhumanly fast, the demon crouched low, then sprang over her head, landing behind her. She spun to face it, but the demon's claws slashed through her leather doublet, exposing a jagged rip in the leather and Kiki's tan skin. Pain flared across Kiki's side, and she cried out before she could stop herself.

The demon howled with victory, its huge mouth a jagged scar extending from one ear to the other. It thrust a long talon at Kiki, but she bent backward out of the way and swung her machete up in a fluid motion. The blade bit into the demon's ankles, severing tendons and producing a spray of green ichor.

The demon crashed into the hard stone, and Kiki followed through with her machete raised over her head. She swung the machete down with a powerful stroke and was rewarded with a horrible crack as the blade bit through bone, cleaving the head from its shoulders. The demon's body shuddered, writhing in pain. The demon's flesh and organs sizzled, and its body exploded into a shower of black ichor.

Kiki flicked the oily substance from her blade before returning it to its sheath.

The sound of pounding feet grew louder, and Kiki glanced over her shoulder to see her Commanding Officer, Solana Ramirez, running toward her. Solana's cheeks were flushed red from the heat, but not a single errant curl escaped the severe bun she pulled her red hair into. Even from across the rampart, Kiki could see the sternness on Solana's face, and she felt her stomach turn. Cowering in her shadow stood Yarixa, her face pale and drawn along with a contingent of Slayers.

Solana spun around in a slow circle, keeping her feet from sticking to the demon ichor that stained the floor and was pooling in the scratches she left in the stone. Kiki watched Solana take it all in. She saw how Solana's eyes darted, and her nostrils flared as she caught the scent of sulfur and charred flesh. The Commander missed no detail and examined the fresh wound on Kiki's side.

"Report," Solana ordered, her tone clipped.

Kiki stood at attention and delivered her account of the events and the deaths of the demons escaping the Cicatrix.

Solana glared at Kiki, and her features formed a stony mask. Kiki felt uneasy in the face of Solana's displeasure, and Yarixa's gaze flitted back and forth between Solana and Kiki.

Solana barked orders to the waiting Slayers, and they snapped to attention and divided into two groups. The first group burst into action as they took up positions along the Wall. The second group set up their climbing gear to scale down the side of the Wall in search of any further disturbances.

"You," Solana pointed at Kiki. "The infirmary. Now."

Kiki motioned to Yarixa to follow along, but Solana grabbed the smaller girl firmly by the shoulder and stopped them both in their tracks. "Where do you think you're going, Yarixa?" The Commander said, her eyes narrowed into slits.

Yarixa swallowed hard before answering. "I was going to escort Kiki to the infirmary."

Solana took a half-step to the side and narrowed her eyes at Yarixa. "Unless you've taken a wound that I can't see, you will remain at your post until your designated time of leave."

Yarixa begged Kiki with her eyes, but Kiki shrugged. Not even Kiki could worm her way out of everything.

Yarixa's shoulders slumped in defeat, and she turned and trudged back to the Wall. She slunk back into position, wrapping her thin arms around her shoulders as she shivered in the cold.

Kiki bit her tongue at the look of satisfaction on Solana's face. She stuffed her hands into her pockets and forced herself to take five even breaths to stop herself from letting loose a string of curses.

She couldn't believe Solana had made such a stupid decision. Everyone knew Yarixa wasn't capable on her own.

With a grumble and clenched jaw, Kiki brushed past Solana and marched off toward the infirmary, her heavy boots thumping against the frozen ground.

The Commander deserved to be brought down a peg or two, but Kiki doubted Solana would even listen. Her head was so far up her own ass she'd probably have to get a Healer to pull it out.

CHAPTER THREE

DISAGREE

KIKI

With a rigid spine, Kiki strode away from the Wall. She placed her palm against her wound and bit her lip as she marched onwards. The wound hurt more than she cared to admit, but she forced her lips into a straight line, her face betraying nothing of her deep pain.

She passed a pair of first-year Attendants on washing duty and gave them a stiff nod of acknowledgment. The Attendants were getting younger and younger each year. This group couldn't have been older than thirteen years old.

"Look, it's the Sicario," one of the Attendants whispered to her friend.

The Sicario. A nickname Kiki had earned in large part due to the rows of stars tattooed along her wrist. Each star was a kill. Before the Cicatrix tore through the kingdom, the sicarios had been hitmen sent to eliminate a threat to the crown. The name now meant much the same except that, now, the enemy was demon-possessed and a lot harder to kill.

The other Attendant looked up at Kiki only to drop the pair of bloodied trousers she'd been scrubbing into the washbasin. Brown water splashed over both her and her friend.

"Stop staring," the first said with an elbow into the second's side.

"Did you know the Sicario took down five demons with one tlazon?" the other said in awe as she plunged her hands back into the soapy water.

Kiki couldn't help but snort. The stories were getting wilder and wilder. Not that she did anything to stop them, either. She had a namesake to preserve, after all.

"No! I heard it was ten," the first Attendant said, her eyes wide.

Kiki pretended not to hear them as she continued toward the infirmary. However, she did push her shoulders back and pulled her hand from her wound. Looking weak didn't suit her reputation. Plus, it would do no good if the Yearlings and Attendants didn't fear her just a little bit.

Kiki passed another group of Attendants on their hands and knees, picking pebbles from the ground. A Drill Slayer stood over them with her hands on her hips and narrowed eyes.

"I don't want to see a single rock near my tent," the Drill Slayer barked. "Clean faster!"

The Attendants panicked and dropped pebbles from their hands faster than they picked them up.

Kiki sighed at the sight. She did not miss the Attendant days, that was for sure. The four hours of sleep she could handle. Even the washing and latrine duties, while disgusting, hadn't been entirely awful. She hadn't been a fan of working in the kitchens, with all the mopping and scraping mold from bread, but at least she'd been able to sneak extra food every now and then. No. It was the unusual and useless punishments that Kiki hadn't been able to stand.

Once, Kiki had failed to pass the fitness test and been made to bear crawl everywhere for a week. Kiki still had dirt stains on her green trousers to prove it. She also never failed another fitness test afterward. Begrudgingly, she could admit that the punishment had at least been effective.

Kiki made it to the infirmary tent, a large green structure that looked more like a circus tent than a proper infirmary. A large emblem of a sword piercing a skull was emblazoned on the side--the mark of the Demon Corps.

The Demon Corps made the tent from old Slayer uniforms that were too worn and damaged to continue being issued out. Still, the Demon Corps wasn't one for wasting and had found a new purpose for the material. The edges of the tent fabric were frayed, and the Demon Corps had patched up some parts of the tent with mismatched green fabric.

Kiki pushed back the tent flap and slipped inside. Pale green light filled the infirmary, and the usual smells of camphor and anise were overpowered by the moldy scent of earth and herbs. Healers walked between cots along both sides of the tent, occasionally stopping to examine an injured Slayer. Only a few Slayers were being tended to that evening, so Kiki meandered between the beds until she reached her friend's section.

Luna was finishing up with a patient when Kiki approached. She looked beautiful, with her midnight black hair pulled into a tangled bun. Her Healer's apron was so starched that the creases in its front looked razor-sharp.

A look of annoyance spread across Luna's face as she surveyed the bloody cut on Kiki's abdomen and the gash in her upper arm. "You're bleeding on my floor," she quipped.

Kiki glanced down at the bloody footprints behind her, leaving pockmarks on the dusty wooden floorboards. "Sorry," Kiki mumbled.

Luna, already pushing up her sleeves, pointed to a nearby cot, the blankets spackled with dried blood. "Over there," she said, apathy in her voice.

It's not that Luna didn't care that Kiki was injured. It was just that when wasn't Kiki injured? That was the real question. There was a reason Kiki was at the top of her class. Being the best also meant taking a wound or two. Sometimes three.

Kiki sat on the practical grey linen of the cot. She ran her hand along the fabric, rough and scratchy from being washed too many times. Stains of old blood splashed across the sheet. Still, the supply officers wouldn't dream of tossing the sheets just yet. To the Demon Corps, the sheets had plenty of life left in them.

The Corps used every resource until it was practically rotting. Even then, unless an item was completely useless, the Corps would find something for which that item could have renewed life and a new purpose. Waste not. The unofficial motto of the Demon Corps.

Luna splashed her hands with water from a nearby basin. She scrubbed her hands thoroughly and dried them on a threadbare towel. She then poured the filthy water into a basin to be repurposed later.

She grabbed a jar of clear liquid from a nearby shelf lined with herbs and mixed pastes before turning towards Kiki.

"Let me see it," Luna said, her voice a sweet melody that directly conflicted with her obvious annoyance with Kiki.

Kiki lifted her shirt for Luna to see the wound, to which she earned a disapproving grunt.

With medical precision, Luna opened the jar. The sharp scent of fermented agave wafted into the air, making Kiki wrinkle her nose in disgust. It wasn't that Kiki didn't enjoy tequila as much as the next person; it was just that she'd enjoyed it a little too much one night after Watch one night and had spent the following day in training puking her insides out. After that, she'd sworn off the stuff.

"Brace yourself," Luna said, and she tilted the contents onto Kiki's wound.

Kiki winced as fire seared through her skin, and the alcohol washed away any impurities that could cause infection. Fresh blood sprang to the surface, poinsettia red.

"Where's Yari?" Luna asked as she grabbed a jar of salve and unscrewed the metal cap. She dipped her finger into the salve and scooped out the smallest amount before smearing it over the clean wound. Though Luna was a magicked Healer, she still needed the entire wound clear of anything that could cause infection for the healing to take hold and not become septic.

"Solana made her stay," Kiki said, not bothering to hide the disdain in her voice. How she hated Solana Ramirez. The Commander was only a year older than Kiki's twenty-one years, but she'd risen through the ranks of the Demon Corps so quickly that when she was only sixteen, she had graduated and became a ranked Slayer in the Corps. Solana didn't let anyone forget that fact, either. She was arrogant and cruel, with the ice of the Lobo Mountains running in her veins.

Luna shook her head as she grabbed another jar and scooped out a white powder that she sprinkled over the wound. She tossed the dirty linen into a bucket full of linen scraps that she'd have to scrub clean later. The Corps couldn't afford fresh linens all the time.

"It's because Solana can't do anything to me, so instead, she picks on Yari. It's not fair," Kiki said between gritted teeth.

Luna placed her palms on Kiki's wound, and the air became thick like molasses. The world seemed to slow, and Kiki felt suddenly light-headed. A warm golden light radiated from Luna's palms as she called on the Healer magic within.

Healers were rare in Ozero before the Cicatrix split the kingdom. They'd become even rarer and harder to find since the darkness had swallowed up entire generations of families and their homes.

Luna was technically an apprentice in the Healercorps. Still, with her innate abilities as a magicked Healer, she'd likely be promoted to Commander upon graduation and be given charge of a regiment of Healers.

Kiki felt like a thousand fire ants were eating at her wound. It made her both squirm and wince with pain. Not to mention that Luna had learned to redirect her magic to take strength from her patient rather than from herself. Magic always had a price, and often there were too many patients for Luna to heal to warrant her being the one to pay that price every time. Instead of giving up some of her strength, Luna had learned to draw strength from the patient she was treating, reserving her strength only for those who had none of their own to give.

The light faded from Luna's hands in a few short moments, and she retreated to the washing station to clean her hands again.

Kiki swayed, and the room spun as ravenous hunger erupted inside her. Such was the cost of magic.

She'd do anything for a bowl of pozole. It didn't matter that the dining hall staff put more hominy and chiles into the stew than actual pork. The smell of cumin and oregano reminded her of home and of her wela. She'd watch her grandmother's wrinkled hands peel the onion and chop it so fine it was almost a paste. Wela had never used a recipe for her dishes either; she'd done it all by how it felt, how the food smelled, and most of all, how it tasted.

The memory of her wela made Kiki's eyes water. That was a long time ago, and there was no use in dwelling on the past. She brushed the corners of her eyes and slid off the cot.

Luna turned as she dried her hands on her apron, now stained with splotches of Kiki's blood. "Where do you think you're going?"

Kiki started to walk away, determination marking her every step. "I'm going back to the Wall. Someone has to keep an eye out for Yari."

"You won't always be there to look out for her," Luna said, disapproval heavy in her voice.

Kiki blew out a frustrated breath and spun on her heel toward her friend. Luna's face could have made kings cry if she'd lived in another time. It was hard for Kiki to stay mad at Luna for long, not just because she was beautiful and her very presence seemed to create a sense of calm, but because Luna was kind and only said honest, and sometimes harsh, things because of how much she cared for a person.

"Speaking of," Kiki said as she crossed her arms over her chest. "Have you put in your assignment request yet?"

Luna's eyes darted to the ground before she turned and busied herself with rearranging the glass jars of salves and poultices. "No, I haven't had a chance. Things have been busy around here, if you haven't noticed."

Kiki glanced around the mostly empty infirmary. "Clearly."

Luna put a jar down too hard, making the glass clang loudly. "You know what I mean."

"I don't, actually. We're graduating in three days. We're about to be free of this hell hole, and if our requests get approved, which there is no reason for them not to, then by this time next week, we'll be sipping frozen margaritas on the southern Wall."

Luna bit her bottom lip as if contemplating whether she should say what was on her mind or not. She seemed to decide on the latter. Luna shrugged and said, almost defeated, "I'll get the request to my Commander in the morning."

Kiki knew Luna was hiding something, and she wasn't about to let Luna stay tight-lipped about it. Not this time. "Don't you want to keep the group together?"

Luna fiddled with the lid of a jar of sludgy green paste. "It's not that," she said, her soft voice quieter than usual.

Kiki huffed in annoyance and took three long strides toward Luna's side. She grabbed the jar and put it back on the shelf.

Luna shifted her gaze, refusing to meet Kiki's stare. "I think I am more use to the Corps if I stay here."

Kiki's mouth dropped open. She hadn't been expecting this from Luna. The same Luna who had nursed her back to health when Kiki had come down with the sweating sickness. The same Luna who still cried at night for her family and snuck into Kiki's bed just so she wouldn't have to be alone.

"You're joking," Kiki scoffed. She searched Luna's face for any sign of jest but found none.

Luna shrugged. "I know we always said we'd stay together, but more people need me here. The southern Wall already has enough magicked Healers. Not enough stay here in the north."

Kiki threw her hands in the air. "Because the north is the actual worst!"

Luna's shoulders slumped as if the world's weight lay across them.

"Fine," Kiki said, anger boiling in the pit of her stomach. "Stay here then. But feel free to join us in the south when you're tired of freezing to death at night and your stomach is empty."

The heat of Luna's stare followed Kiki out of the infirmary, stinging more than the cold wind that whipped across her face.

"If you go back out there, Solana will put you on latrine duty for insubordination," Luna called after her.

Kiki waved a dismissive hand in the air. "We're graduating in three days. Solana Ramirez can make me cut the grass outside her tent with my sewing shears for all I care. After graduation, I'll never have to see her stuck-up swine face again."

Kiki pulled the collar of her Slayer leathers up as she stepped out of the infirmary tent. Motes of snow swirled around her, catching the moonlight. She made her way towards the armory to replenish her supply of tlazons and jade-tipped arrows. Come to think of it; she could pick up a sharpened machete while there. Maybe even grab a sharpening stone if she was lucky.

Of course, when was Kiki ever that lucky.

CHAPTER FOUR

HAPPY TOGETHER

KIKI

T he wind roared past, whipping Kiki's chin-length hair against her face. Snow crunched beneath her feet as she walked away from the infirmary. No matter how much the cold bothered her, she wasn't taking any chances; there were still plenty of Yearlings and Attendants buzzing around the camp, and she refused to show weakness.

Kiki looked at the night sky; broad swaths of white radiating from the moon swallowed the Slayer camp in a wash of eerie shadows. Though it was near the witching hour, the night was still young in Slayer terms. It wouldn't be until the sun peeked across the horizon that everyone could release their anxious breaths.

Most demons attacked when the sun was setting or completely dark. Once it was day, they seemed more reluctant to face the sun's harsh rays. Still, Slayers couldn't afford to relax, even during the day.

Kiki reached the supply building on the outer edge of the fortress. It was a sad excuse for a building, probably built a generation ago, and should have been condemned. However, it was the warmest place in the Norceran base camp.

Kiki pushed against the rotting wooden door of the supply building with her whole body. The hinges groaned as she burst inside and a gust of cold air swept through the solitary halls.

The torches that lined the length of the supply hall flickered as the wind from outside rushed in and whipped around Kiki. The hall was lit by roaring wood fires along both sides, bringing comforting warmth to her face. She quickly shoved the door closed again.

At the end of the hall, a young man was hunched over the supply counter, his full attention on the task in his hands.

Kiki stopped in her tracks when she saw who was on duty. She considered going back out again and braving the cold again. Even from this distance, she could tell the officer on duty was her previous boyfriend.

The supply officer lifted his head to see who'd come into the hall, and a smile split his face.

Kiki groaned internally. There was no going back now. If she ran, she'd only look like a coward, and, of course, that was not acceptable.

Kiki pressed her shoulders back and adopted that false bravado she had become accustomed to wearing.

"If it isn't the Sicario herself," the officer said, a look of mischief glinting in his blue eyes.

Kiki steeled her spine. She had the biggest soft spot for guys with hair blacker than Slayer leather and eyes as bright as sapphires. "I'm here for supplies, Turi. Not to flirt." Kiki removed her machete from her belt strap and let it fall onto the supply counter with a resounding thunk.

Turi Artchete grinned with a devilish tilt to his full lips. "That's too bad." He gave her one last meaningful look before turning to the crates of supplies kept behind the counter.

Kiki felt a flutter in her stomach at the look in Turi's eyes. He'd always had such an effect on her. It had been that reason alone that she'd broken up with him over a year ago. She couldn't afford another distraction. She had enough to worry about. Keeping Luna off the front lines. Making sure Yarixa didn't get another tooth lodged into her neck. Watching out for her own hide. No, the split had been the right decision. Even if Kiki still wondered whether she could have made room in her heart for one more person.

As Turi rummaged through the crates, Kiki eyed the obsidian tlazons sitting just behind the counter. Their edges glinted in the flickering torchlight.

She'd come here for supplies. No sense in not restocking. She helped herself to the fresh tlazons and slid them into the straps wrapped across her chest.

As she tucked the last tlazon into its spot, she noticed what Turi had been working on when she'd first walked in. It looked like a clash between a set of knuckle rings and a spiked garrote. Only the spikes were forged into the shape of four claws.

Turi had always liked to tinker and make new weapons. It looked like he was back to his old antics. Though, to be fair, most of his weapons were familiar and offshoots of weapons that were already part of the Slayer arsenal. This, however, was new.

Kiki's fingers itched to take hold of the new weapon.

"Don't even think about it," said Turi, his back still turned to her.

Kiki cursed under her breath. Turi knew her too well. Regardless, she swiped the claws off the counter and examined them. "I see you've been experimenting again." Kiki turned the set of claws over in her hands, admiring the craftsmanship and attention to detail.

"I could say the same for you." Turi returned to the counter with a gleaming obsidian machete, the edge razor sharp. "You cut your hair again."

Kiki ran a hand through her chin-length hair. "I needed something more practical," she said, feeling self-conscious. She'd had waist-length hair when she'd dated Turi, and he had always commented on how pretty it was. She felt dumb for thinking his opinion mattered, but she knew she still cared about what he thought.

"It suits you," he said, sliding the machete and a new sheath over the counter.

Though she knew she had no right to feel it, Kiki couldn't help the ripple of satisfaction that rushed along her neck.

Turi offered her a sweet smile, and a light of hope sparkled in his eyes.

Eager to change the topic, Kiki held the claws up. "These are nice."

Turi reached out and took them from her. "They're not ready yet. I still have some adjustments to make."

"When are you going to transfer to engineering? You're wasting your talent here."

Turi returned to tinkering with the claws with a set of metal pliers. "I like it here. My friends are here. There's always work to do. What's not to like?"

Kiki scoffed. "How about the freezing cold? Or the fact that there's never enough meat at dinnertime? Or the fact that more Slayers die along this strip of the Cicatrix than anywhere else?"

Turi looked up at her, his blue eyes catching the light from the torch flame. "You're here," he said, his voice soft and inviting.

Kiki sobered immediately. Her face turned cold, and she became all business. The last thing she needed was a distraction. Her main priority was keeping Yari, Luna, and herself alive. An assignment to the southern border wouldn't hurt. Nothing else mattered. Even boys with blue eyes and devilish smirks.

"Not for long," she said, grabbing the machete and turning on her heel.

Turi groaned from behind her. "What did I say now?"

Kiki paused for a second. Her shoulders suddenly felt heavier as she rotated to face Turi. Why he bothered with her, she would never know. She was an overprotective control freak most days and a pain in the ass the rest of the time.

"I have my priorities," she said with a shrug.

Turi sighed, the light in his eyes faded, and the mischief on his lips soured. "I've just never been one of them. Have I?"

Kiki opened her mouth to respond, but Turi cut her off.

"Don't. I can't hear another excuse out of you."

Kiki clenched her fist and began to walk out of the supply hall. "Thanks for the gear." She yanked the door open only to find Solana Ramirez on the other side with her arm outstretched.

Kiki cursed under her breath. Well, damn.

Solana's usually blank expression turned to ice at the sight of Kiki. "Quirera," the Commander said. Her quick gaze took in the fresh supply of tlazons strapped to Kiki's chest and the freshly oiled machete sheath. She tilted her head the way a jaguar might in the middle of a hunt. "Where do you think you're going?"

Kiki tried to step around the Commander. "Nowhere," she said with a fake smile. "Back to the barracks, of course."

Solana narrowed her eyes. "Which is it then? Nowhere or the barracks?"

Kiki resisted the urge to roll her eyes. "Actually, I don't know why I said that. I'm starving. So it's to the mess hall for me." Kiki tried to move around Solana again, but the Commander clapped a firm hand on her shoulder and steered her back into the tent.

"You wouldn't be restocking your supplies to return to the Wall, would you?" Solana said, her tone sharp and her grip even sharper. "Because, if you were, you'd be disobeying direct orders, and I'd have no choice but to charge you with insubordination."

Kiki groaned.

Solana moved her back to the counter where Turi stood, his eyes trained on the counter in front of him. "Put it back," Solana ordered.

Kiki begrudgingly removed the new machete and tossed it onto the counter. Turi kept his eyes down as he grabbed the machete and made it disappear beneath the counter.

"If you were anyone else, I'd hold you back a year for your clear inability to follow orders," Solana said in a monotone.

Kiki felt a surge of rebellion burning in her chest. "But I'm not just anyone. Am I? I'm the most decorated Slayer in the Corps. You couldn't hold me back even if you tried."

Solana sneered. "You're not a Slayer yet."

Kiki waved a dismissive hand in the air. "Technicalities."

Solana's eyes took on a hard gleam. "I may not be able to hold you back a year, but I can keep you from the graduation carnival tomorrow night."

At that, Kiki's false bravado wavered. Miss the party? The only thing she'd been looking forward to for months? Kiki felt the blood drain from her face. "You wouldn't."

Solana smirked and released her hold on Kiki. "One more act of defiance, and I won't hesitate." She pushed past Kiki and started to talk with Turi, acting as if Kiki weren't even there.

Kiki felt a seed of unease unfurl in her stomach as she walked out of the supply tent. Solana Ramirez would be the end of her; Kiki was sure of it. Kiki didn't know what she'd done to make Solana hate her so much, but whatever it had been, Kiki was certain that Solana had deserved it.

CHAPTER FIVE

GLITTER AND GOLD

KIKI

K iki fidgeted on the wooden stool she'd stolen from the mess hall. She leaned forward and braced her hands on the cracked, enameled surface of the sink in the girl's washroom. Her face looked pale in the mirror, except for dark rings under her eyes. She sighed.

Yarixa stood over her with a paintbrush in hand. An assortment of paint pots lay open and teetered at the edge of the sink behind her.

"Stop fidgeting, or I'll never be done in time for the carnival," Yarixa scolded, her face a mask of concentration as she continued to draw. She used wide, long strokes to apply a thick layer of white paint over Kiki's entire face.

The wet paint smelled of ammonia and turpentine. Kiki resisted the urge to cough. "It smells funny," Kiki complained.

"I'm almost done," Yarixa said as she stepped back to examine her work.

Behind them, a group of Attendants had started the showers, and a chorus of yelps erupted in the bathroom when ice-cold water blasted their bodies.

Kiki glanced at her reflection in the frosted mirror and pursed her lips. Yarixa turned and dipped a new brush into a paint pot of deep red. She swiped it across Kiki's lips and nodded in approval.

Yarixa was a visionary with a paintbrush. She could remold a person into any creature, both real and imagined. For the carnival tonight, she decided to paint Kiki into the visage of a Katrina sugar skull.

Even though it wasn't technically the day of the dead, it was Demon Corps tradition to honor those who hadn't made it to their final year by throwing a graduation carnival that rivaled the autumnal day of reverence. There would be a live band, games, and drinks to share tonight. Kiki wished there would be food, too, but that was hard to come by on a normal day.

"You look amazing," Yarixa said as she stepped out of the way for Kiki to get a better look in the mirror. "I wish we could have found you a dress. It would look so much better with the right clothes."

Kiki inspected her face in the mirror. Yarixa had done it again and somehow managed to transform the macabre into that which is beautiful. Even though Kiki looked like a deathly version of herself, she had never felt prettier.

Kiki smoothed out the front of her green uniform, her eyes catching on the old dirt stains on her knees. It was either this or Slayer gear, and her leathers were still getting washed from the previous night.

"Oh, wait, I want to add one more thing," Yarixa said as she corralled Kiki back onto the stool.

Kiki sat down and watched as Yarixa pulled a cloth from her pocket. She unfolded it to reveal a handful of glittering shards. "They're cast-offs from the welders," Yari explained as she handled the pieces of jade with care. "I sanded down the edges as best I could to shape them."

"Yari," Kiki gasped as she watched her friend dab the back of a gem with some leftover paint. "They're beautiful. Don't waste them on me. Wear them yourself."

Yarixa shook her head, "They won't match what I plan to do for my makeup. Besides, you never let me do this, so I'm taking advantage."

Yarixa leaned over Kiki as she carefully placed each gem one at a time.

Kiki tried to stay still to avoid ruining Yarixa's plans and instead focused her attention on the ugly necklace around her friend's throat. "Why do you still wear that thing?" Kiki asked.

Yarixa paused to touch the tooth hanging from the leather strap around her neck. "It's my good luck charm."

"I don't see how wearing the tooth that nearly killed you symbolizes good luck. Seems more like a bad omen to me."

"It reminds me that I'm never alone." Yarixa's eyes grew distant, and a smile lifted the corner of her lips. "It's lucky to me because I'm lucky to be alive. If it weren't for you and Luna, I would have died that day."

The memory of that night on the Watch returned to Kiki as if it were happening all over again.

Kiki, Luna, and Yarixa had been second-year Attendants. They were on Watch that night under the supervision of a ranked Slayer when a horde of demons burst from the tree line. The Slayers on duty had been competent enough to eliminate most of the threat, but that hadn't stopped demons from breaching the Wall.

Yarixa had always had a strong freeze response when it came to danger. When the first demon climbed over the parapet, she'd remained glued in place as a silver demon bear lumbered towards her. Kiki had been in the middle of eliminating her own threat when she heard Yarixa's blood-curdling scream.

Yari had been rammed into the ground by the demon bear, its massive paw on her chest. It sank its teeth into her throat, and Kiki felt like her whole world split in two. Before she knew what she was doing, Kiki was atop the back of the demon bear with a jade-tipped arrow in one hand and a tlazon in the other. She stabbed the bear multiple times until it howled, tossed her off its back, and bounded back over the Wall to the Cicatrix.

Luna scrambled over and started to heal Yari immediately. Her skin turned ashen as she pulled from her own life force to heal their friend. Luna collapsed from the effort, and a second later, Yarixa's eyes flew open, a silent scream on her lips. There was nothing left of the wound save for a dislodged bear tooth lying next to Yarixa's head.

Yari grabbed the tooth and had worn it ever since.

Kiki shook her head to rid herself of the memory. "You'll never be alone again." She reached out and grabbed Yarixa's hand, reassuringly squeezing it.

Yarixa smiled, returning Kiki's gesture, then went back to adding the jade pieces to her masterpiece.

Just then, a Yearling rushed into the washroom. Upon seeing Yarixa and Kiki, the Yearling bent over her knees and inhaled deeply. "From Commander Ramirez," she said between panting breaths. She held a folded parchment out to Yarixa.

Yarixa set down her brush before taking the paper from the Yearling. Kiki watched her friend's eyes travel the page and felt a pit open in her stomach when Yarixa's face fell.

"What is it?" Kiki stood and angled her head to read for herself.

Yarixa released a heavy sigh before handing the paper over.

Kiki read Solana's message and promptly crumbled it in her hand. "She can't make you miss the party. She's just punishing you because she can't punish me!"

Yarixa shrugged, her mouth turned down in a sad line. "It's okay. With all the seniors off from Watch tonight, I understand."

"You're a senior too!" Kiki kicked the wooden stool into the corner.

Yari started to put the lids back on her paint pots. "I don't mind. Truly. You know I like getting ready for parties more than I actually enjoy attending them. Besides, there'll be so many people in one place. So loud. All that pushing. The music." Yarixa made a show of shuddering. "I'm not bothered by it."

"Well, I am!" Kiki said as she slammed a palm against the sink. She faced the mirror; this time, what looked back at her wasn't just beautiful. It was also terrifying. "This is all we've been looking forward to for the past three months. It's a symbol of our freedom from this hell hole. Solana can't do this to us!"

Yarixa approached Kiki slowly as if she were a feral animal that would dart when anyone got too close. "She can, and she just did. Please, don't make a big deal out of it. Don't do anything rash, and definitely don't use this as an excuse to pull a prank just to get revenge."

Kiki silently cursed Yarixa for knowing her far too well. After all, all it would take was for Kiki to get a Yearling on latrine duty to look the other way while Kiki stuffed Solana's boots with a nasty little surprise.

Yarixa continued. "Just imagine I'm back in the barracks reading a book. Pretend like I chose to stay behind. Honestly, I might have, anyway. Everyone is going to be at the carnival tonight. I can't think of anything more suffocating than Yearlings pushing and prodding each other on the edge of the dancing because they're too afraid to join everyone and all the seniors fumbling around from too much alcohol."

Kiki crossed her arms over her chest, distinctly aware that the gesture made her look like a child throwing a tantrum. "I'd be fine with that if only it were true. But you're on Watch. The Wall is too dangerous right now. Have you not noticed the attacks on the Wall have been increasing? It's not safe for you out there."

Yarixa closed her paints. "It's sector seven, Kiki. It's the safest place on the Wall. Besides, you can't always be there to watch my back. At some point, I have to learn how to take care of myself."

"No. I made a promise that I'd always watch over you. I keep my promises," Kiki said as she pulled her friend into a bone-crushing hug.

"That was fifteen years ago, Kiki. I'm not a baby crying for her mother every night. Neither is Luna, for that matter."

Kiki mumbled under her breath.

Yarixa pulled away and leveled her with a steely gaze. "Go to the party. Enjoy yourself and tell me everything when I get back from Watch."

#

Kiki took a sip of her bitter drink as she stood on the outskirts of the party. The crowd was large and loud, and, as Yari had predicted, the Yearlings were circled on the edge of the dancing crowd but refused to join the throng of moving bodies. Seniors howled like wolves as they moved to the rhythm of the music, their hips swaying and their arms were thrown carelessly to the wind.

Kiki loved to dance, but without both of her best friends, the carnival seemed utterly pointless.

Not only had Yarixa been ordered to the Wall tonight, but Luna had been called away to a Demon Corps base over twenty miles to the south. Apparently, there had been a large breach, and demons had killed several Slayers. The ones left were seriously injured, and only a magicked Healer could help bring them back from the brink of death.

Kiki allowed herself to sway to the music when the band started to play her favorite song. As she took another sip of her drink, she saw a familiar pair of blue eyes gazing at her from across the party.

Turi painted his face like an angel of death. His black hair and blue eyes contrasted with the white paint covering most of his face. Seeing her, Turi started to weave his way through the crowd. Even in his basic uniform of green trousers and shirt, Kiki thought he looked impeccable. To be fair, she was not the only one who thought so as the Yearlings he passed giggled behind their hands to one another.

"Care to dance?" Turi asked when he reached Kiki.

"Not particularly," Kiki said, forcing an air of aloofness into her voice even though she really did want to dance. Especially with him. But it wasn't fair to keep playing these games with him.

"It's your favorite song," Turi said in a sing-song voice. His eyes glinted with the invitation.

"I thought you were mad at me," Kiki said, finishing the rest of her drink.

Turi shrugged. "I can't stay mad at you for long."

Kiki gave him a doubtful look.

"You've been nothing but honest with me. You don't want a commitment. I can accept that."

Kiki sighed in frustration. Why did he have to make this harder than it already was? "It's not just that."

"I know," Turi said. "You have Yari and Luna. They're your family, and your main priority is to look out for them. I'm not saying I want to break that up or anything. I actually envy you for it. I wish I had friends like that."

Kiki supposed she couldn't blame him for being so honest. Though, the fact that he was so honest only made it harder for her to keep the obsidian wall around her heart in place.

Turi moved closer. "I care about you, and just because we broke up doesn't mean I suddenly stopped caring. I know you better than you think. You push people away because you feel like you have to take care of everyone. But you don't have to take care of me. I've taken care of myself for this long, haven't I?"

Kiki considered his words for a moment. She didn't like the fact that Turi had seen right through her ruse so easily. He had an unnerving way of seeing the walls she had built around herself and scaling up them anyway. He'd been a good boyfriend and a better friend than she'd deserved since their breakup.

She sighed, feeling the ice around her heart begin to thaw. Plus, she couldn't deny that she still cared about him, too, no matter how much she said otherwise.

Kiki motioned toward the dance floor. "If the offer still stands, I'll take that dance now."

Turi beamed and held out his arm to lead her to the dance floor.

As they began to dance, Kiki felt herself relax in Turi's embrace. His hand was warm against her waist, and his chest was firm against her cheek. She sucked in a deep breath of his soap and slowly exhaled. His heartbeat was like a second drum, pounding in time with the music. It felt good to be in his arms again. She had missed this feeling of closeness and intimacy.

Kiki felt a lightness in her chest that she hadn't felt in months. Maybe Turi was right. Maybe she didn't have to take care of everyone all the time. She could allow herself to be cared for too.

Turi rested his chin on top of her head and gently rubbed her lower back in lazy circles.

Kiki's pulse raced at the sensations he was stirring up inside her.

They danced like that for some time, neither of them speaking, just enjoying being close to one another again. Finally, Turi broke the silence. "I've missed you, Kiki."

Kiki looked up at him and smiled sadly. "I've missed you too, Turi."

Kiki's face was so close to Turi's that she could feel his breath on her lips. Her pulse quickened as he gazed into her eyes. He leaned in closer, his eyes searching hers, and she held her breath. His lips touched hers, warm and soft, just a whisper at first.

Her heart pounded in her chest, and heat flushed her cheeks. She drew a ragged breath, pulling away from him. "We can't," she whispered.

Turi traced his fingers along her face, his touch feather soft. "Why not?" he asked, his face twisting in anguish.

Frustration burst through Kiki's chest like an inferno, and she scowled. "This was a mistake," she hissed.

Turi ran a hand through his hair and groaned.

Kiki was ready to tell him off for weakening her defenses, but the warning beacons surrounding the fortress flared to life, and long bellows of horns echoed along the wind.

Kiki spun to see sector three's flares ablaze. Then sector two. Then sector one. Kiki prayed to any god or spirit that would listen. Sectors five and six bloomed with flame at once. She held her breath as flames pulsed in the distance until every warning beacon was lit one by one.

All but sector seven.

Around her, the carnival descended into chaos as the ranked Slayers sprang to action and raced for the Wall. Most of the seniors ran for the sectors that were already alight with flame. But Kiki ran headlong toward sector seven.

Please don't light. Please.

The first of sector seven's beacons burst with fire, and it wasn't long before the remaining beacons also exploded with light.

Kiki forced speed into her legs as she raced toward Yarixa's sector. The sound of fighting grew louder as Kiki rushed toward the Wall. Slayers were fending off demons of all sorts. Three-headed beasts with tongues for arms.

Demon-possessed wildlife. Rabbits with red eyes and jagged teeth leaped from the Wall and down into the camp, leaving destruction in their wake. Deer with mangled horns and serrated hooves bucked Slayers off the Wall and into the attacking horde.

Kiki rushed past it all with only one thought on her mind. Keep Yari safe. She could only hope that she wasn't too late.

CHAPTER SIX

DARKSIDE

YARIXA

Yari crouched down behind the parapet, her knees knocking together against the cold stone Wall. The frigid air stung her cheeks and nose, turning her face bright red. The night was black, a thick blanket of velveteen. Snow had fallen during the day, covering the Wall and the land beyond in sheets of pristine white. A silvery moon hung low on the horizon, casting an eerie glow over everything. Yari pulled her cloak tighter around her shoulders and shivered.

The raucous music from the carnival was faint, like a frenzied whisper. She could see only vague, jumbled shapes and the occasional flash of torch lights through the trees.

Something in her stung at the thought of Kiki, who would be celebrating her graduation tonight with Luna. She should have told her best friend that she would not graduate this year. She'd even meant to tell Kiki the truth tonight, but, like every time before, the words had frozen on her tongue. Instead, like a coward, she had let Kiki believe Commander Ramirez had put her on patrol tonight.

Yari groaned, her breath huffed out in a billowy cloud before being swept away by the fierce wind. Shivers raced up and down her spine as she ran trembling fingers over the rows of tlazons strapped across her chest. Once, when she was a Yearling, she had thought the tlazons were beautiful--a treasure to be admired and worn by heroes. Now she knew better. The palm-sized spears were tools for survival. Formidable weapons in capable hands. Only, she wasn't one of those deemed competent. Sighing, she double-checked that the obsidian machete at her hip was clear in its sheath and blinked away the frost crusting her eyes.

Yari moved to the next parapet and nodded to the boy on guard there. He was breathing rapidly, his brown eyes wide. He clutched his machete with white knuckles and swiveled his head back and forth, taking in every shadow and nook.

No doubt this was his first night on Watch, and he was questioning whether or not he was ready. But no one could ever be ready for what came crawling from the Cicatrix. Yari knew well the fear that snaked up one's spine at the slightest flicker of movement in the shadows. The ever-present anxiety that tonight would be her last.

Yari was yanked from her brooding thoughts when a beacon of fire lit up the leftmost flank of the Wall. Moments later, the rightmost beacon roared to life. She saw the other Slayers and Attendants pause in mid-motion, their eyes darting to one another in tense apprehension. Yari gripped the stone railing with white knuckles, her eyes straining into the night. One by one, the beacons of each sector lit up until sector seven was the only one that remained dark.

Yari gasped as she saw the first demon emerge from the dark abyss. Clawed hands sank into the mud, and it reared back, an inhuman screech piercing the night. Behind it, a horde of writhing demons crawled forward and paused along the treeline as if taking up battle positions. The first demon lifted its head slowly and stared at Yari with black eyes. Its mouth opened to reveal row after row of jagged teeth, and it hissed as it bounced like a cat, racing toward the Wall. The pack of demons rushed forward, their screeches echoing in the night, sending vibrations rattling her bones.

Yari crouched behind the parapet and held her machete at the ready. She heard the bellow of a horn signaling the start of the battle and knew there was no turning back.

She fumbled for a tlazon and sent one flying towards the approaching pack. Her fingers were slick with sweat, and it flew half the distance it should have. She wasn't cut out for this life; she shouldn't have made it as far as she did. Yari retreated backward.

Kiki was the one who had made a name for herself, the Sicario. Yari was nothing more than a liability, the shadow which trailed behind. The heat of shame brought a wave of tears to her eyes, and she angrily wiped them away. Only a true failure could feel this way, and it was no time to wallow in her own worthlessness. She had bigger problems, like the demons racing across the no-go zone. The squelch of mud filled the night with a dark symphony as the demon's talons and claws ripped through the earth.

Yari hurled another tlazon towards the approaching onslaught, her gaze focused on a scarred and horned demon shambling towards her. The foul creature had claws for hands and horns that shot out from its forehead. Red spikes covered its grey skin like jagged armor. The jade-tipped tlazon struck the demon's shoulder, and its mouth opened in a soundless scream as it grabbed the shaft sticking out of its shoulder.

The next few seconds happened in a blur. One moment Yari was throwing tlazons with wanton abandon, the next, her body was flung like garbage as the demon furiously hurled Yari into the Wall. Her head hit the stone with a crack, and her eyes locked on the ever-gaping maw of the beast. It glared hungrily at her and spat out a glob of foul saliva as it hunched over her. It leaned in closely, its black eyes the only things visible through the darkness of its cowl. Its lipless mouth revealed jagged teeth dripping with blood. The demon grabbed her with its claws and lifted her off the ground easily. Bony hands wrapped around her stomach as it threw her over its shoulder. Crouching low, its spider-like limbs bending at odd angles, the demon lurched back over the Wall, taking Yari with it.

A scream died in her throat as she struggled under the creature's vice grip. The demon sprinted across the no-go zone, its long skeletal limbs carrying her with inhuman speed toward the Cicatrix's dark, swirling mist.

Yari came to her senses and reached for a tlazon but found no more strapped to her chest. Frantic, she considered her options and ripped the bear tooth from her neck. Not that the tooth would kill the demon or even seriously maim it. But she had no more weapons and couldn't let herself die without a fight. She brought the tooth to her lips and kissed it tenderly like an old friend. Her heart thundered, and her senses came to her in sharp focus. She whirled around and plunged the tooth deep into the demon's neck; it shrieked and recoiled, dropping her into the cold mud.

Yari scrambled to her feet but slipped on the still-wet ground. She grabbed onto a branch and tried to get her balance but lost it and crashed into the ground. A cloud of mud surrounded her as she struggled to get back up. Claws gripped her ankle and yanked her back. The demon raced toward the Cicatrix, its claws and tusks flashing in the moonlight.

Yari dug her hands into the mud but only managed to uproot handfuls of soft wet earth. She slipped across the ground as the demon dragged her toward death. Then, her head collided with something hard, and everything went black.

Chapter Seven

PLAYGROUND

Kiki

K iki's leg throbbed from a shallow stab wound, and she bit her lip as she limped along the Wall's parapets. Fire and chunks of blackened stone scorched the Wall and hard turned the ramparts into some macabre demon playground.

The breach hadn't been easy to contain, and the Demon Corps had paid a heavy price for their victory. Broken bodies of hundreds of Slayers littered the Wall; their bodies ripped to shreds, and their eyes glassy with fear.

When Kiki reached the Wall last night, the attacking horde of demons had been thick and never-ending. Kiki's Slayer training had kicked in, and she'd joined the frantic efforts to defend the Wall.

A torrent of guilt washed over Kiki. She'd defended the Wall, but what about Yari? Who had defended her?

Kiki bent down over a Slayer and pressed her hand to their eyes, closing them forever. She hadn't known this Slayer. However, a distant part of her was grateful that she hadn't. Still, she whispered a blessing for this soul and moved on in search of Yarixa.

Each step Kiki took along the Wall made her feel heavier as if she were moving through honey. She moved very slowly, checking everybody she passed to see if a distraught Yarixa were under any of them. Hope sprouted in her stomach with every pair of eyes she closed that wasn't Yarixa's.

Thanks to Kiki's failure to find Yarixa immediately, she had the grim task of searching through the dead for her friend. Kiki ran through the events of last night and the early morning over in her head. Yarixa hadn't been among the huddle of survivors at debriefing. Nor had she been in the infirmary. No one had seen her, and no one knew where she could be.

The Wall was the only logical place.

Kiki fought back the tears that welled in her eyes. She wasn't ready to accept the truth. Not yet. Even though this—horror—was the nature of their job. None had any real choice once they aged out of the orphanage. They'd had two choices, the Demon Corps or panhandling on the streets.

Kiki paused in her task and faced the darkness stretched across the horizon. She cursed the Cicatrix and all the pain it had brought into her life. All she'd wanted was to keep her friends safe.

And she'd failed.

Kiki knelt next to a dead Yearling. Her obsidian machete gripped tight in one hand. Kiki pressed the dull eyes shut and stayed for a moment to pray. She hadn't prayed in years. But she'd done so twice within the last twenty-four hours. She figured now was as good a time as any to start.

Once Kiki had worked through sector seven with no signs of Yarixa, she moved on to the other sectors. It was nightfall by the time she finished sector one, and she still hadn't found her friend.

Kiki trudged through muddied snow as she made her way toward Commander Ramirez's tent to file her report. A familiar voice called her name, and Kiki spun around to find Luna racing to catch up, her long black curls bouncing in time with her steps.

"I heard what happened and came as soon as I could," Luna said as she bent over her knees to catch her breath.

Kiki's heart clenched at the sight of her friend. How was Kiki supposed to tell her about Yari? How was Kiki supposed to even tell herself? Feeling lost and a little disoriented from the lack of sleep, Kiki patted Luna stiffly on the arm and continued to carve toward Commander Ramirez's tent.

Confused, Luna grabbed Kiki's hand and pulled her to a stop. "What happened to your face?"

Dumbfounded, Kiki touched her face, the movement slow and hollow. When she pulled her hand back, white and black paint covered her fingertips. A sense of loss made her chest ache. "Yari painted my face for the carnival."

Luna turned her head left and right as if looking for someone. "Speaking of, where is she?" Luna asked.

Kiki's eyes watered at the question, and she hung her head. She didn't know. That was the problem. There was no body. Nothing on this side of the wall or the other. That was perhaps the worst part. She didn't have the answer.

"Kiki?" Luna asked and stooped down to see Kiki's eyes.

Kiki couldn't face her friend. It was too much. She shook her head.

Luna stood there, frozen, as a wave of understanding washed over her, dropping her jaw and crumpling her face into one of misery. She pressed a hand over her mouth to stifle the wail that escaped.

"No, please, no," Luna gasped as she started to run towards the Wall.

Kiki pulled her back. "She's not there."

Luna looked around frantic as if doing so would somehow manifest their friend.

Kiki glanced around herself, feeling lost. "She isn't anywhere."

Luna began peppering her with questions. Had Kiki checked the infirmary?

Yes.

What about the other sectors?

Yes.

What about the supply building? Kiki could have missed her.

Yes. And no one had seen Yarixa since. Kiki had asked.

Luna gripped the sides of her head with both hands. "I don't understand."

But there wasn't anything about their situation that was hard to understand. Not really. It was just that neither Kiki nor Luna was willing to face the truth. Not until they saw a body. Not until they had no choice but to accept it.

Inside the Commander's tent, a frenzy of activity reigned. Kiki shoved her way through the crowd of Slayers, Attendants, and Yearlings standing, talking, and yelling in the Commander's tent. They were waiting for their assignments.

She found the Commander's second-in-command standing in front of the Commander's desk. He looked harried as he balanced a notebook in one hand and scribbled notes with the other. He didn't notice Kiki's approach.

"Captain Bernat," Kiki said, approaching the burly man. "I need to speak to the Commander. It's important."

Bernat stopped what he was doing and gave Kiki his undivided attention. "I'll make sure you see her, but now isn't a good time."

Behind Bernat, an oak table sat in the middle of the tent. On the table, an Attendant spread a map of the Norceran base camp across its surface. Solana traced her fingers along the path of the breach adding colored flags to mark the breach points. A cold gust of wind blew through the tent, sending the flags flapping wildly.

Solana stood with her hands on her hips, her head tilted to one side, listening to a Slayer with long braided hair explain what they knew so far. Kiki waited patiently for the brief to end, but she decided she couldn't wait any longer.

"Commander Ramirez," Kiki interrupted the Slayer briefing Solana.

"Wait your turn," Solana said, not even looking up to acknowledge Kiki.

"The camp in Dolores reports similar numbers," the Slayer continued.

Kiki's anger boiled in her stomach. She needed answers, and she needed them now! Kiki slammed her hand against Solana's desk. "Listen to me!"

Solana peered up and pursed her lips. "Slayer Xochicale?" she said, her voice dripping with annoyance.

If it had been any other time, Kiki would have felt a small victory over Solana using her new title. But this was not the time for ego.

"Yarixa is missing," Kiki announced as she fought back the tears that threatened to spill over.

Solana's usually stoic demeanor faltered for a moment before she quickly recovered and donned her typical mask of detachment. "Thank you for reporting in. She'll be honored with the rest of our Slayers killed in action."

Kiki couldn't believe what she was hearing. "No. She's not dead, Commander. She's missing."

Solana's eyes narrowed. "There is no missing, Quirera. There is killed in action, and there is wounded."

Kiki shook her head violently. "No, I've searched the whole camp. I went through the entire Wall. She isn't here."

Solana seemed to contemplate for a moment. "If what you're saying is true, then perhaps there is a third explanation for her disappearance. One that you aren't bothering to consider."

Kiki and Luna exchanged a confused look. What was Solana getting at?

Solana moved a square piece from the map in front of her. "If Yarixa isn't anywhere in camp, and she's not one of the deceased. Then the only logical explanation is that she deserted." Solana tossed the wargaming piece off the map and let it roll to the ground.

Kiki felt like she'd been punched in the gut.

"She'd never do that," Luna spoke up. "Yari was loyal to the Corps."

Solana examined them both with her steely gaze. "She was also a shoddy Slayer and wasn't going to graduate this year."

Kiki and Luna exchange another confused look. "What do you mean she wasn't going to graduate?" Kiki asked, a sense of dread rising in her chest.

"Didn't she tell you?" Solana turned from the map to retrieve something from behind her. "I thought the three of you were close?"

"Tell us what?" Kiki growled as she stepped around the desk that separated her from within strangling distance of Solana.

Solana looked down on Kiki, a glimmer of pity in her eyes. "I issued Yarixa a notice of delayed graduation weeks ago. I'm surprised she didn't share this."

Kiki felt as if Solana had poured ice-cold laundry water on her head. "No." Kiki took a stunned step away. Even if Solana was telling the truth, Yari wouldn't—she couldn't. "I don't believe you."

Solana shrugged at that moment, and no other gesture of dismissal had ever infuriated Kiki more. "I don't know what else to tell you. The facts are there as plain as day. Now, if you'll excuse me, I have larger problems to deal with." Solana brushed past Kiki and resumed talking with the Slayer who'd been briefing her earlier.

Kiki let Luna lead her out of the tent. Once in the cold, Kiki whirled on Luna. "Did you know?"

"Me?" Luna asked with a hand pressed to her chest as if the question was offensive. "Of course not. I wouldn't keep something like that a secret."

"Wouldn't you, though?" Kiki felt like her world was spiraling.

"No." Luna drew back from Kiki, the hurt clear on her face. "If I had known, I would have convinced her to tell you." At the look of distrust on Kiki's face, Luna added. "I. Didn't. Know."

Kiki growled in frustration. "She wouldn't desert. That's not possible." She started to walk at a brisk pace. She didn't know where she was going. All Kiki knew was that she had to keep moving, or else the truth would catch up to her. And that was the last thing she wanted at this moment.

"Let's stop and think about this a minute," Luna said, breathless to catch up to Kiki.

"She didn't do it," Kiki snapped.

"I agree with you," Luna said, pulling on Kiki's arm to make her stop. "But we need to think about this logically. What sector was she assigned to last night?"

"Seven."

"And you said you checked the whole sector?"

"Yes. I checked and double-checked."

Luna contemplated this for a moment, her eyes moving as if seeing events unfold in her mind's eye. "Did you check the no-go zone?"

"Yes," Kiki said, throwing her arms in the air out of sheer frustration and the need to move. "The bodies that were down there were brought up. She wasn't among them."

"No. I mean. Did you go down there yourself? Physically?"

Kiki shook her head. Admittedly, she hadn't thought of that.

Luna's face brightened. "Then that's where we start."

Kiki followed Luna back to sector seven and allowed a flutter of hope to blossom in her chest.

Chapter Eight

TWISTED

Erasmo

Throughout his life, Erasmo Ozetero had acquired a handful of names. To some, he was a Prince of Ozero, a protector and Lord of the Eastern Territory. Other names weren't quite so flattering, but he loved them all the same. His enemies called him the Bastard of the East, and his personal favorite was the Demon Prince.

Perhaps he shouldn't have taken such pleasure in being called a demon prince, but it was the truest name of them all. After all, as each year passed, more and more of his humanity slipped away. As he'd seen with all the male members of his family, one day, he'd stop being a human and roam his shattered kingdom as a mindless bear.

Erasmo stood on the edge of a platform that jutted from the top of the northern tower. He looked down at his men as they milled about and shouted orders. The light breeze tugged at his shoulder-length hair, which Erasmo tied back with a strip of black leather. The wind carried the smell of freshly tilled soil, which led all the way to the southern fields, where his people were hard at work.

A small measure of pride blossomed in his chest. The Eastern Territory was the single largest stretch of undisturbed land, a sliver of what had once been the Ozero kingdom.

Erasmo caught movement out of the corner of his eye. His cousin, Mauricio, stood behind him with his fists balled up and several red blotches on his blue tunic. Erasmo turned and inspected his cousin's knuckles crusted with blood.

Erasmo raised an expectant brow. "I take it you failed?"

Mauricio scowled as he wiped a bead of sweat from his brow. "The bastard is tough. I'll give him that."

Erasmo huffed and pushed past his cousin, making his way toward where they'd set up the interrogation room.

Rows of windows lit the manor house from top to bottom. The four-story home had high ceilings, a large kitchen, three sitting rooms, and was large enough to house all of his family, which consisted mostly of males related to the Ozetero clan.

Erasmo passed a pair of men who were pointing and shouting. Within moments, an audience gathered as the men continued to argue. Erasmo shook his head and kept walking. There was only so much he could do to prevent in-fighting. Besides, once the two landed a few punches, they'd likely forget the reason for their quarrel and go down to the dining hall and get drunk on pulque.

As they drew nearer to the interrogation room, the air around them rippled with rippling shadows.

Erasmo turned to look at his cousin. Swirls of darkness radiated from his cousin's shoulders.

"Cut it out," he snapped.

Mauricio's jaw clenched, but Erasmo held his silence as he looked into his cousin's eyes.

They were glowing red.

Erasmo rolled his eyes at Mauricio's lack of control. At least when Erasmo's shadows came out, it was because he wanted them to.

Erasmo glared at his cousin. "Do you have no control? Tuck them away," he growled. "Now!"

Mauricio's forehead creased with anger, but the color of his eyes returned to their normal brown. "I can control it," Mauricio snarled. "But I'm not about to apologize for a little taste of blood."

Erasmo sighed. "Next time, try to wash the blood off your hands."

Mauricio nodded, but Erasmo caught him licking his knuckles like a cat lapping warm milk. "You're twisted," he said to his cousin before he opened the door to a dimly lit room and strode inside.

The walls were covered in grey peeling paint, and some chipped away to reveal patches of sheetrock underneath. Spiders had built a web across one corner of the room, where a few broken plates lay scattered on the wooden floor.

The only sound was the crackling flame of a lantern tucked into a corner.

A skull-faced man sat hunched in a rickety chair, his hands bound behind him with rusty iron shackles. Blood spotted the man's shirt and soaked the wooden slats under his chair. Bright purple bruising spread along the length of his jaw, and dried blood caked the gauze bandage wrapped diagonally across his face.

A small grin tugged at the corner of Erasmo's lips at the sight of the man's battered form. It had been a long time since he'd dealt with a stubborn captive. He could only hope this one would live up to his high standards.

Mauricio wasted no time in yanking the prisoner to his feet by his hair.

The man cried out in pain, and his head fell forward, the back of his skull connecting with Mauricio's chin. Mauricio hissed, his teeth bared in a feral grin.

The man lifted his head, and Erasmo got his first good look at the captive. His orange hair was a tangled mess, and scars marred his dirt-covered face.

This man was no stranger to battle, Erasmo could tell.

He lifted his left eyebrow in curiosity when he caught sight of the man's eye. A metal device covered the entire socket in the shape of a five-pointed star. The metal seemed inlaid with gems, and he could tell that the parts pressed into the skin around his eye were sharp and pointed. The man's left eye had been replaced with a metal replacement, but it hadn't been cheap.

Erasmo's lips curved up into a feral grin.

A low rumble left the prisoner's throat, and Erasmo rolled his eyes at the growl.

"You're the one who set fire to Arcediano." It was a statement, not a question.

Arcediano had been a flourishing village before the warlock had wreaked havoc upon it. Now, it stood in ruins and was nothing more than a memory.

The man lifted his dark gaze but said nothing.

Erasmo waited for the flash of fear he was sure he'd see. It always happened. No matter how strong a man was, there was always a moment of terror when he realized that he'd come to the end of his rope at the hands of the Demon Prince, and there was no hope of escape.

No fear flashed in those dark eyes.

Erasmo couldn't help the frown that formed on his face. It was a shame that he couldn't scare the man. The blood was sweeter when they were afraid.

Erasmo walked to the far end of the room and leaned on the cold stone wall, his arms crossed. "I can't help but wonder why you're so loyal to my brother." He arched an eyebrow when met with silence.

Erasmo lunged forward and knocked the metal star free with a single blow.

The man hissed, and his head fell forward.

Erasmo grabbed the man by his hair and yanked his head up.

The man's good eye widened, and he tried to jerk away, but Erasmo's grip was too strong.

"What is my brother planning?" Erasmo asked loudly and watched as the man's throat bobbed with a dry swallow.

"I will not betray the King," the man said hoarsely.

"There are no kings anymore," Erasmo scowled. "I'm not going to ask you again." He didn't wait for a response. He lifted the man from the chair and slammed his back into the wall. Erasmo grabbed the man's right wrist and turned it upward.

A black bear tooth was tattooed on the man's wrist. This was one of his brother's men, and Erasmo had no qualms about bleeding him dry.

Erasmo willed his claws to extend from his fingers. The man let out a pained grunt as he tried to pull away from the sharp pressure of Erasmo's claws singing into the back of his skull.

"Tell me, and you will be rewarded with a quick death. If not--well, I'm sure you can imagine," Erasmo said as he turned his gaze to Mauricio.

Shadows swirled around Mauricio, enveloping his frame in a black mist. His eyes glowed red again, and his teeth lengthened, revealing their razor-sharp points.

"My cousin likes to play with his food if you know my meaning," Erasmo whispered in the captive's ear.

"Long live the King," the man wheezed as he glared daggers at Erasmo with his remaining eye.

Erasmo growled as he hurled the man toward his cousin. "Have fun," he sneered as he stormed from the room.

"Always do," Mauricio purred.

As Erasmo closed the door behind him, the sound of flesh being ripped from bone filled the air, along with an agonized scream.

Erasmo pulled a handkerchief from his pocket and cleaned the crimson from his claws before retracting them.

"Bastard." A small growl clenched the center of Erasmo's chest. "But perhaps I should give my brother some credit. His people are loyal to his cause," he muttered as he headed to the dining hall. He needed a drink. And a stiff one at that.

There had been a time when Erasmo would have joined Mauricio in torturing the man, but not anymore.

He'd grown weary of war.

He'd grown weary of death.

He'd grown weary of fighting.

As he walked, an obsidian tooth bounced against his chest. The totem was warm and heavy in his hand as he tucked it back under his shirt.

It was only a matter of time before the totem stopped preventing the shift. But the alternative was somehow worse. If Erasmo wanted to be free of the curse, he'd have to fulfill the prophecy, and he'd long ago abandoned the idea.

He grunted when he shoved the door open to the dining hall. It was hot and humid, smelled like roasted meat, and the boisterous voices of his family members filled the room. Female voices were confident and ringing, and male voices were low, rumbling, and heavy.

Erasmo ducked his head and wove his bulky frame through the crowd, leaving a low-hanging bough of cigarette smoke in his wake. He picked a smaller table hidden in the shadows and plopped down onto a rickety chair, the wood groaning under his weight. He folded his hands behind his head and leaned back on the two back legs.

A serving boy hurried forward and placed a wooden tankard on the table. It was full to the brim with bubbly yellow liquid, and the smell of fermented agave filled the air.

Erasmo extended his hand for the glass when he felt a burning pain in his wrist and then yanked it back. A thin welt, shaped like a crescent moon, was raised on his wrist.

He placed the glass to his lips, ignoring the sharp ache in his hand. He choked back a cough as the bitter liquid scorched his throat. The burn intensified, and he squeezed his hand into a fist as he silently cursed it.

It had been a while since the mate mark had flared with life. A sharp pang of fear that wasn't his own wormed into his heart. He shoved the feeling aside with a sneer.

For as long as Erasmo could remember, he'd been plagued with feelings that were not his own. The feelings of his mate. Whoever she may be.

He smirked at the cruelty the mark represented. His love was a curse, a death sentence to the woman he was fated to love. The only way to end the Ozero curse was to sacrifice one's mate. A final punishment for the crimes of his father.

The prophecy was why Erasmo abandoned the idea of breaking the curse altogether. Because to kill one's mate was an unthinkable betrayal. It was akin to carving one's heart out with their bare hands. There was no worse pain than losing one's mate.

Erasmo drained the rest of his drink and slammed the glass on the table too hard. It shattered in his hand, splintered glass slicing into his palm. His face twisted, and he shouted a curse as crimson blood dripped onto the stained wood.

It didn't matter what his mate was feeling. He had to endure it. Ignore it even.

He had larger problems to deal with. Whatever his brother was up to, he had to end it.

CHAPTER NINE

DOOM DAYS

KIKI

K iki stood on the lip of the Wall and leaned forward as far as she dared. Luna slowly scaled down its length, her hands clumsily finding finger holds in the crevices between stones. A rope wrapped around her waist, and the other end tied to a stone parapet kept her from falling to her death.

Light snow danced in the air, gathering on the tips of Kiki's hair and eyelashes. A strong wind sent chills up Kiki's spine, and she hissed at the sting reddening her cheeks. Flurries spiraled in the air, casting a blanket over the no-go zone.

"Would you hurry up?" Kiki called down. "You're going to get us caught."

Luna's eyes were two blazes of fire as she glared back at Kiki. She made a rude sign with her hand and continued her descent.

Kiki glanced over her shoulder to check for any passersby. The surviving Slayers and trainees cleared sector seven and removed the bodies of their comrades for burial. A skeleton patrol kept Watch, despite the long previous night. All it would take was for one person to walk along this way and catch Kiki and Luna going into the no-go zone.

Kiki was talented at worming her way out of most situations. Still, she wasn't looking forward to squirming out of another, especially one that could get her and Luna sent to the dungeon for insubordination.

The Demon Corps deemed the no-go zone forbidden to enter without special authority. Usually, a Commander would supervise an excursion into the no-go zone so the Attendants could retrieve as many tlazons and jade arrows as they could find. After all, the Demon Corps didn't waste resources.

Luna yanked on the rope, and Kiki glanced back down. She'd made it down, her face smudged with brown, dried mud. Kiki stifled the urge to laugh.

Kiki scaled the length of the Wall in less than half the time it took Luna. Of course, Kiki had trained as a Slayer for the last four years, and Luna had joined the Healer Corps after two years as an Attendant. It wasn't a fair competition, but Kiki took pride in her accomplishment.

Kiki's heart pounded as she looked at all the blood on the ground. She saw faint shoe prints leading away from the Wall, bent twigs, bits of torn fabric, and tiny shreds of leathery-looking flesh.

Luna, too, started to examine the ground looking for clues. Though there were no more bodies on this side of the Wall, there were plenty of signs of struggle.

Kiki knelt and touched a track left in the mud. It was too large to be Yari's, but it had once belonged to someone. That thought alone sobered her enough to search the ground thoroughly. Every track, every divot in the mud, had once belonged to a fellow Slayer.

To someone who had dreams and aspirations. Someone who'd gone to bed hungry as Kiki had done on more nights than she could count. Someone who had joined the Demon Corps because they'd had no other choice.

Kiki continued to search. She stepped into a crater the size of ten Slayers laid down head-to-toe. What had caused such a large indentation? Kiki shuddered at the thought of a leviathan demon rushing from the woods. Fear pricked her spine, and she quickly squashed it back down. Now was no time for fear.

"Kiki!" Luna shouted from across the field. "Come."

Kiki turned on her heel and ran headlong toward her friend. A jolt of hope pierced her heart. Mud splashed up the length of her trousers and splattered her face.

Kiki skidded to a halt alongside Luna. There, squashed into the mud, lay Yari's bear tooth necklace.

Kiki gingerly lifted it from the mud as it made a sucking sound from the extraction. Kiki's lungs constricted as it suddenly became hard to breathe. Where was the body?

Kiki clutched the tooth to her chest as if, in doing so, she was holding onto Yari as well.

"Look," Luna said, her fingers pointing toward a set of deep gouges in the mud.

Kiki followed the trail with her eyes first. A casual observer might not have been able to notice the patterns carved into the mud. Thankfully, tracking was part of Slayer training and was one of Kiki's specialties.

Kiki slowly followed the trail, careful where she stepped as she scanned the field. A leviathan demon had pressed a large set of prints into the sludge. Alongside the paw prints were the distinctive divots of boot markings, as if someone had dug their heels in.

Kiki imagined the scene in her head. She pictured a four-legged creature with paws the size of a pig dragging a Slayer through the mud. The Slayer had put up a fight, and they'd tried anything at their disposal. They'd grabbed onto that root just over there. The root held until the Slayer's grip slipped. The previous night's story was all laid out in the mud, carved into it like a grim report.

Kiki paused in her imaginings and followed the rest of the trail. The markings continued well into the no-go zone. Kiki had to know for certain. What lay at the end of the trail?

Luna spoke suddenly, breaking Kiki from her dark thoughts. "Kiki," she hissed. She jerked her head to the red flags waving in the wind along an invisible line that separated the no-go zone from the Cicatrix. Despite the border markings, the actual Cicatrix still lay fifty paces away.

The wind kicked up, and the red flags flapped violently in the wind.

Kiki suppressed a shudder as the gale whipped through her hair. She told herself the cold made her shiver, not because she was this close to the Cicatrix.

Darkness moved between the trees of the Cicatrix like a mist of smoke. A feeling of dread dropped in Kiki's stomach the longer she stood near the border.

Kiki pressed the toe of her boot along that forbidden line. Even from this distance, she could tell that Yari's trail continued well into the heart of the Cicatrix.

Luna began to sob uncontrollably. "She's gone." She covered her face with both hands and sank to her knees. "I can't believe it."

Neither could Kiki. Not without a body. Not without absolute proof. "We have to find her."

At that, Luna lifted her face from her hands. "You can't be serious."

Kiki knelt in the mud to join Luna and took her friend's hands. "She's alive. I can feel it. We have to find her."

Tears drew a path down both sides of Luna's face. She opened her mouth to say something, then seemed to think better of it. She pulled her hands from Kiki and started to get up.

"I hate it when you do that," Kiki said, an edge to her voice that she'd never used with Luna.

"Do what?" Luna wrapped her arms around herself as if doing so would protect her from the harsh realities they faced.

"Shut down on me." Kiki pointed an amusing finger at her friend. "You have something to say? Then say it!"

Luna shook her head and started to walk away. "We should get back before someone notices."

Kiki wasn't going to let this go, not without a fight. Why was she the only one fighting for Yari here? "Stop doing that!"

Luna ran both hands over her face in pure frustration. "Doing what?"

Kiki took two long strides toward her friend, the air around her feeling full of energy as if the wrong move could ignite the air and set the world on fire. "Walking away. You can't turn your back on this. We have proof that Yari was here. In this spot. Those are her tracks." Kiki pointed aggressively at the trail. "She's probably hurt and scared. We have to find her!"

Luna released a heavy sigh. "We don't know any of that. You're just seeing what you want to see. Those could be anyone's tracks."

"And the necklace?" Kiki held Yari's bear tooth up by its leather string.

"It could have fallen off and been trampled by anyone." Luna chewed the inside of her cheek and whispered, "Or something."

"Or she could have left it here as a clue for us to find."

"Now you're not even making sense." Luna turned and started back toward the Wall.

Kiki shouted after her. "She'd never leave this behind. Not by choice."

But Luna pretended she didn't hear.

Kiki turned to face the darkness of the Cicatrix, a lone figure against the darkening landscape. She felt an uneasiness unfurl in her gut. It was a feeling she wouldn't be able to shake, even hours later.

K iki made the long walk back to camp alone. She went over the tracks time and time again in her mind. Yet they told her the same story no matter how she looked at them. How could Luna not see the same thing?

Frustrated and heartsick, Kiki scaled the Wall and, once within the inner walls, made her way to the wash house. Her green uniform was covered in ichor, blood, and mud from the long battle the night before, not to mention all the sloshing around in the no-go zone. She smelled like a raw fish market, and her hair stuck to her face.

Kiki pushed past her peers as she walked through the camp, ignoring their stares and the whispers they made beneath their breaths. She finally saw what the rest saw when she reached the washroom and stood before the line of sinks and the frosted mirrors hung above.

If she had looked like a beautiful nightmare just a day ago, then today, she looked like a hellish monster straight out of the tales the seniors would tell the Yearlings to keep them in line.

Yarixa's paint had smeared into a ghostly grey. Kiki's hair stuck to her scalp with blood and ichor, and her eyes dripped with black paint.

Fully clothed, Kiki stepped into the nearest shower stall and turned on the faucet. Ice-cold water splashed against her skin and seeped into the filthy green fabric of her uniform.

Kiki preferred a hot shower, but the frigid water was a stark reminder of where she was and who she was. After all, Kiki Xochicale was a Slayer. And a damn good one at that. She'd failed her best friend and yelled at her other best friend, all in a matter of twenty-four hours.

Kiki scrubbed her face until it was red and raw. Her shoulders shook from the cold, and she stared at the way the blood of her fallen peers swirled in a pool at her feet. She promised herself at that moment that she'd find Yarixa. Even if that meant deserting the one thing she'd dedicated her entire life to.

CHAPTER TEN

THE MIGHTY FALL

KIKI

K iki returned to the barracks to find her Slayer gear folded neatly on her bunk. She made a mental note to thank the Attendants on wash duty.

She peeled off her drenched green uniform and tossed it into the nearest wash basket. Not that she'd be coming back for it.

She tugged on the black leather of her gear and pulled the straps tight as she fit the machete onto her belt. She then slipped from the barracks into the shadows.

Kiki wasn't sure how she planned to get out of the camp. She knew she'd have to scale the Wall again, but doing so at night was more challenging than during the day. She supposed she should have left while she had been in the no-go zone, but she'd decided against that plan. After all, she couldn't just stroll into the Cicatrix without so much as a single weapon on her. What she was about to do was ridiculous and borderline insane, but she wasn't entirely stupid.

Kiki crept around the edge of the camp, keeping to the shadows and keeping her footsteps light. She didn't want anyone seeing her and wasn't in the mood to develop a plausible cover story.

Kiki wove through the green tents and cut a path toward the supply hall. She didn't have any belongings to speak of, but she needed more gear to last more than a few days in the Cicatrix.

Kiki crept along the outer wall of the supply hall, trying to quiet her footsteps as she headed around the corner to the back entrance. She tensed at the flickering light of a torch, but a pair of Yearlings rushed toward the mess hall, and the light faded along with their hurried footsteps.

She reached the back door and opened it on grit-covered hinges. Torchlight guttered from the storage room, their rosy light casting shadows on crates stacked atop one another and weapons piled on tables.

Kiki crouched over a crate to examine the contents. She contemplated taking a bludgeoning mace but decided against it. The mace, a fantastic close-combat weapon capable of severe damage, was too heavy and would slow her travel. Kiki found some tlazons, not freshly made nor as sharp as she would have liked, and wrapped them in some canvas cloth. She wouldn't have an Attendant picking up her tlazons and would need to keep a healthy supply on her at all times.

Kiki's heart jumped into her throat when she heard the whisper of boots on the stone floors. She spun, a tlazon in her hand, ready to send the lance flying at whoever had entered. She breathed a sigh of relief when she saw who it was.

Turi Artchete held a soldering iron and a piece of bread in one hand. His mouth fell open at seeing Kiki, and before he could say anything, Kiki rushed him, knocked the tool from his fingers, and pressed a hand over his mouth.

Turi's blue eyes widened as Kiki shoved him against a stack of crates, his eyes begging for an explanation.

"I'm leaving," Kiki said, her voice calm. "Tonight."

Turi tried to respond but couldn't get a word out with Kiki's hand over his lips.

"Promise you won't sound the alarm." Kiki hesitated a moment as she watched Turi's head nod in agreement.

She released her grip, and Turi let out a breath. "What are you thinking?" he asked. His eyes quickly scanned her, taking in the extra weaponry she'd secured for herself.

Kiki pressed a finger to her lips to remind him to keep quiet. "I'm going after Yari. She's still out there. I'm going to find her and bring her home."

Turi was speechless for a moment as her words slowly sunk in. However, his silence quickly shifted into a storm of confusion. "The

Commanders will charge you with desertion. If they catch you—"

Kiki ran a hand through her chin-length hair in exasperation. "I don't care. Doesn't anyone get that?"

"Why are you doing this?" Turi's eyebrows knitted together in concern.

"Because my best friend is alive. Because she'd do the same for me if roles were reversed. Because — because — I promised. I promised I'd always look out for her," Kiki said in a torrent of words.

"I know you're grieving," Turi said, his voice a comforting hum. "But you have to accept the truth. Yarixa is—"

"Don't you dare say it," Kiki said, pointing an accusatory finger in his face.

"Please don't do this," he said as she stepped closer. He placed his hands on her shoulders and gently squeezed. "This is a suicide mission," he whispered, pressing together in a grimace.

"I have to," Kiki said as she shook herself from his grip. "I can't let her go without knowing for sure."

Turi's shoulders sagged in defeat. Shaking his head, he said, "If you're going, I want you to have something." He left Kiki in the storage room and returned a moment later. He held the claws he'd been working on the previous day. "Take them. You'll need them where you're going."

Kiki pulled the claws onto her knuckles and made a swiping motion in the air with each one. Despite their size, the claws were perfectly balanced and felt like an extension of her own hands than a cumbersome addition.

"Thank you," she said as she tucked the claws into her belt strap. She hoped Turi knew how much she truly meant it. "I never deserved you. You're a good friend." With that, she kissed Turi on his cheek and slipped from the supply hall.

Kiki had one last stop before she left the camp. She made her way toward the infirmary, where she was sure to find Luna. She owed her friend an apology. She couldn't leave things the way she had in the no-go zone.

As Kiki slipped from shadow to shadow, she felt the unnerving sensation of being watched. Kiki paused and searched the darkness for any sign of someone following her. But the camp was a constant hum of activity, and no one seemed to notice Kiki lurking in the shadows.

Kiki shook the feeling off and continued towards the infirmary. It was probably nothing. Just nerves. After all, she was committing the highest form of treason in the Corps. It wasn't something she did lightly, and the nagging feeling in her gut was probably from the sense of guilt gnawing at her.

Kiki ducked into the infirmary tent through the back, much like she'd done to get into the supply hall. A sheet of linen was hung on a line to dry and provided the perfect cover. Kiki peered from behind the sheet to get a better view.

Healers tended to the wounded Slayers and Attendants who'd been injured in the recent breach of the Wall. They moved from cot to cot; their faces pale with exhaustion, and their white aprons smeared with blood stains and body fluids.

Luna's face was white in the dim lamplight, her worry lines deep. She fell to her knees beside an injured Slayer, who was curled on her right side on a hard cot. The girl's breathing was fast and shallow and blood-encrusted one nostril. Luna's hands hovered over the girl, her lips, pressed tight together, trembled as she used magic to ease the Slayer's suffering. The Slayer's hand twitched, then moved no more.

A tingle of fury pricked Kiki's skin. Clearly, Luna had been drawing on her own life force to heal these Slayers. Kiki couldn't help but feel that Luna shouldn't have to do that. Sure, it was her job, and Kiki knew that Luna did it willingly, but damn the Corps for not having a better solution than this.

Kiki tried to catch Luna's attention but was afraid to do something too noticeable. The last thing she needed was for the other Healers in the tent to take notice of Kiki as well.

Luna stood from the cot and wiped her hands on her apron. She whispered something to a nearby Healer and walked toward the back of the tent where Kiki lurked.

Kiki dove back into the shadows and pressed against a wobbly wooden table. Glass bottles of healing salve and poultices clinked together at her sudden weight. Kiki winced at the sound and hoped it wasn't too loud for anyone else to hear.

Luna ducked behind the sheet, and before Kiki could announce her presence, Luna said into the darkness. "Whatever you're about to do, I hate it already."

Kiki cursed under her breath. Did all her friends have to know her this well? Kiki slowly stepped into the light.

Luna crossed her arms over her chest. "What are you up to now?"

Kiki had the sense to cast her gaze to the floor. Now that Luna was here, the shame of having yelled at her friend washed over Kiki in waves. "I came to say I'm sorry."

Luna unfurled her arms. "I know."

Kiki crossed the space between them and opened her arms. Luna returned the embrace and, after a few seconds, let go. "Don't do it," Luna whispered.

"You don't even know what I'm doing," Kiki said, annoyance dripping through her voice.

"I don't have to know exactly what you're about to do to know that it's probably very stupid and most definitely dangerous." Luna pierced Kiki with her firm gaze.

Luna wasn't wrong. Kiki could accept that much. "Then you won't be surprised that I've come to say goodbye."

Luna shook her head, the lines on her face deepening. "Please don't go. Stay. We'll go to the South. Like we always planned. Just—" Luna swallowed the lump in her throat. "Just don't do this."

Kiki hugged her friend again. "I have to know the truth."

Luna's shoulder's shuddered as she began to cry.

"I'll come back for you," Kiki whispered into her friend's hair. "I promise."

Luna broke away. "The second you leave, they'll charge you with desertion. You can never come back here."

Kiki had thought of that. Of course, if she returned with Yari in tow and the story of her retrieval, surely the Corps would reverse the charges. At least, that's what Kiki told herself. It was either that or live the rest of her life regretting not following Yari's trail and never knowing what really happened.

"I will return," Kiki said and hugged Luna. "I promise."

"Don't make promises you can't keep," Luna sniffled.

Kiki broke the hug off and stepped back into the shadows. "I always keep my promises."

Kiki looked over her shoulder one last time before leaving the infirmary tent. Luna's eyes brimmed with unshed tears that she refused to let flow. Kiki felt a tug at her heart. This would be the first time they'd be separated in the fifteen years of knowing each other.

Kiki gave her friend an encouraging smile and ducked out of the tent before she lost her nerve. But Kiki wasn't expecting something, or rather someone, to be standing right outside the tent flap. She collided full-bodied into another Slayer dressing in full battle gear.

An apology died on Kiki's lips as she recognized the eyes that stared down at her.

Solana Ramirez's face was a mask of righteous fury. Kiki felt her stomach drop into her feet at the look on her Commander's face.

Well, damn.

Before Kiki could run for it, Solana grabbed Kiki by the collar of her Slayer gear and took Kiki down with a swipe to her ankles. Kiki fell to the cold hard ground with a grunt.

"I knew you were up to something," Solana said as she pressed her knee into Kiki's back.

"You're always up to something, Quirera. I didn't expect treason out of you."

Kiki turned her head just enough to look into Solana's cold gaze. "I've given my life to the Corps. This doesn't change that."

Solana sneered at Kiki. "We'll let a court-martial decide that."

Luna burst from the back of the tent at hearing the commotion but stopped short when she saw Kiki being detained by Solana. Luna seemed as if she was contemplating stepping in, but Solana stopped that, too, before Luna could incriminate herself. Solana drew her machete and pointed the tip at the center of Luna's chest. "If you know what is good for you, you'll turn around and go back to your job."

Luna opened her mouth to speak, but Kiki stopped her before she could incriminate herself. If Luna admitted to knowing Kiki's intentions, she could be court-martialed too. "It's okay," Kiki said as she pleaded with her friend. "I'll be fine."

Luna stood there for a moment, seeming to consider her options. Her eyes traveled down the length of the machete and the murderous gaze of Solana at the end of it.

Luna backpedaled into the tent without another word, letting the flap mask her from view.

Solana disarmed Kiki quickly, taking the tlazons, machete, and iron claws from her.

Solana inspected the claws. "These look like Artchete's work," she mused.

"I stole them," Kiki said quickly. She couldn't let Turi be dragged into this too. She cursed herself for putting her friends in danger. But more than that, she cursed herself for getting caught.

Solana clicked her tongue and glared down at Kiki. "How the mighty do fall," she said, her voice like icicles stabbing her back.

Kiki cursed herself and her stupidity. She should have paid more attention. She could have sworn someone was following her. She should have doubled back and made sure. Now, she'd put herself in prison, put friends in danger, and could never help Yari.

CHAPTER ELEVEN

HEATHENS

ERASMO

I n the deep mountains of the Eastern Territory, where the last glimmers of sunlight fell to the tops of trees and reflected on the earth like gold coins, men sparred with their blunted practice swords. Each man fell into a trance as he focused on his strikes, breathing in time to their swings. The air was full of barked commands and clashing steel. Their bodies were bruised by combat, and their spirit was hardened by determination.

Shadows crept across the square, growing longer and longer with the approaching twilight. Erasmo wiped his brow with a trembling hand and inched backward, panting. He turned his face to the cobalt blue sky, blinking at the afternoon clouds. The air smelled like fir needles and frost, filling his lungs with much-needed air. His muscles ached, and he pressed his hands to his knees to keep from falling.

Across the sparing square, Mauricio threw his sword down and sagged against the wall, breathing heavily. Clouds of dust swirled around him as he rolled over onto his hands and knees, trembling and coughing as he struggled to catch his breath.

"Tell me again," Mauricio shouted over the din of sparring men, "why you like to torture me." His cousin winced as he pulled himself to his feet.

"You rely too much on the shift," Erasmo chided. "You must learn to rely on your sword instead of the bear."

"I get that. What I don't get is why we have to train before dinner?" Mauricio whined.

Erasmo straightened and assumed a fighting stance. "Because you're out of shape and need the exercise," he snarled. "Stop stalling and fight me."

With a powerful swipe, Erasmo lunged forward, bringing his sword down to his right. Mauricio leaned back and barely avoided the blade, raising his sword to defend himself. The clashing of their blades sent sparks flying.

Erasmo turned and delivered a headbutt that forced his cousin to stagger backward and to the ground.

"Enough," Mauricio huffed, holding his hand up in defeat. "I can't take it anymore."

Erasmo held out his hand to help his cousin stand. "How that must injure that ego of yours."

Mauricio snarled, baring elongated canines.

Erasmo tipped his head back and laughed. "You're such a baby," he said, shaking his head. "Come on, let's go eat."

Mauricio leaped to his feet, suddenly full of energy. "Finally! That's what I'm talking about."

Erasmo tugged at his cousin's sleeve and pulled him across the training yard toward the dining hall. They each took a long sniff; the smells of warm bread and roasted meat wafted over them.

Mauricio's jaw dropped as he stepped into the room. The large dining hall looked like a cathedral decorated for a feast day. Tables were covered with heaping platters of fajitas, racks of succulent pork, towering pyramids of enchiladas, and platters overflowing with tortillas. The aromas made Erasmo's mouth water.

Mauricio's stomach gurgled audibly, and with a mischievous grin, he raced to grab a plate. Erasmo followed after his cousin, plucking a hot coil of carne asada from the grill and set it on his plate. He grabbed a stack of steaming tortillas and covered his food in chiles.

Erasmo led them to a long table and sank into the worn bench, his muscles protesting every movement.

Without warning, Erasmo's vision narrowed. The room's noise faded away, and all he could hear was the beating of his heart. A sharp pang of despair flooded the mate bond, causing him to freeze mid-bite and drop his fork. His eyes widened as a storm of pain and anguish coiled around his chest.

Erasmo had never felt such strong emotions trickling down the bond before. He tried to shove the bond away, but it was like trying to swim against a riptide. The bond pulled him under until all he could feel was the crushing weight of despair. His heart clenched in his chest, and he felt like he couldn't breathe.

Mauricio's face wavered in and out of focus as tears rose in Erasmo's eyes. He could feel his mate's pain as if it was his own, and it was almost too much to bear. Erasmo was suddenly filled with the need to reach out and comfort his mate. To ease her suffering. Blinding rage filled another part of Erasmo at whatever was causing her such anguish. He clenched his hands into fists, his knuckles turning white.

Against his will, Erasmo staggered to his feet and started towards the door, the compulsion to answer his mate's call overriding all else.

Mauricio pulled on Erasmo's sleeve, his face etched with worry. "What is it?" Mauricio asked, his hand going to the hilt of his sword.

Erasmo shook his head, not trusting himself to speak. The bond was pulling at him, insistent and demanding. The east. She was on the other side of the darkness. Unreachable.

A growl escaped his lips, and he braced himself against the table, the wood groaning under his weight.

"It's my mate," Erasmo said, his voice breaking into a sob. "Something's wrong."

Mauricio's eyes grew wide with fear and his mouth twisted into a grimace. "What do we do?"

Erasmo pushed past the pain, determination steeling his spine. "Where's Aurelia?"

His cousin, Aurelia, was the only member of his family who could safely cross the darkness.

Mauricio shrugged helplessly. "She hasn't returned from her last crossing yet. Knowing her, she's probably blazed out of her mind, gambling away our profits."

Erasmo clenched his teeth together so hard that it hurt. "Find her," he growled. Another pang of grief flooded the mate bond, nearly driving him to his knees. "Find her!" he roared.

Erasmo had tried to ignore the mate bond his whole life. But whatever this was, he could not in good conscience ignore. His mate needed him. Something primal within him ignited, and a roar of fury rumbled from his throat as he grabbed the table's edge and flipped it over, sending plates crashing to the ground.

The dining hall fell silent, and his family paused mid-conversation to stare at him.

Mauricio tried to pull Erasmo away, but Erasmo ripped his arm away. His breath came in ragged gasps and the air vibrated with swirling shadows. "Go now," he gasped. "Bring that weasel back. I don't care if you drag her back, kicking and screaming. Bring Aurelia to me."

Mauricio nodded and raced from the room, shouting commands as he went. The dining hall erupted into action as Mauricio called his men to him in search of their cousin.

A flood of rage filled him, and he felt the sudden need to spill blood. Whoever had hurt his mate would pay. Dearly. He'd savor their suffering for daring to lay a hand on her.

CHAPTER TWELVE

SARCASM

KIKI

Kiki shivered as a gust of wind spiraled through the dungeons. She tucked her knees to her chest and wrapped her arms around her knees to stay warm. The dungeon was a dismal place and full of criminals and traitors.

Kiki supposed she shouldn't complain too much. At least she had a view. A single window with iron bars was at the top of the far wall and was the only natural light source. Even though frost coated the bars and crept over the sill, Kiki still caught glimpses of the torches and fires sprinkled around the Norceran base camp. It was more than she could say for her fellow inmates cramped into their cells like cattle.

The dungeon was dank and dark. Torches lined either side of the narrow hallway, flames sputtering anytime the wind howled outside.

Kiki could hear other prisoners complaining about the cold and needing an extra blanket. She also heard other prisoners telling the complainers to keep their mouths shut or else. Admittedly, Kiki was part of the latter group. There was no sense in complaining about her situation. She'd put herself in it, after all.

The only thing Kiki was truly concerned about was whether or not Luna was being interrogated at this very moment. What about Turi?

Solana wasn't the kind of person to leave any stone unturned. When it came to Kiki, this was especially true.

What a mess. If only she'd have been smarter. Been more watchful. Then, Solana wouldn't have caught her.

A voice slithered through the darkness. "Don't see your kind here often."

Kiki peered through the bars of her cell and strained her eyes to see who spoke to her.

A girl about Kiki's age pressed her back to the cell directly across from Kiki's. Her hair was jet black, and her eyes were the color of the moon. Kiki felt a chill run up her spine at the sight. Those kinds of eyes weren't natural. Kiki wasn't sure what eyes like those meant, but she didn't think any good could come from them.

"So," the stranger drawled. Her accent was strange and lazy, as if she couldn't be bothered to form the sounds of words completely. "What did you do to get yourself tossed into this hell hole?"

Kiki narrowed her eyes at the question. Though she'd been an idiot to try going after Yari, that act alone didn't suddenly make her a criminal. Not like this girl who clearly was just that.

Though the lighting was dim, Kiki could still see enough of the silver-eyed girl. The stranger's clothes were a ragtag mashup of patterns and colors. To make matters worse, it was clear the girl hadn't washed her clothes in quite some time.

"Hello?" The girl said, turning towards Kiki. "Did they cut your tongue out or something?"

Kiki wasn't going to dignify that with a response. Kiki moved away from the bars and tucked herself further into the corner of her cell. If Kiki just ignored this girl, she'd likely give up.

"Hmm, shame. You know, the guards threatened to cut my tongue out too, but I guess they decided against it since my tongue is still flapping." She chuckled, and the sound echoed through the empty hall.

"I haven't had a decent conversation in weeks," the girl groaned. "Would have been nice to talk to someone new. Get some updates." There was a shifting sound like cloth against the stone.

Kiki peered through her side and saw that the girl had moved closer to the bars.

"Hey, I do have one question. You can just nod or shake your head. It's really a 'yes' or 'no' kind of question."

Kiki resisted the urge to roll her eyes at this impossible girl. She shrugged her shoulders in answer.

"Did the Protectorate ever handle that lice situation down in Oros?"

Kiki had no clue what this girl was talking about. Lice? In the capital? The Protectorate would never allow such a thing.

The girl didn't wait for an answer. She shuddered as if her skin were alive with crawling mites. "Terrible thing, lice. I had a bad case once when I was passing through Charloxtl. You don't even want to know where you can get lice." With that, she pointed to her nether region, and Kiki felt revulsion bubble in her chest.

At least the Corps had demanded good hygiene and clean clothing, even if those clothes were second-hand and held on by threads.

The girl seemed unfazed by Kiki's reaction as she continued to prattle on, "By the time I reached Gonzala, I'd gotten rid of them. Which was a good thing too because—"

The girl continued to talk, but Kiki was stunned by what she'd just heard. Oros? Charloxtl? Gonzala? Each of those cities was thousands of miles apart, not to mention that Gonzala was on the other side of the Cicatrix.

If she'd been in Charloxtl first, she'd have had to go all the way around to get there. That kind of journey could take weeks on horseback.

Kiki couldn't help her sense of curiosity. Who was this girl? And how did she end up on this side of the Cicatrix?

"You wouldn't believe the food they have in the West," the girl said as Kiki turned her attention back towards the other cell.

"Oh, what I would give for a churro." The stranger pressed her face to the bars. "But like a real one. Not one of those sad excuses for churros you have here in the East. I want one with real sugar and cinnamon."

At that, Kiki's ears perked up. Sugar? Cinnamon? Those were forbidden commodities; even then, only the very wealthy could afford both the cost to procure them and the bribe required by the Protectorate to turn their head at the transaction.

Kiki looked at the girl once again, and realization dawned on her. "You're a smuggler."

The girl didn't seem phased by the accusation. Instead, she seemed to take it as a compliment, which only served to fluster Kiki more.

"The best in all of Ozero," she said proudly. "Hey, you can talk! That's a relief; I was kind of getting tired of my own voice. But now that you can talk, we can be friends. It gets awful lonely down here."

Kiki felt annoyance surge in her gut. "I'm nothing like you, and I will not be your friend."

The girl scoffed at that. "I see your Slayer gear. Yet, you're still down here with me. Whatever you did, you got caught doing it."

Kiki felt anger coil in her stomach. "I was trying to save my best friend. That's a lot nobler than your sorry excuse for an existence."

The girl chuckled at that. "A girl has got to eat. There aren't many options for orphans. You would know since you're clearly one too."

Kiki drew back from the bars of her cell as if she'd been stung. "You don't know me. For all you know, I could come from one of the noble families in Oros. I could be a distant cousin to the royal family."

The girl shrugged at that. "Sure. You could be. But you aren't."

Kiki growled in response. She'd had enough of this conversation. It wasn't going anywhere, and she'd rather drown in the sorrow of her own thoughts than have this tit-for-tat with a criminal.

"So you were trying to help a friend," the girl prodded after a long silence. "What's so bad about that?"

Kiki pressed her lips closed.

"Oh," the girl said in a knowing tone. "It was that kind of friend, huh? Who were they? The partner to one of the Commanders?"

Kiki was shocked at the stranger's innuendo that Kiki had a fraternizing affair with a higher-ranking officer.

"Oh, no!" The girl continued. "Were you helping the General's partner? "Her strange eyes widened in shock. "Wow, tough beat, my friend. It was worth it, right?"

Kiki finally had enough. "I did not engage in a fraternizing relationship with a superior officer. And I resent the suggestion that I'd do anything like that."

"Touchy." The girl snickered. "Okay, then, what did you do?"

Kiki sighed in defeat. This girl would never shut up unless Kiki told her. At least, that's the lie Kiki was willing to let herself believe. Perhaps she'd die of being talked to death, and she wouldn't have to face the court martial after all.

Secretly, Kiki was glad to pour out everything she'd been carrying the last few days. She told the stranger in the cell across from her everything. From her last night on watch with Yarixa, to the showdown with Solana, to the graduation carnival, to the breach, and the moment Solana caught Kiki going after Yarixa in the Cicatrix.

It did feel good to let it all out. Once Kiki was done, she took gasping breaths and wiped the tears from her eyes. At some point, she'd started crying. Kiki hated crying in front of people, and the embarrassment of having cried in front of some random girl washed over Kiki like a wave.

"That's some serious stuff," the girl said. "You've had a crap week."

Kiki didn't need some stranger to make her feel validated in her decisions from the last week, though, if she were being entirely honest with herself, she did feel some small pleasure in someone else's approval.

"I just want to know what happened to her," Kiki said after a few moments had passed. "I feel like a piece of me has been ripped away, and I can't let Yari go without knowing if she's still out there or if that piece of myself is truly gone."

"Yeah," the girl said, sounding thoughtful. "You know, if your friend did survive the other night and was dragged into the Cicatrix, then she's never going to be able to make it back out."

Kiki blew out a frustrated breath. "You too? I thought you were on my side here."

"No! That's not what I mean—"

The girl was cut off when a metal door burst open, and a lone figure swept into the hallway. The girl quickly ducked into the shadows of her cell and hid from view.

Kiki's mouth dropped at recognizing the person standing in the dungeon. "Luna?"

Luna drew closer to Kiki's cell and knelt in the dirt to be eye-to-eye with Kiki. "I'm going to get you out of here."

"Absolutely not." Kiki hissed as she frantically searched the darkness for any guards. "You're going to get caught and thrown in here right next to me."

"It's okay. I have a plan," Luna said as she pulled a jar of clear liquid from her apron pocket.

Suddenly, the walls shook as an explosion on the upper levels of the dungeon went off. Small rocks in the ceiling shook free and fell to the ground in a puff of dust.

Luna tossed an annoyed glance upwards and quickly poured the liquid onto the metal hinges of Kiki's cell door.

"What was that?" Kiki asked, eyes still cast upward as the sounds of shouting and boots against stone echoed through the stone passages.

Luna shrugged. "Just a small part of the plan going off a bit early."

Kiki stepped back in shock. "You didn't...." Kiki couldn't find the words. What had she dragged her friend into? What had Luna just done?

The hinges to Kiki's cell started to smoke and sizzle as the iron slowly melted away. An acrid scent wafted into the air, burning Kiki's nose.

"What is that stuff?" she asked Luna, covering her face with her hand to filter the worst of it.

"Trust me," her friend replied, screwing the top back onto the jar. "You don't want to know."

Another figure careened around the corner. Before Kiki could warn Luna that someone was coming, she recognized the newcomer as none other than Turi.

Luna whirled on him. "What happened to following the plan, Turi?"

Turi wiped a bead of sweat from his brow. "You said once they were all in position to set them off!"

Luna groaned. "I didn't think you'd place them so quickly. And what's with all the shaking? The jalapeño bombs shouldn't cause so much commotion."

Kiki's head whipped back and forth between her friends as they bickered.

Turi rubbed the back of his neck and grimaced. "I may have accidentally placed one too close to a support beam, and it may have started a chain reaction."

Luna's mouth fell open. "How bad of a chain reaction?" she growled.

Turi winced. "The administration office may be caved in at the moment."

"You idiot!" Luna screeched.

Kiki shook the bars of her cell and growled. "Can someone please tell me what the hell is going on here?" she shouted to be heard over the sound of distant rumbling. "What's Turi doing here? And what is a jalapeño bomb?"

"I'll explain later," Luna said, pointing to the melting metal hinges. "The solvent is almost done, and we'll have to haul out of here or risk being crushed to death. No thanks to someone," she said, casting Turi a scathing glare.

A voice chimed in just then, and both Luna and Turi wheeled around to face the stranger in the cell across from Kiki.

The silver-eyed girl smiled coyly. "You wouldn't happen to have a little extra of that magic juice, would you?"

Luna fixed the girl with a glare. "And who are you exactly?"

With a flourish of her arms, the girl scrambled to her feet and announced, "Aurelia Ozetero, at your service."

"Don't pay her any attention," Kiki spoke up. "She's a smuggler."

"You wound me, friend," Aurelia said as she placed her hands over her heart in feigned hurt.

Luna whipped her head between the cells. "I see you've been busy," she said to Kiki, her brows knit together in disapproval.

"I am not friends with that girl," Kiki pointed at Aurelia. "She nearly talked me to death when I was minding my own business."

Luna snickered at that. "Wow. Got a bit of your own medicine, I see."

Kiki saw the humor dancing in her friend's eyes and quickly pressed her lips together to hold back her retort. However, she did stick out her tongue instead.

The solvent finished its job, and Turi helped Luna to pull the metal door off the hinges. "What's a girl like you doing in a place like this?" Turi said with a mischievous glint in his eyes as he offered her a hand up.

Kiki took the proffered hand and wiped the dust from her gear. "Don't think flirting with me for a second will get you off the hook. I still demand to know what you're doing here."

Turi grinned. "Proving that I'm not the one who needs rescuing."

Kiki ground her teeth at his response.

"Wait," Aurelia said as Kiki and her friends started to leave. "Take me with you!"

Luna hesitated, but Kiki pushed her friend forward. The last thing any of them needed was to add breaking out a real criminal from Demon Corps custody.

"I can help you find your friend!" Aurelia shouted, her voice desperate and frantic. "There are many ways into the darkness, but only one way out if you don't want to become a raving demon-possessed creature! Trust me, I've seen it happen. You can't just walk out the same way you walk in. The curse will take you!"

Kiki exchanged a worried glance with her friends. Luna's eyes were wide with fear, and Turi's face was no better.

"Do you think she's telling the truth?" Turi asked in a whisper.

"Not in a million years," Kiki said in a huff. "But I'd rather be wrong than risk not bringing her."

Kiki held her hand out to Luna for the jar with the solvent and returned to Aurelia's cell, her face a storm of murder.

"You won't regret taking me; I've crossed the darkness hundreds of times. I'm an expert," Aurelia said in a blur of words.

"Shut it," Kiki said between clenched teeth. "If you double-cross me, I swear—"

Aurelia placed a hand over her heart. "I'll help you find your friend and get you safely out."

As the solvent went to work on the iron hinges of Aurelia's cell, Kiki couldn't help the feeling that this was a bad deal and that she would regret making it. In any case, it's not like she had all that many options, to begin with.

Chapter Thirteen

UNSTEADY

Yari

Groggily, Yari opened her eyes. Groaning, she clenched her fists and breathed deeply, coughing at the putrid air. She wrinkled her nose at the rotten stench of decay. She ran trembling hands over her arms and recognized the texture of stringy hair stuck to her battle leathers. Her mouth was sticky, and her tongue was coated with a bitter taste, resulting from a full stomach emptying into the dirt.

She blinked against the fading light and was confronted with the sight of scalped heads, protruding ribcages, and sodden flesh sprawled

139

in the snow as a host of demons feasted on the bones of the dead.

Yari waited for them to attack, but instead of attacking, they circled her slowly and hissed. She saw their fangs and the thin, worm-like tongue that flicked between their clawed fingers. When she turned her head, she saw a swarm of bugs and maggots crawl through the dirt behind a demon and follow it as it walked. The insects covered its feet and toes, wiggling up and down in the dirt next to the demon.

The demons' bodies were gray and scaly, chunks of fresh meat and dried blood covered their jaws, and their eyes were wide with hunger.

Yari flinched as they bound her hands behind her back and wrapped a thick rope around her waist. The rough fibers cut into her flesh, and she groaned as the rope dug deep into her skin.

The demons barely noticed Yari as they walked around her and sniffed the air. One of them, with black, wrinkled skin, a forked tongue, and beady eyes, stepped close to Yari and wrapped a scaled hand around her throat.

She choked and gasped for air, thrashing wildly at the rope binding her hands.

Just when Yari felt her vision blurring, an immense shadow the size of a bear shot from the darkness fast and with a thunderous roar. The bear ripped the demon's hands from her throat, and she gasped for air.

The shadow looked back at Yari, bright blue eyes glistening in the moonlight, and she saw that it was a bear. Shadows swirled around the bear's massive frame, its silver fur glittering in the moonlight.

It stood on its hind legs, towering above the demons, and flexed its claws as it bellowed, the sound shaking the snow from the branches above.

The bear ripped through the demons, twisting its claws in their chests, tearing their heads from their necks, and squishing them flat. The sound of bones breaking and bodies ripping as if they were made of paper was sickening. Deep inhuman growls echoed from the massive shadow as it carved a path through its enemy.

The bear slashed one demon across the chest, slicing through skin and muscle like it was made of cheese, and then crushed another against a tree with its forearms, flattening the demon's face and spraying the snow with black ichor. Huge black-clawed hands pulled three more demons by their necks into the air and snapped their spines with a resounding crack.

Entrails spilled from the bear's teeth as it tore through the demons until none remained.

The bear lumbered forward, and Yari looked away, so she didn't have to meet its gaze. She heard the bear's heavy breathing and winced her eyes shut. She readied for the attack, her whole body tensing. The inside of her mouth became dry, and her throat tightened.

She didn't want to die. But she was trapped, and the more she struggled against her bindings, the tighter they became.

A strong hand cupped her face and pulled her chin forward. Yari's eyes fluttered open and met a dazzling pair of blue eyes. A man pressed his rough, calloused hand to her cheek.

"You're safe," the man said, his voice a deep rumbling melody.

Yari's head felt light, and her vision blurred, darkness wrapping around her, taking with it the man and his brilliant eyes full of concern.

Chapter Fourteen

UNCONSOLABLE

Kiki

With Aurelia and the others in tow, Kiki, Luna, and Turi inched down the dark corridor. The flickering torches cast only a meager circle of light, so they had to inch their way through the dark passageway and take great care not to stumble. As they advanced, the air grew colder and danker. Soon they were surrounded by the smell of damp stone and mildew.

Kiki wrinkled her nose and breathed through her mouth. "The Corps should be ashamed of the state of this place," she whispered.

The group rounded two corners without running into any patrols or guards on duty. But they still had three more turns to make before they reached the main landing, and there were the rumbling walls to deal with.

"We're almost there," Turi said under his breath, casting anxious looks over his shoulder.

"Quiet," Luna said, her voice barely above a whisper. "I hear feet."

Kiki's heart dropped through her middle and landed somewhere in the pit of her stomach. Her mouth went dry, and her tongue stuck against the top of her mouth.

Luna crouched on one knee, motioning for the others to do the same. The footsteps drew closer still, and Luna held up a finger to hush them. Kiki could only hear her own heartbeat as it pounded hard against her ears. The footsteps halted, and the team held their breath.

A voice rang out—a throaty, low voice—and Kiki's blood turned to ice. Solana Ramirez sure had the worst timing.

"Turi?" the voice said, echoing off the walls. "Is that you?"

Turi's eyes grew round with fear, and he shook his head in reply.

Luna nudged Turi forward, forcing him around the corner and right into Solana's path.

"What are you doing here?" she asked, looking over his shoulder.

Kiki stood as still as a stone statue. She didn't dare move a muscle or breathe too hard lest Solana would hear the three of them hiding around the corner.

"I was just—"

"You were visiting Xochicale, weren't you?"

Turi grunted his response, and Kiki silently cursed him for freezing up like a doe in the hunter's sights.

Kiki had no idea how Solana would react if she knew that both Luna and Turi were trying to help Kiki. One thing she did know was that Solana would throw her friends into the dungeon and that she'd never be able to see any of them ever again. They would likely be separated, maybe even executed. Aurelia would be taken in for questioning, and Kiki had no idea what kind of lies the smuggler might tell.

"You could do better than her, you know," Solana mused. "Either way, it's none of my business. I'm glad I ran into you. Go upstairs and assess the damage. You're good with engineering, and it'll be a few days before the Engineering Corps receives our message for help."

Turi hesitated, and Kiki prayed that he didn't look over his shoulder, pinpointing their exact location.

"Now," Solana barked, her voice echoing through the stone halls.

"I—I just have a few questions," Turi stammered.

Solana grunted and crossed her arms over her chest. "Fine."

Turi started to fire off a series of statements full of facts and figures that made Kiki's head spin.

Time ticked by ever so slowly as Turi prattled on. How long had it been? Minutes? Seconds? It was all the same if Solana peeked around that corner—all of it would be over.

From the corner of her eye, she saw Aurelia sneak back the way they had come. Aurelia held a finger to her lips and a smile on her face.

What was she doing? Kiki wanted to yell at the girl, tell her that whatever half-baked idea had popped into her head would get them all thrown right back into the dungeons. But her throat wouldn't move.

Turi kept up his run-on sentence, and Solana's voice suddenly rang out again.

"I'm sorry, Turi, I don't have all night. I don't know all the specifics. Right now, I need you to go upstairs and do what you can to stabilize the building."

"Yes, Commander," Turi stuttered. "At once."

"As you were," Solana said, her tone clipped as she headed down an adjoining hall.

Kiki's breath caught in her throat as the Commander's footsteps receded, leaving a lone silence that was broken only by the pounding of her heart. She let out a long sigh as Luna rose from the ground and Turi rounded the corner to meet them.

"That was close," Aurelia whispered.

"Hey, where did that girl go?" Turi asked, eyes scanning the darkness for the smuggler.

Suddenly, there was a reverberating clang as a metal door slammed shut.

"What the hell?" Solana said, her voice like ice.

Aurelia ran down the hall, a battle cry sailing from her lips as she ran straight for Solana and raised a glass jar into the air. It was the jar of solvent that Luna had brought with her. Only now, it glowed with the light of the noonday sun.

"That's not good," Luna mumbled.

Solana whirled at Luna's voice, and her eyes locked on Kiki. "You," she seethed.

Kiki lunged, snatching Luna's arm and yanking her into the safety of the darkness. Turi chased them, stumbling over his own feet until Solana caught him around the waist and threw him to the ground. She caught up to Luna and grabbed her hair, yanking her off her feet.

Kiki stopped dead in her tracks and pulled her machete free. "Let them go."

Solana clenched her fists, and the corners of her lips were turned down. She glared with such intensity that Kiki's insides cowered away. "What is the meaning of this?" Solana said in a low growl. "Turi? Luna? How could you?"

Just then, Aurelia caught up to them and skidded into the hallway, the bright light from the jar engulfing them. Solana shielded her eyes, and her grip slipped on Luna's hair.

"Duck!" Aurelia yelled and threw the jar of solvent ahead of her.

Kiki threw herself to the ground, pulling Luna with her. Solana and Turi weren't as lucky. A flash of light and a plume of smoke hit them, and then a split second later, the hissing burn of solvent splashed over their bodies.

Aurelia raced forward and yanked on Luna's arm. The two of them ran towards the opening of the corridor ahead, leaving Kiki and Turi to fend for themselves.

Kiki couldn't see Solana through the dark gray miasma that now swept down the corridor like a slow-moving wave. Turi groaned in pain, drawing Kiki to his side.

The moment she touched his shoulder to help him up, warning bells rang through the dungeon, the sound so loud that it knocked Kiki to her knees. She covered her ears to muffle the sound, but it didn't help. It kept getting louder until she was sure her head would explode.

"Kiki!" Luna called out through the ringing in her ears. "The exit, now!"

Kiki staggered to her feet, her limbs feeling heavy. "We're not leaving him!"

Kiki pulled at Turi's uniform, desperate to get him away from the vapors.

"Help me!" Kiki cried to Luna, who came running back and grabbed hold of Turi's shoulders just as Kiki grabbed his feet.

Solana rolled on the ground, her face contorted with pain. Steam rolled off her as the acid ate through her uniform.

"You'll pay for this," Solana said. "I swear it." Solana's hand darted out and snaked around Kiki's ankle.

Kiki screamed at the contact from Solana's hand on her ankle. Her skin burned and blistered at the touch. Kiki yanked her leg away.

"We have to go!" Luna cried as she yanked on Kiki's arm.

"What about her?" Kiki said, her conscious rebelling against her. Solana was many things, but she didn't deserve this.

"Leave her."

"We can't!" Kiki tried to pull her arm away, but Luna's grip was like a vice.

"L—let's go!" Luna pleaded. "We have to."

Kiki glanced backward one last time. The skin of Solana's face bubbled, and her eyes were bright red. Still, that didn't stop the Commander from pulling herself together and lurching to her feet.

A sense of awe filled Kiki at how Solana staggered forward as if she intended to pursue them still. As if she weren't minutes from death.

Aurelia was already running ahead, Turi's arm draped over her shoulder as she dragged him with her.

"There's the exit," Luna cried.

As they emerged from the dungeon, the sky above was pale and hazy. There was a faint sulfuric smell of burned stone as she stumbled into the Demon Corps camp.

Kiki's mouth was full of bitterness she couldn't quite make out. It was the sour taste of nausea and the bitter flavor of acid in her throat. What had she just done?

There was no coming back from this, not after leaving Solana like that.

Despite the fatigue that pulled at Kiki's very bones, she knew they had to push on. The Wall and the Cicatrix were close, and a storm was brewing. There was nowhere left for them to go except forwards in this new world.

for her. But watching as the solvent ate through Solana's uniform—the way her skin had blistered and bubbled. It was enough to make bile rise in Kiki's throat.

"Are you okay?" Luna asked as they slowly picked their way through the tangled brush.

Kiki hung her head until her chin touched her chest. "What happened back there—it was messed up."

Luna shivered as if the mention of it gave her the chills. "We had no choice."

But that wasn't entirely true. They did have a choice, and Kiki knew that. At the very least, Kiki could have faced her sentence. It was the right thing to do, and her choice to skirt the law had ended up in Turi getting hurt and Solana's death.

"I don't like this place," Luna said, bringing Kiki back to the present.

The Cicatrix was a line of blackness that rose against the pale winter sky. Its cadaverous edge was like an hourglass, an abyss on the horizon.

Kiki had never been this close to the Cicatrix before. The closest she'd come was the other day when she'd toed the line of red flags set out by the Corps. They'd crossed that forbidden line several hundred paces back, and Kiki had been on edge ever since.

Kiki tried to slow the hammering of her heart, but it was no use. Something about being this close to the darkness made all of her senses turn on high alert.

Luna, for her part, looked like she was going to be sick. Her footsteps were hard and heavy, like they were full of lead. The rhythm of her steps thudded like a syncopated heartbeat, erratic and anxious. Even her pace slowed as they neared the swirling mists of darkness.

"Do you smell that?" Kiki whispered to Luna as they drew closer. The very air around the Cicatrix smelled burnt, like sulfur, and the sickly sweet smell of decay. Kiki licked her dry lips and instantly regretted it. The air itself tasted vile. If evil had a taste, it would be this.

Luna rubbed her arms with her hands. "I-I don't think we should do this."

Kiki didn't blame her friend. Kiki thought much the same. With every step, it felt like a spider inched down her spine.

A branch snapped behind them, and Luna's face paled. She whirled around as if she expected to meet her death.

Kiki put out a hand to brace her friend. "Calm down. It's just Turi and Aurelia."

Luna's eyes were frantic as she nodded, but Kiki could tell that her friend was still on edge. She stopped walking, and her shoulders shook.

Aurelia caught up to them with Turi's arm slung over her narrow shoulders. "You feel it, don't you?" she asked, looking over Luna's shivering form. "It's the darkness. Don't let it get to you. It'll feed on you if you let it." Aurelia pushed forward and led the way.

Kiki didn't know what Aurelia meant by that. How could the Cicatrix feed off of anything? Kiki thought the darkness was just a bunch of swirling mist that divided the kingdom. That's all they'd been taught about it in the Corps. The darkness came, and the monsters with it. End of story.

"Maybe this wasn't such a good idea," Luna said in hushed tones so that only Kiki could hear. She still hadn't moved and seemed like she was seconds from bolting.

Kiki was starting to wonder the same thing. Maybe this whole thing had been a mistake. Kiki shoved that thought into the back of her mind and took a moment to evaluate the situation.

Maybe this *was* a mistake. But it was a little late to consider that now, especially when they were so close to the Cicatrix. Right now, all that mattered was getting to the other side.

Kiki placed a hand on Luna's arm, hoping the mere contact would comfort her friend. She was careful with her words, afraid that if she spoke too loudly, she might further spook Luna. It was as if Luna were a frightened deer caught in the hunter's sight.

"I'm scared too," Kiki said, her voice hushed. "Remember why we're out here. We must try if there is any hope that Yari is out there." Kiki felt like she was saying this as much to herself as to Luna.

Luna met Kiki's eyes with her own. Within them, Kiki could see a shadow of darkness swirling as if Luna were trapped in a living nightmare. Kiki felt a shiver run the length of her spine at seeing the terror in Luna's eyes.

"We'll do it together," Kiki said and held her hand out.

Luna was slow to take Kiki's hand but eventually did, and together they staggered toward the expanse of the Cicatrix looming ahead. As they approached, the mists within started to move like a wave swelling as if in greeting.

The air thickened, and Kiki could almost feel the heavy press of dark energy against her body as if someone had thrown a blanket over her.

"Just push past the feeling," Aurelia called back to Kiki and Luna. "Once we pass the boundary, it'll fade."

The darkness grew heavier and thicker as if a tidal wave was racing toward them. Every instinct in Kiki's body told her to run. This was a place of evil. With each step she took, that feeling magnified tenfold until every breath became a chore.

"Don't let go," Luna whispered. She tightened her cold fingers around Kiki's in a death grip.

"We're almost there," Aurelia said up ahead. "Just a little further."

The darkness crashed over them like a curtain drawn over a window. Kiki could no longer see the light of day or feel the sun's warmth on her skin. The sensation of the dark energy pressed in against her, and she could barely see her own hand in front of her face.

"What's happening?" Kiki called ahead to Aurelia. She could no longer see the other girl.

"Keep moving!" Aurelia shouted back. "None of it is real. It's all part of the illusion."

Kiki didn't know what to think of that. Her heart hammered in her ears, and her skin prickled with gooseflesh.

Kiki blinked hard, trying to get her bearings. She pulled Luna closer until she linked their arms. Whatever happened, she could not let go.

Up ahead, there was a glint of metal in the distance, a glimmer of something pure. Whatever was up ahead sparked hope in Kiki's heart. All she had to do was get to that glowing beacon of light. Everything would be okay if she could only reach that point.

Kiki's legs and heart worked in unison. She could feel the surge of hope pulsing through her limbs as she pulled Luna to catch up to Aurelia and Turi.

The only thought in Kiki's mind was that she had to reach that pureness beyond. Still, she could feel the darkness trying to break her resolve, and every step was like fighting against quicksand.

In the distance, Kiki caught sight of fireflies flittering around, dancing with each other in the darkness. The light from the fireflies illuminated a small figure dressed in Slayer leathers.

Kiki could hardly believe her eyes. "Yari!" Kiki called out, convinced that the apparition before her was, in fact, her friend.

Out of the darkness, Aurelia and Turi staggered towards Kiki and Luna, having doubled back. "Keep up," Aurelia chastised. "Trust nothing."

Though Kiki heard Aurelia, she also felt like a thread was tugging her toward the figure in the shadows. Kiki pulled Luna toward the figure she was so sure was her friend.

Aurelia held out an arm to stop her. "Don't you listen? It's not real. Fight the feeling." Aurelia yanked Kiki's arm and pulled her away from the illuminated shadow.

Kiki wanted to scream and run back to that figure. It was Yari. She was sure of it!

"Keep moving!" Aurelia shouted as she tugged on Kiki's arm and dragged her forward.

"I can't leave Yari behind." Kiki tried to resist, but Aurelia's strength was inhuman. Her friend was there. She had to go back!

"That is not your friend," Aurelia shouted into the darkness. "It's the curse trying to trick you and trap you here."

A black hand reached out of the darkness and wrapped around Kiki's ankle. The hand sure felt real despite what Aurelia said about nothing being real. The grip tightened around Kiki's ankle until it felt like her bone might break. That, too, felt real enough.

An inhuman wail pierced the air, like a wolf howling at the moon, only this was colder and darker. Terror like molten tar poured through Kiki's veins. If she gave in to this feeling, it would harden into amber, and she'd be stuck in this feeling forever.

The hand from the darkness grew stronger, pulling Kiki back. "Help me!" It wailed with Yari's voice. Kiki's heart clenched at the sound.

"Don't listen to it," Aurelia said, her own voice strained and cracking.

A black tentacle whipped out of the darkness and wrapped around Aurelia's ankle, trying to pull her back.

"Don't do this," the voice said to Aurelia, only this time, it was a man's voice.

Aurelia shouted, "Leave me alone!" She kicked at the tentacle, and it swirled into mists of smoke.

Luna screamed as a swarm of black tentacles wrapped around her leg, pulling her back as well.

"RUN FASTER!" Aurelia yelled.

Kiki held onto Aurelia as if she were a lifeline and ran headfirst toward what she hoped was the exit. She kept her grip firmly on Luna, afraid that she'd never see her friend again if she let go.

Tree limbs and shrubbery tangled at their feet, slowing their progress and clawed at them as they ran. They ran until they couldn't breathe. The darkness was seemingly never-ending, the pull of the Cicatrix relentless.

They ran for what felt like an eternity but kept their feet moving at Aurelia's insistence to keep going.

Just when the darkness felt suffocating, like a sack had been thrown over Kiki's head, and the air was running out, her group broke through the barrier and stumbled into a clearing.

Kiki fell to her knees along with Luna. Their hands were still clasped, and their breaths were heavy, misting into the cold air.

Aurelia and Turi were crouched as well, their own chests heaving for breath.

"We made it!" Aurelia exclaimed.

Yes, they'd made it out alive. Kiki felt instant relief as the feeling of despair and terror slowly faded away. She'd never felt more scared in her entire life.

Next to her, Luna started to cry, and Turi looked pale and ashen as if life had been sucked from him.

Aurelia, on the other hand, looked unshaken. Once she caught her breath, she rose to her feet and started to stretch her arms over her head.

How could she be so calm? They'd almost died!

Anger suddenly flared to life inside Kiki's chest. She stumbled to her feet and staggered toward Aurelia, a look of murder in her eyes. "You never said it was going to be like that!"

Kiki stared at Aurelia, who appeared completely calm. "You never asked," Aurelia responded with a shrug.

Anger radiated from Kiki's eyes in waves. "The Cicatrix could have killed us back there!" Kiki shouted.

Aurelia looked at Kiki coolly, clearly unbothered by Kiki's outburst. "False," Aurelia stated, her tone matter of fact. "None of that was real. It's all part of the illusion to warn people away and keep them in. Nothing you saw or felt back there could actually hurt you."

Kiki sighed heavily and leaned forward, hands on her knees. "You're unbelievable. I should have never trusted you."

"Think what you want of me. But I got you through, didn't I?"

Kiki and Aurelia stood toe to toe as they argued in the middle of the clearing.

Luna headed over to Turi, who was still sitting on the ground, and tenderly touched the blisters on his hands from the solvent splashed onto him.

Sticks and leaves covered Turi's head in tangles of black hair, and his usually vibrant blue eyes were dull.

"It'll be okay," Luna said to him, her voice a soothing melody.

She placed her hands on Turi's worst blisters, and the ground beneath her feet withered as she drew on the forest's energy to heal him. The blisters on Turi's skin faded with Luna's healing magic, and his skin became smooth once again. Turi sighed with relief as the pain finally faded away.

"What now?" Kiki asked Aurelia, her rage still simmering beneath the surface. Aurelia didn't seem to notice or care.

"I know someone who might be able to help find your friend. It's a long way from this part of the Cicatrix, though, so we should find a safe place to make camp for the night," Aurelia answered as her eyes scanned the forest, getting her bearings on their location.

Kiki didn't like the idea of trusting Aurelia to lead her and her friends to someone who might be able to help. There were too many variables to consider. The first and foremost of those being Aurelia herself.

Kiki silently cursed herself for having trusted the smuggler for even a second.

Kiki's brooding thoughts were suddenly interrupted when Turi's body started to glow with radiant energy that covered them in an aura of golden light.

Luna gasped, and both Kiki and Aurelia stepped back in shock.

"What's happening?" Turi cried as the glow engulfed his hands and traveled up his body until it overtook his face. The light grew brighter as if the sun itself were growing inside him.

"You've got to be kidding me," Aurelia said, her voice full of disbelief.

"What's going on?" Kiki asked. Turi was on the ground, and instinct told her to stay back, but concern for her previous boyfriend forced her forward a few inches.

Quickly, Luna scrambled backward and crouched down, her hands shaking and her eyes wide with fear.

Aurelia held Kiki back with an arm. "Watch, and you'll see."

See what? What was happening to him?

Kiki wanted to help but didn't know how. The glow surrounding Turi was blinding, growing to five times his size. It began to move as if it were alive, sending a chill up Kiki's spine.

Kiki placed her hand on her obsidian machete as fear coiled around her heart like a vine. She didn't know what was happening, but whatever it was, she'd be prepared to fight it. That, at least, she understood.

When the light around Turi faded, a leviathan bear stood in his place. It stood on its hind legs, like a human, and swiveled its black eyes around as if confused. Its muzzle was long, and its fangs were impossibly sharp. A black tongue hung from its mouth as it started to move around.

"I think your friend has some explaining to do," Aurelia said as the three girls watched the bear grunt and huff as if trying to communicate.

Kiki's mouth fell open. What had she gotten herself into?

CHAPTER SIXTEEN

THE VIOLENCE

ERASMO

T he tavern's shutters were pulled shut, and the light from an oil lamp hanging from a beam above the bar cast long shadows over the smoke-filled room. The barkeep was slumped in his chair and dozed with his head propped up on one arm. The barkeep's mouth hung open, spilled drinks stained his shirt, and he snored softly. Dropped coins rolled around on the floor. Drunkards and prostitutes murmured to each other while they discussed the recent disappearances that had taken place at the edge of town with surprising indifference.

Erasmo sat in a corner booth, his mug of pulque untouched as his fingers drummed over the sticky tabletop.

The tavern door creaked open, jingling the bells hanging beside it, and a lean man with brown hair walked in, his four companions in tow.

Erasmo signaled at Mauricio, who sat at the bar. He motioned toward the stranger, and Mauricio nodded his understanding.

Not taking his eyes off the man, his cousin threw back a glass of tequila and ground out his cigarette in a half-eaten plate of nachos.

Erasmo watched as Mauricio strode to the man and pointed toward where Erasmo was waiting.

The man sighed with a pained expression and slumped towards Erasmo. When he reached the booth, he scowled. "If it isn't the Bastard of the East. To what do I owe the pleasure," the man sneered.

"Tomás," Erasmo said with a nod of his head. "Word has it that you've been dealing with my cousin again."

Tomás spat onto the dirt floor. "That snake? I'm done with Aurelia. She still owes me four hundred pieces of gold for her last failed crossing, and she better hope I don't catch up to her on the road because if I do, she'll disappear so quietly that no one will ever find her again."

Erasmo sighed and reached into his waistcoat, rummaging past the dagger and throwing lances. He withdrew a small velvet pouch and shook the contents, the coins jingling together. "This should cover it," he said as he tossed the pouch onto the table.

Tomás eyed the bag of coins as he pulled one out, then brought it to his mouth. He pressed the coin between his teeth. Satisfied with its authenticity, he flipped the coin in the air and caught it with a wicked grin. "When are you going to tire of covering for that piece of filth?"

Erasmo clenched his teeth. Aurelia was many things, but she was still his family, and no one was allowed to disrespect his family that way. "I'd watch my mouth if I were you," Erasmo said as he snapped his fingers.

Six of Erasmo's men slithered from the shadows, their swords drawn and pointed at Tomás' men. The tavern fell silent, and a few patrons skittered out the main door. Mauricio drew his knife and held it to Tomás' throat.

Tomás sputtered and held his hands up. "I meant no offense," he mumbled, eyes watching the edge of Mauricio's blade.

Erasmo pushed away from the table, the legs of his chair screeching in the silence of the tavern. "If that were true, you wouldn't have said it," Erasmo drawled.

"What do you want?" Tomás snapped. "No man in his right mind goes looking for his debts. What are you after?"

Erasmo drew closer to the smuggler so that their noses were inches apart. Then he extended his talons from his hand, trailing them down the man's face. "Where is she?"

Tomas blinked in confusion. "Aurelia? Hell, if I know!"

Erasmo glanced at Mauricio, who flicked his blade, opening a crimson slice against the soft flesh of Tomas' throat.

Tomás squirmed. "Last I saw her, she was crossing near the Norceran basecamp."

"Now, why would she go there?" Erasmo asked, his voice turning lethal.

"I don't know, I swear!" Tomas cried as Mauricio nicked another cut into the man's skin.

Mauricio groaned as the blood trickled down Tomás' neck. "His fear smells delicious," he said, red swirling in his brown eyes. He licked his lips as he sniffed the air again. "If we can't get the scum to talk, he'll make a nice snack."

Tomás' eyes went wide, and he whimpered. "Okay, I'll tell you. Just keep this psycho away from me!"

Erasmo signaled Mauricio to back off, and his cousin reluctantly released the man. Erasmo grabbed Tomás by the collar and tossed the smaller man into the booth.

"Talk," Erasmo ordered.

Tomás wrung his hands in his lap. "I will, but you have to promise not to kill me."

Erasmo raised a single eyebrow. "What makes you think I won't?"

The smuggler blanched. "I offered to clear Aurelia's debt if she could procure Slayer weapons."

Erasmo clenched his fists at his side. Only a fool would take up an offer like that. Aurelia must owe a lot more than Tomás was letting on. "How long ago did she cross?"

Tomás looked down at his hands and counted out on his fingers. "Three--no--four days ago." His eyes darted toward Mauricio, lingering in the shadows. "That's all I know. I swear."

"Very well," Erasmo said, signaling to his men.

Mauricio snickered as he grabbed one of Tomás' men by the collar. He slashed the man's throat open in a single, smooth slice. Blood spurt across the table and Tomás' face.

The smuggler sputtered and looked accusingly at Erasmo. "I thought you said you wouldn't kill me," he cried.

"I didn't make such a promise. But for your help, I'll spare you," Erasmo said as the sound of tearing skin and panicked screams filled the tavern.

Erasmo reached into his jacket again and procured another pouch of coin. He tossed it onto the bar counter and tilted his head at the barkeep. "For the trouble," he said as he stepped over a body and walked out.

The cool night air kissed his face, and he wiped the specks of blood from his skin with the back of his hand.

Suddenly, a pang of fear sliced through his chest, bringing him to his knees. His mate.

Pure unbridled terror rippled down the mate bond, and Erasmo raced toward the stables where he and his men had left their horses. Without another thought, he mounted his giant black stallion and raced from the town center.

A tug toward the easternmost part of his territory directed his path. It was as if the mate bond tied a string between him and his mate and it was being pulled taught, threatening to snap.

His mate. She was here. She'd crossed the Cicatrix.

Chapter Seventeen

REAPER

Solana

Solana's eyes fluttered open. She lay in a cot that was not her own. Tinkling glass, whispering voices, and rustling sheets filled the air. She turned her head and saw a nearby cot covered in blood.

Morning light spilled through the infirmary tent, piercing her eyes. Healers moved around, attending to the sick and injured.

She glanced down at herself and noticed that dirt covered her hands and face, and soot covered her uniform. Her hair was out of place and hanging loose over her shoulders.

The sound of explosions and screams still echoed in her ears. She closed her eyes and tried to remember what had happened. Kiki and her friends had escaped the dungeon. That much, she was certain. It was what happened after that was still unclear.

Solana tried to sit up, but a wave of nausea and dizziness hit her. She felt the back of her head. There was a large bump with dried blood caked on it. She touched her face and winced. Her lips were swollen, her face was bruised, and her skin was chafed and raw from where the acid had splashed.

The tent's flap opened, letting in a shaft of sunlight. Solana squinted and saw a familiar figure. "Bernat," she said, her voice rough and cracked.

Bernat knelt in front of her and put a hand on her forehead. His azure eyes narrowed as if he was going to say something, but he just shook his head and stood up. "You're alive," he said, slow and deliberate, full of emotion.

Solana was surprised at the relief that she heard in Bernat's voice. And she couldn't help but smile. "I'm alive," she repeated in a whisper. "I'm alive."

"What happened?" Bernat asked, looking away from Solana. She couldn't help but wonder if he was looking away because he couldn't stand to look at her. Was she really so hideous? Solana pushed that thought deep down in the space where she buried all her other feelings. It didn't matter what Bernat thought; she scolded herself. He was her second-in-command and nothing more. Any feelings she may have for him were a sign of her own weakness.

"Sol?" Bernat's eyes were full of worry. His eyes had a way of locking onto things yet still being aware of everything around him. It was as if he was always watching, taking everything in so that nothing could get the jump on him.

"There were explosions. The walls shook, and there were screams from the lower levels. I went down to see what was happening and found Slayer Xochicale. Healer Luna and Officer Artchete had freed her. They had some kind of acid. It burned through the iron hinges." Solana recounted what she had seen with precision but faltered when she came to the last part. "The acid burned through my uniform.

Xochicale escaped and left me for dead. Then, the whole building—"

Bernat cut her off. "The explosions in the upper levels started a chain reaction. The Attendants who found you barely got you out before the roof caved in."

Solana frowned, and a wave of sadness washed over her as the fragmented memories pieced together. The crash of stone against stone. The screams. The flames. The calls for help. She'd been powerless to help those that had been trapped inside.

Solana hated that feeling. It was a feeling she'd vowed she'd never fall victim to again after the Corps had taken her in off the streets. The memory of sleeping in cold alleyways and fighting off rats for scraps returned fresh and raw. How she'd searched for her parents, her aunts, and uncles but had found no one. How her cousins had tried to stick together, but, in the end, it was everyone for themselves. No one could afford another mouth to feed.

Solana knew that her story was anything but unique. Once the darkness had split the kingdom in two, there were more orphans than the kingdom knew what to do with. There was no use in wallowing in self-pity for her lot in life. It was the same lot that most of her subordinates also faced. All she could do was bottle those memories up, stuff them into the darkest corners of her mind, and pray they'd never resurface and get in her way.

Solana tossed off the sheet that had been tucked around her and sat up, determination fueling her every move. The past was the past, and she had larger problems at hand. Like getting her regiment in order. Learning how many were trapped in the dungeons and extracting them as quickly as possible. "How many?"

Bernat cast his eyes to his boots. "We're not sure yet."

"That's unacceptable, Slayer," Solana said as she pushed herself to a stand. The world tilted sideways for a moment, and she grabbed Bernat's arm to steady herself. "Give me something to work with," she demanded.

Bernat stared at her, not speaking for a long moment.

Solana plowed past his silence. "We know how many were in the upper levels—how many were in the dungeons, in the barracks, on the Wall. We have rosters for a reason. Call a muster. Do a roll call. It's not that hard."

Bernat opened his mouth to speak but closed it again. He seemed to be struggling with something. Solana narrowed her eyes. "Bernat?"

"Sol, I think you should sit down."

Solana suddenly became aware that she was still holding onto Bernat for balance. He smelled like campfires and Slayer leathers. It was a smell that was unique and distinctly his. It made Solana long to reach up and take a deep inhale. She wanted to lean in and rest her head on his chest. Being this close to him sent her heart on double time.

Bernat seemed to also become aware of their prolonged contact. His eyes traced the sweep of her lips, and hers did the same. His gaze slowly searched her face as if seeking permission.

Solana wanted to lean forward and close the distance between them. To run her fingers through his midnight-black hair. To touch the stubble along his jaw. She could feel his heart beating through his chest at twice the usual rate. She longed to close the chasm of responsibility and duty that separated them.

But to do so was an abuse of her rank, and she would do no such thing.

Solana abruptly broke the contact and sat back on the cot's edge. "Spit it out, Bernat," her voice had an edge to it that she didn't usually use with her second.

The light in Bernat's eyes dulled for a moment at the sudden distance between them. But Bernat quickly replaced it with his typical efficient exterior. "It's not just the people who are trapped," Bernat blurted out.

"What do you mean?" Solana's stomach turned over. She didn't like the look on Bernat's face. It was the same look he'd had when he'd told her about the breach the other night.

"There was another attack last night. After the dungeon collapsed. There have been—disappearances."

She curled her hands into the sheets until she could feel her nails pressing into her skin. All of these half-answers and tip-toeing around her like she was some fragile doll. "Just give it to me straight," she snapped.

Bernat frowned and turned his eyes to the floor. He took in a deep breath as if to steady himself. Trying to look calm, he explained,

"Reports from the Slayers and Attendants who responded to the breach indicated that the demons were taking people. The demons appeared to drag them back to the Cicatrix."

Solana's heart dropped into the pit of her stomach. The world slowed as his words settled on her. "They're—what? Taking our people? Into the Cicatrix?" she repeated, her voice brittle with fear. She would have thought it was impossible, but the look on Bernat's face said otherwise.

"That's what witnesses are saying," he replied, his eyes cautiously watching her as if waiting for her to explode into action. "But we don't know why the demons are doing it."

Solana looked down at her scarred hands. Fear of what the demons were doing combined with the worries of what they would do in response, and the people trapped in the dungeons... It was all so much. Her mind was whirling with thoughts of people being captured and what was happening to them now. Bile surged in her throat at the thought.

Solana had to do something. Those were her people out there. Her responsibility. They deserved action on her part, not this pathetic wallowing. Solana felt a rush of determination ignite inside her soul.

"Gather our gear, Bernat. Meet me at the supply hall in fifteen minutes. We're going after our people." Solana rushed to her feet and immediately tipped forward.

"Take it easy!" Bernat admonished, catching her in his arms and slowly setting her back onto the cot. "You're in no shape to be going anywhere."

"Are you my second or my babysitter?" Solana snapped. Shame at showing such physical frailty clawed at her insides. This was not who she was. She was the youngest Commander in the history of the Demon Corps. She had rows of stars on the insides of her wrists to prove that she was more than capable of taking down demons. She'd risen from gutter slum to what she was now. It shouldn't have bothered her so much to be in such a weakened state, but it did nonetheless.

Bernat pursed his lips and crossed his arms over his chest. He didn't say a word, but his eyes said it all. She wasn't going anywhere until she was fully healed.

Solana's shoulders slumped in defeat. "Damn it all," she muttered. "Get me a Healer. The sooner I'm on my feet, the better."

"Like you had any other choice," Bernat said, a small grin tugging at the corner of his lips. He turned on his heel to get the attention of the nearest Healer leaving Solana to consider everything she'd just learned.

Solana signed as Bernat's words still echoed in her mind. She was still having trouble with the news he'd shared. The demons were actually taking their people. Why would they, she wondered. What were they doing? Were her people even still alive?

She stared at the rows of stars lining her wrists, one for each kill, and shook her head. It didn't matter. She would get them back, or she would die trying.

CHAPTER EIGHTEEN

DEAD MAN WALKING

KIKI

At first, Kiki couldn't believe what she was seeing. A giant black bear stood before her, its mouth opening and closing as if the sharp rows of teeth within its maw were too big. Black claws dug into the dirt, leaving gouge marks an inch deep.

Kiki's hand drifted to her obsidian machete as the bear began to pace around the clearing, all the while making strange grunting and squeaking noises. Her fingers curled around the hilt of her weapon, but she didn't unsheath it.

She'd seen Turi become the bear. One moment he'd been a human, the next, he'd shifted into a bear. She didn't understand how such a thing was possible. Until the bear gave her a reason to attack, she refused to be the one to draw first blood.

Perhaps Turi was still in there. Inside the bear. Somehow.

Standing to her right, Aurelia was laughing, barely able to hold it in.

"What's so funny?" Kiki snapped, her ire building toward the smuggler.

Aurelia's eyes gleamed with mischief. "I think your friend has some explaining to do," she said, a grin tugging at her lips.

Kiki scowled at the silver-eyed girl and took a hesitant step toward Turi. "Turi? Is that you? Are you in there?"

The bear turned its large head and fixed her with a burning stare. Its large, blue eyes glinted, and a low rumble built within its throat. Kiki's breath caught in her throat. She stood perfectly still for a moment, then swallowed and forced herself to hold the bear's gaze.

"Of course, that's Turi," Aurelia said, taking three long strides to reach him. She looked the bear square in the eyes and made a "hmph" sound in her throat. "You know, I thought you looked familiar. You have the eyes, sure, but anyone can have blue eyes. It was your nose that should have been the giveaway."

"Hold on," Kiki said, taking another step forward. "What do you mean? What was a giveaway? Why aren't you freaking out right now? What are we doing standing around here? Turi is a bear!"

Aurelia crossed her arms over her chest, the smirk never leaving her face. "I'm talking about the lost Ozero princes."

Kiki placed her hands on her hips and glared at the smuggler. "We don't have time for this," she said, "if you know something, then you better start talking."

"You don't know?" Aurelia asked, looking at Kiki as if she had grown a second head. "Really? I thought even people outside knew the histories."

Kiki's jaw tightened, and her fingers tightened on her machete. If the smuggler didn't start talking some sense soon, Kiki was of half a mind to sink the blade into the other girl's chest. "By all means, educate us."

Aurellia tossed her hands in the air and began to pace. "I guess it makes sense that you don't know. Huh, I just sort of assumed it was one of those stories people grew up with."

Kiki tapped her foot in impatiently on the ground. "Still waiting."

"Right," Aurelia said, a tone of sarcasm in her voice. "Well, it's kind of a long story. We might want to find a safe place before it gets dark. We may have crossed the barrier alright, but the demons still come out at night."

Luna squeaked at that. Her eyes were wide with fear, and she exchanged an uneasy glance towards Turi.

"Yeah, the Cicatrix is nothing compared to what roams this forest. You haven't seen anything yet," Aurelia said. To Turi, she said, "I promise I'll explain everything. For now, you have to be a good bear and follow us."

Turi made a move to swat at Aurelia for talking to him like he was some kind of pet, but Aurelia dodged his paw and instead let out a gleeful laugh. "I can't wait to tell the others," she said with a smile that made her look unhinged.

"Others?" Kiki quipped. "What others?"

But Aurelia ignored her question and instead turned toward the trees and began muttering to herself. "Let's see, we're on the eastern side of the river." She looked up to the sky and put her hand alongside the sun. She studied the sun's position and suddenly said, "Got it!" Turning to Kiki and Luna, she said, "I know where we are, and I know just the place for us to hunker down in."

Aurelia walked quietly, eagerly leading them down a narrow path through the dense trees. Leaves crunched underfoot, and the air hissed with each branch they pushed past. The trees were tall, their trunks thick and covered in a white bark that crackled when touched. Luna squirmed uncomfortably, her body jerking against Kiki as she struggled to keep up the smuggler's quick pace.

Finally, they entered a small clearing surrounded by a copse of white-barked trees. The air smelled like decay and sap as if the forest had been overtaken by fungus and mold.

"We'll be safe here," Aurelia said as she pointed to markings carved into the trees. "These are boundary spells. They only work on small spaces and aren't much help if a horde is after you, but it should hold up for the night so long as we don't draw too much attention to ourselves."

The carvings in the tree bark looked crude. She traced the ridges on the bark with her finger, fascinated by the hundreds of small grooves carked into the bark. The grooves formed a pattern that twisted up and down the trunk but looked like no language she had ever seen before. "These marking are supposed to keep us safe from demons?" she asked, her lips pursed in disbelief.

Aurelia plopped down to a seat and glanced at Kiki with a look of mischief. "There are a lot of things in this world that you have no idea about, Kiks." She patted the ground next to her. "Come, take a load off."

Kiki balled her hands into fists and remained standing, if only because doing so was the opposite of what the smuggler had suggested. "I want answers, and I want them now."

Luna moved toward the smuggler and sat down slowly, curling her knees into her chest and setting her head on her knees. A sob escaped her throat, and Kiki couldn't help the pang of annoyance that ripped through her chest.

Just another thing she had to deal with.

But before Kiki could go to her friend, Aurelia jumped up and raced to Luna's side.

"Hey, hey, hey," Aurelia said, her voice soft and soothing while her hand rubbed circles on Luna's back. "Don't worry, it's going to be okay."

Luna shook her head in defiance, tears streaking her cheeks. "No, no, no," she said. "I can't do this. I can't do this. I can't be here. I have to go. I have to go." She spat the words out in a violent whisper.

"Wait, what?" Aurelia said. "We just got here."

Luna flinched at the mention of 'here' and began to sob harder. Aurelia wrapped her arms around her and hushed her.

Kiki scowled and threw Aurelia a death glare. She didn't know where the smuggler thought she had the right to console Luna, let alone touch her, but for the moment, Luna seemed to calm down, and that was enough for Kiki. "Just tell us what's going on already."

Aurelia ignored Kiki and took Luna's hands into hers, and waited for some sort of response.

Luna's head snapped up, and she stared at Aurelia with a mix of anger, distrust, and an odd kind of sadness. The two stared like that for a while.

Aurelia spoke first. "Hey," she said softly, her voice barely audible over leaves rustling in the distance. "I'll make you a promise. Okay? I know this place. I grew up in these woods. I've given so many demons the slip you wouldn't believe it." At the word, 'demons, ' Luna started to cry again. "Look, I get it. It's scary. But I won't let anything happen to you."

Luna merely nodded, and she dropped her face into her hands. Her shoulders shook with quiet sobs.

Aurelia sat back on her heels and turned to face Kiki and Turi. "So, for starters, how much do you know about the darkness? How it started and what happened."

"Pretend like we know nothing." Kiki's voice took on a hard tone, like a sharpened nail scraping against bone. The smuggler was really starting to get on her nerves.

"We'll start from the beginning then," Aurelia said, settling into a more comfortable position.

"Please," Kiki drawled, impatience icing her words.

"Calm down. I'm getting to it. Can't tell a story without the right tools." Aurelia grabbed a twig and started to draw in the earth. Kiki stiffened at the gesture and how much it reminded her of Yarixa.

Her heart ached at the thought of her friend, and that only served to stiffen her resolve. She had to find Yari. Save her. Bring her home.

Aurelia finished her sketched and opened her palms to the drawings. "Eons ago, the barrier between the human world and the demon realm ripped open. There was a war between the humans and monsters, and eventually, the humans won. The demons were banished back to their realm, and peace fell on Ozero once again."

Aurelia drew out stick figures and eight-legged monstrosities into the earth. "Fifteen years ago, King Alejandro wanted to expand his kingdom. So he searched for ways to build the largest army ever seen. Larger than even during the Demon Wars. He discovered an old spell that would open the gateway between our world and the demon realm."

Aurelia drew a door and the image of a demon crawling out. "King Alejandro thought he would be able to control the demons and make them do his bidding, but he was wrong. So wrong."

Kiki huffed. "Can you get to the part that explains why Turi is a bear?"

Aurelia rolled her eyes. "You can't rush the magic, Kiks."

She clenched her hands into fists but managed to stay silent.

Aurelia continued, seeming to grow in confidence as she told the tale. "Queen Valentina, upon discovering what her husband had done, created a spell that would contain the demons and punish her husband. But the spell was flawed. In cursing her husband, she also cursed all the males in her family line. Before the spell could take effect, she sent her four sons away, each to a separate part of the realm, in the hopes that the curse would never reach them. As the darkness fell on the land, trapping the demons inside, the Queen died having linked her own life to the containment spell so that it would be strong enough to keep the monsters inside."

Aurelia paused for what seemed to be dramatic effect and turned her silver gaze to Turi. "Two of her sons made it out of the barrier, but my cousins, the twins, did not." She paused again, and her voice took on a note of awe. "Turi, you're one of the lost princes. The curse wouldn't be affecting you if you were anyone else but Arturo Ozero, youngest son to King Alejandro and Queen Valentina."

A low growl vibrated from Turi's chest, and Kiki suddenly had the urge to comfort him. She reached a hand toward him and hovered her palm over his shoulder. Taking a deep breath, she closed the distance and pressed her palm into his soft fur.

At her touch, Turi instantly relaxed, and Kiki felt warmth radiate into her palm.

"On the bright side, you're only a bear during the day," Aurelia added as if it was an afterthought. She looked toward the sky and the setting sun above. "You'll shift back into a human once the sun goes down fully."

Chapter Nineteen

THE OTHER SIDE

Kiki

O verhead the sun slowly sank behind the horizon, painting the sky in hues of orange and purple.

Kiki bit her lip as Aurelia spoke about curses and demons and sacrifices. Already, Turi was pacing the clearing, careful to stay within the protection runes. A low growl vibrated in his throat as his claws dug into the dirt. Kiki was grateful that she wasn't the only one to seem overwhelmed, but it was all too much. Her mind reeled as she tried to make sense of Aurelia's tale.

Luna sat next to Kiki with her knees drawn up and her hands wrapped around them. Her eyes were glazed, and she stared at nothing as she wrung her hands. Kiki had never seen her friend so rattled before. She'd seen Luna face an entire infirmary of injured Slayers before, blood coating her apron and hands. Nothing had ever made Luna cringe before. No wound was too gory. No amount of puss disgusted her. Whatever Luna had seen while they were crossing the Cicatrix had made her retreat deep into herself.

To make matters worse, the second Turi crossed through the Cicatrix; he'd transformed into a bear. Kiki ran a hand over her weary eyes. She was used to facing many decisions at once. Most of those decisions were matters of life and death. But this? Luna breaking and Turi being cursed? Kiki had no frame of reference for how to deal with any of it.

The sunset drenched the sky with color. It wouldn't be full night for another hour, which meant Turi would be a bear until then. But that was too long for Kiki's tastes. She needed answers. Now.

Turning her raptor gaze to Aurelia, Kiki spat, "You said what's happening to Turi is a curse. How do we break it?"

Aurelia cast her silver gaze to the ground and lifted her shoulders to her ears. "I don't know. My cousins have been trying to break the curse their whole lives. Every year that passes, they lose more and more of their humanity until, one day, they'll be more bear than men." She shook her head with a sigh. "Most of the men in my family haven't shifted into their human form in years. It's only a matter of time before the same happens to the twins."

Kiki's heart dropped into her stomach. She couldn't just sit around and accept that Turi was part of some family curse. Not when it was her fault that he had come into the Cicatrix. He'd be safe on the other side if it weren't for her. He'd be clueless to his heritage, to the curse, and definitely wouldn't be pacing the forest in the form of a bear.

"So that's it?" Kiki snapped, her hands curling into fists. "He's stuck like this for the rest of his life?"

Aurelia sat on her heels next to Turi, examining his black claws. "My cousins found a spirit woman who helped them stop the shift during the day. It's not a permanent fix, though. The second they take their totem off, they shift back into bears."

Hope fluttered in Kiki's chest. She refused to believe that Turi was doomed to a life of slowly losing his humanity. "How do we find this spirit woman?"

Aurelia shifted in her seat as she picked at some dirt beneath her fingernails. "The spirit woman doesn't help people out of the kindness of her heart. Rumors say that she was a powerful mage before the curse spread and corrupted her powers. Her help comes at a steep price."

Kiki bristled at the mention of a cost for help. Nothing in this life was free. Why would she think any different in this cursed land? "Fine, I'll pay it."

Aurelia shook her head slowly, her silver eyes glinting in the dimming light. "You won't be paying with gold, Kiks."

Something in Aurelia's voice sent a shiver down Kiki's spine. Despite the unease unfurling in her gut, Kiki leaned forward and stared the smuggler in the eyes. "I said I would pay it." Aurelia swallowed hard and cast her eyes toward Luna, avoiding Kiki's gaze. "But first, we find Yarixa. Is that something this spirit woman could help with also?"

Aurelia's eyes widened. "You want to ask her for two favors?"

"What choice do I have?" Kiki asked, blowing out a frustrated breath. She grabbed a twig from the ground and snapped it in two.

Aurelia chewed her bottom lip in thought. "My cousin might be able to help. He's the Prince of his own territory and has soldiers and mages at his disposal. He might even know something."

"It's been almost two days since Yarixa was taken. I can't waste any more time." Kiki broke the twig into smaller pieces and tossed them to the ground. "Where is your cousin in relation to the spirit woman? If he's close, maybe we'll stop in for supplies."

Aurelia picked up a stick and began drawing a rough map in the soil. She drew an "x" marking their current location east of a wide river and a set of jagged mountains. On the other side of the river and mountains, Aurelia drew a triangle to mark the location of the spirit woman. On the side of the "x", she drew a circle to mark her cousin's territory. If the map was close to scale, Kiki estimated it would take at least a week of hard travel to get over the river and through the mountains. That was if she were alone and had no one else to worry about. But Luna and Turi weren't used to such physical demands. So make that three weeks.

Blowing a breath between her teeth, Kiki followed the trail between their "x" and the single peak at the circle's center. The distance was, at most, a day.

Kiki pointed to the peak. "What's that? A mountain?"

Aurelia gave Kiki a non-committal nod. "It's not so much a mountain as a fortress." In the dirt, Aurelia drew out a sweeping estate that towered over the surrounding land on the flat part of a plateau. Three layers of walls guarded the perimeter while leviathan brass pulleys and levers lifted steel enclosures from the bottom of the plateau to the outer wall. "We call it La Aguilera, or the eyrie."

Kiki didn't like going to Aurelia's cousin for help. So far, Aurelia had guided them into the Cicatrix, but Kiki couldn't shake the sense that the smuggler was hiding something. She was too eager to help. No one was ever that helpful unless there was something in it for them.

"The good thing is we're near his territory. It should only take a day to reach him," Aurellia said with a smile.

Kiki didn't have it in her to return the gesture. So much had happened in the past couple of days alone. She feared what another day would bring.

As if sensing her thoughts, Aurelia spoke up. "Erasmo, that's my cousin, will help you. It'll be better for us if we seek him out."

Something in Kiki raised an eyebrow. Why was Aurelia pushing this so much? "Why do you want us to go to this Aguilera place so bad? What's in it for you?"

Aurelia scoffed, looking towards Turi, who could offer no commentary as a bear, and Luna, who was still unresponsive. Shaking her head, she turned her unnerving silver gaze to Kiki. "You're so self-absorbed. All you care about is your friend, but what about your other friends? They need you too."

Kiki's checks heated at the mention of Luna and Turi.

Aurelia jutted out her chin. "Just like you need me." Kiki scoffed, and Aurelia narrowed her eyes into slits. "If you want to get out of the Cicatrix alive, you'll have to learn to trust me. Because I'm the only one who can get you out."

Kiki sucked her bottom lip between her teeth, calming her thundering pulse. "Why? How come you're the only person? That seems a bit convenient, wouldn't you agree?" Kiki snarled, her fists clenching in her lap.

Aurelia's silver eyes seemed to darken until they were two molten pools of pewter. "I went to the spirit woman myself when I was eighteen. The harvest yield had been low for too many seasons. Our silos were depleted, and our people were on the brink of starvation. We weren't going to survive the winter. So I went to the spirit woman and asked for help." Aurelia's gaze glossed over as if she was reliving that day. "The thing you have to know about the spirit woman is that she will help you, but not in the way you expect. And the payment she takes will reflect that."

Kiki crossed her arms over her chest, hardening her heart to Aurelia's sob story. She couldn't afford to let Aurelia inside her walls. It was crowded enough already.

Aurelia wrung her hands in her lap. "I asked for a way to save our people. I should have been more specific. The next thing I knew, I couldn't see how I used to. Everything had become blurred shapes and colors. People I thought I knew were surrounded by these auras, coloring their intentions and desires. Not even night was full of darkness. Everything had an inner light, and I could finally see it for what it was."

Luna had unfolded her arms from her knees and was staring at Aurelia, her mouth slightly agape. Kiki resisted the urge to groan, just what she needed, Luna feeling like she had to fix this broken girl.

Kiki kept her face impassive as she quirked her head. "What a sad little story you've got there. What's it have to do with getting us back through the Cicatrix?"

Aurelia's lips thinned into a tight line as if she were holding back an insult. "I told you all that because I can see the rifts in the darkness. The tiny pockets that allow a person to slip through without the curse taking you and turning you into a demon."

Kiki's stomach turned to lead. There was so much the Demon Corps didn't know about the Cicatrix. This information was among them.

Shaking her head, Kiki said, "Fine, I can accept that we need you. But we came in here with one goal. To find and save Yarixa. Not so that you can have a little family reunion."

Aurelia snarled. "You're so selfish! I'm not doing any of this for me. Nothing I've ever done has been for me. I'm doing this for my family. Even though I just met him, Turi is my family. That may mean nothing to you, but it means everything to me."

Kiki curled her fingers into fists, her knuckles whitening. Aurelia had the gall to think Kiki was being selfish. Yari and Luna were her family. That's why she was here. That's the only reason she ever did anything.

As if sensing the need for a truce, Turi lumbered to his feet and nudged Kiki with his nose. His azure eyes sparkled with understanding as if he were saying that he knew Kiki wasn't trying to be so single-minded. That he knew her reasons and didn't fault her for them.

In a moment of weakness, Kiki ran her hand through his silken black fur, the warmth from his body warming her palm. Even as a bear, he was a better friend than she deserved. "I'm sorry," she murmured. "You know I want to help you. I just--"

Turi nudged her again as if to say that she didn't need to explain, before settling next to her, his giant shoulder pressed against her thigh.

Aurelia seemed to calm down as well. She leaned forward so she was at eye level with Kiki. "My cousins, Erasmo and Arlando, have been under the curse longer than Turi. It might not be long before they stop shifting and become simple bears. I think Turi should be able to meet his brothers while he still can."

Kiki hadn't thought of it like that and knew that if she had a chance to see her own family again, she'd take it. No matter the cost. Who was Kiki to deny Turi that chance?

With a heavy heart, Kiki nodded, agreeing to Aurelia's plan. She just hoped she wouldn't regret letting another person inside her walls. There was only so much of herself she could parse out. Eventually, she'd have nothing left of herself but a sliver, and she'd be no help to anyone.

Chapter Twenty

IRRESISTIBLE

YARIXA

Yarixa found herself in a sun-dappled forest. She lay on a bed of soft moss, and all around her were trees towering up to the sky. Birds sang in the branches, and a light breeze rustled the leaves. Yari sat up, dazed by the beauty of her surroundings. She couldn't remember how she got here, but she knew that it must be some kind of magical place.

She stood up and looked around, trying to get her bearings. Suddenly, she heard a noise behind her and whirled around to see a massive bear standing there, looking at her with intelligent azure eyes. Yari's heart leaped into her throat, but the bear didn't seem *threatening. It simply regarded her for a moment before turning and loping away into the forest.*

Yari watched it go, wondering what kind of place she has stumbled into. She decided to follow the bear and see if she could find some answers. She walked for hours, but the forest seemed to go on forever. Every time she thought she must be getting close to the edge, she came across another stretch of trees.

She was beginning to tire, and her stomach growled with hunger when she saw a light up ahead. She quickened her pace, drawn towards the light like a moth to a flame. As she got closer, she saw that it is coming from a small cottage nestled among the trees.

She approached cautiously, but there didn't seem to be anyone home. She knocked on the door and called out, but there was no answer. After a moment's hesitation, she decided to go inside.

Yari's eyes fluttered open, and she found herself in a lavish bedroom with a four-poster bed, the sheer curtains cascading over the bed and creating the illusion of a forest. A fire roared from the hearth, its warmth radiating into the room.

Her body was sore as if a herd of horses had trampled her, and her stomach rumbled with hunger. When was the last time she'd eaten? She remembered having eaten with Kiki and Luna in the dining hall. There was more rice and beans in the stew than actual meat, but they'd made the best of it as usual. Then Luna had been called away, and Yari had started on Kiki's makeup for the carnival. But what happened after?

Yari pushed to her elbows as the cobwebs cleared from her head. She winced at the sharp pain in her side and lifted the ivory sleeping gown to reveal white bandages wrapped around her torso. Even her arms bore white bandages crisscrossing over her shoulders and extended to her wrists.

A jolt of panic swept over Yari as she finally remembered the breach in sector seven. Demons had hurtled over the wall and slammed into Slayers, doing their best to hold the line. Yari blinked several times, clearing the memory from her mind. Had the mysterious man brought her to this place?

Yari pulled the feather-light downy comforter from her legs and slipped her feet over the edge of the bed as she took in more of her surroundings. The room was larger than her entire barracks, and the ceilings were vaulted high to accommodate a sparkling crystal chandelier. The stone floor was covered in plush fur rugs, the white and grey complimenting the simple yet warm decor of the room.

Yari was about to get to her feet when the door to the room swung open, and a slender man with greying hair and deep-set brown eyes walked into the room. Flinching, Yari retreated into the bed, pulling the covers over her body. This was not the man she saw in the forest that day.

"Ah, you're finally awake," he said, stopping at the foot of the bed. "The master was beginning to worry."

"W-who are you?" Yari asked, her voice trembling.

"My name is Sergio," the man replied as he bent at the waist in a bow. "My master brought you here after rescuing you from the demons."

Yari looked around the room again, still trying to wrap her mind around what was happening.

"My master says you were on the brink of death," Sergio continued. "You're lucky that the master found you when he did."

Yari nodded, recalling the demon that had taken her from the Demon Corps base camp.

"You needn't worry. You are safe here." Sergio turned and walked to the door. "I will let the master know you're awake," he said before walking out of the room and closing the door behind him.

Yari sat silently before getting to her feet and exploring the room more. There was a white wood wardrobe tucked into the corner of the room. She opened the drawers and found white silk underthings, soft wool socks, and an assortment of fur-lined gloves and earmuffs.

Opening another drawer, she found neatly folded stacks of wool-lined shirts and leggings. Taking items out of the drawers, Yari shed the white sleeping gown and draped it over a nearby chair. She dressed in the beautiful clothes, noting the delicate silver embroidery at the cuffs and along the collar of her blouse.

Another wardrobe with twin doors invited her to explore its contents. She found rows upon rows of fur-trimmed ponchos, each fabric more decadent than the last. She ran her fingers along one made of white wool with grey fur around the collar and at the bottom edges. It was the finest thing she'd ever seen, let alone touched. Tenderly, she pulled it from the wardrobe and draped it over her shoulders. Standing before the nearby full-length mirror, Yari almost didn't recognize herself.

Next to Luna's otherworldly beauty and Kiki's striking features, it was hard for anyone to stand out. Yari was all soft lines. Her upside-down mouth made her look perpetually pouting, and her soft cheeks made her look younger than her twenty years. She'd often wished for Kiki's high cheekbones and her stubborn chin. How many times had she painted her own eyes so they slanted upwards like Luna's or added kohl to her brows to make them look bolder.

Yet now, as Yari looked upon her reflection, she didn't shrink away in despair. Her brown hair had been cleaned and brushed while she'd been asleep. Her soft brown curls cascaded over her shoulders, ending just below her shoulder blades. Sleep had banished the ever-present dark circles that plagued her deep brown eyes. The heat from the fire brought a pink flush to her cheeks, making her look vibrant and energized. For the first time in her life, Yari felt beautiful.

A knock at the door pulled Yari from her thoughts. "Come in," she called out, not wanting to keep whoever was on the other side waiting.

The door opened, and a stunning man walked into the room. He had long silver hair that fell past his shoulders in loose curls. His skin was burnished gold, and his eyes were the deepest blue. He wore a simple tunic and pants tucked into knee-high leather boots.

The man smiled at seeing Yari awake and dressed. "Hello," the man said, crossing the room to stand before her. "My name is Arlando Ozetero. I'm the one who saved you. Welcome to the Winter Keep."

Kiki's cheeks warmed at his closeness. "Thank you," Yari said, averting her gaze from Alrando's intense blue stare. "For everything."

Arlando's lips stretched into a warm smile, his eyes crinkling at the sides. "It's no trouble at all," he replied with a wave at the room. "Really, it's the least I could do after all you must have been through."

Another knock at the door announced Sergio's entrance, holding a food tray. "As requested, my lord," he said with deference to Arlando. He walked into the room with a bowed head and set the tray down on a small table near the fire where two plush chairs waited.

Yari's stomach growled at the sight of so much food. The silver tray was laden with foods she'd never seen before. Small buns with pink and yellow frosting sat piled high on a porcelain dish. Next to the buns were palm-sized turnovers with steam wafting into the air. Yari's mouth watered, but she resisted the urge to run toward it.

Sergio politely excused himself, telling Arlando that he would return shortly.

Arlando motioned to the table with a casual sweep of his arm. "Please, will you join me?"

Yari almost tripped over her own feet as she moved towards the food. Her eyes darted from the buns to the steaming turnovers. Which should she try first? Yari reached for a bun and her eyes closed as sweetness burst inside her mouth.

Arlando chuckled across from her as he crossed one leg over the other and settled back into the chair.

Panic filled Yair's chest at seeing he wasn't eating. Swallowing a mouthful, Yari put the bun down. "Aren't you going to eat?"

Arlando's eyes crinkled with kindness. "I already ate this morning. This is all for you. You must be famished." As if in answer, Yari's stomach growled loud enough for him to hear. "Please, eat."

Yari didn't have to be told twice. She probably looked like a wild animal devouring its prey, but she didn't care.

Sergio returned shortly with a second tray. He set it down on the table and poured them a cup of piping hot chocolate before retreating from the room.

Arlando leaned over, taking his cup between his hands, and blew the hot liquid to cool it.

Yari washed down her meal with the sweet drink and, with a full belly, leaned back in her chair.

Arlando hadn't spoken the entire time Yari had eaten, only sipping his drink occasionally. Now that Yari was finished, he set his cup down on the table and leaned forward, his elbows resting on his knees. "I'm sure you've had a harrowing journey," he began. "So I hope you'll forgive me if I have some questions."

Yari blinked at the gentleness in his tone as if she were a deer that might bolt. "Of course," she said, her voice barely above a whisper. "Whatever you want to know, I'll answer."

Arlando's brows lifted, and he quickly said, "This isn't an interrogation," he said his tone earnest. "I just want to know who you are. What were you doing in the woods? Where did the demons take you from? I'm sure you're family is worried sick."

Yari was speechless for a moment as her mind whirred with his questions. But her mind snagged on one question only. Her family?

Seeing her confusion, Arlando smiled softly. "I'm sorry. You've been through a lot, I'm sure. These questions can wait until you're feeling better. Please forgive me." He got to his feet and gave her a polite bow of his head before walking towards the door to leave.

"Wait," Yari called out. She didn't want to be alone and wanted to answer his questions. "My name is Yarixa. I'm an Attendant with the Demon Corps assigned to the camp at Norcera. There was a breach of the Wall, and in the melee, I was abducted by one of the demons and dragged through the Cicatrix."

It was Arlando's turn to blink in confusion. He returned to his seat, his black brows furrowed. "So, what you're telling me, is that you're from the other side of the darkness. Or, as you called it, the Cicatrix?"

Yari nodded, her mouth slightly agape. "Are we inside it?"

Arlando nodded, his own lips parted as his eyes scanned her in curiosity. "You said you were part of something called the slayers?"

"The Demon Corps," Yari corrected. "I'm in training," she added sheepishly. "I haven't graduated yet."

Arlando quirked his head. "How old are you?"

"Twenty," Yari answered, averting her gaze to her hands in her lap. She knew she looked younger and was often accused of behaving like a mousey child. She often thought she was made from a softer material than her friends.

Where Kiki was made of obsidian and Luna was as beautiful and strong as jade, Yari was like the mud beneath their boots. A lamb among wolves.

Arlando's lips curved into a smile, revealing his bright smile. "Well, Yarixa, I'm sorry that we had to meet under these circumstances, but I'm glad that I was the one to find you and provide a safe haven. Would you consider joining me for dinner this evening if it pleases you? There is much to discuss, and you should get some rest in the meantime."

Yari's cheeks bloomed with heat, and it wasn't because of the fire. When he smiled at her like that, she felt a flutter inside her stomach, making her pulse race. Why did she feel so shy around this man? Maybe the fact that he was the most attractive man she'd ever laid eyes on had something to do with it.

Her reply caught in her throat, and she stiffly nodded. With a gentle smile and a respectful bow, Arlando left the room. Left all alone, Yari twisted the fabric of her poncho between her fingers. She was grateful for the warm room and the food, but she couldn't stay here long. She had no family to speak of, at least not blood relatives. But Kiki and Luna were as good as sisters. If Yari really was in the heart of the Cicatrix, she could only imagine that Kiki was beside herself.

There was one thing about Kiki that Yari knew without a doubt, she'd burn the world to cinders in order to protect those she loved. Feeling a spark of hope blossom in her chest, Yari knew that she topped Kiki's list. Despite all of her own failings, Kiki saw only Yari's best qualities and would stop at nothing to see that Yari was safe.

That thought brought a tear to Yari's eyes as she settled between the soft fur blankets of the feather bed. Where were Kiki and Luna now? She hoped they were okay and that they were safe.

CHAPTER TWENTY-ONE

MADNESS

KIKI

K iki tossed another stick into the fire and took in a deep breath. Night had finally descended upon the land, and with it, Turi had shifted into his human form again. The moment he could speak, he'd peppered Aurelia with questions about his family, which she was all too ready to answer.

Kiki should have been happy for him, but there was an ugly, twisted part of her that was a little jealous. When she was just a Yearling, she'd dream of the day the Cicatrix fell. She liked to imagine that her parents would walk out of the mists with open arms, their faces bright with joy at seeing Kiki again. But as each year passed and more demons crawled from the darkness, Kiki had tucked such fantasies into the darkest corners of her mind, never revisiting them. Until now.

She pushed her self-pity into a dark corner of her mind and curled onto her side, using her arm as a pillow. She served no one by wallowing in childish hopes. So she might as well keep her mouth shut.

Turi and Aurelia continued talking long into the night, their excited chatter grating on Kiki's ears. Though she tried not to listen to them, she couldn't help it. Her own heart ached with sorrow. Sorrow because she knew her parents were dead and she'd never see them again.

Aurelia watched Kiki with a thoughtful expression before she spoke. "What's on your mind, Kiks?"

Kiki bristled at Aurelia's continued disregard for her name. It shouldn't have bothered her as much as it did, but Kiki was the name she'd chosen. Not Quierera. Her mother's name. She'd reforged her identity around Kiki Xochicale. The Sicario.

"I think it's late, and you two should quiet down so I can get some sleep," she hissed. She instantly regretted the words at the way Turi flinched in response. If Aurelia was affected by Kiki's harshness, she didn't let the sting show.

"Apologies," Aurelia smirked. Turning to Turi, she whispered, "We'll talk more in the morning," placing her hand on his arm and giving it a gentle squeeze.

With a nod, Turi moved off and found a spot near Kiki. He settled into a comfortable position, his long, lean form sprawled out on his side. He let out an embarrassed cough before he spoke. "I'm sorry," he said, swallowing hard.

Kiki frowned and turned her dark eyes on him. "It's natural for you to want to know about your family. I'm just tired."

His expression eased somewhat. "Talk to me," he said quietly. "What's wrong?"

Kiki stared at him for a long moment before she finally let out a frustrated breath. "It's stupid," she muttered. "childish."

"What is?" he asked as he reached out and put his hand over hers.

Kiki's breath hitched in her throat, and she quickly pulled her hand free. She couldn't give him the wrong idea. "It's every orphan's dream to have a family that's been looking for them," she whispered, keeping her voice low so Aurelia couldn't overhear. "And I'm happy that you're living that dream. I am. Truly."

"But?" Turi prodded.

She looked away, not wanting him to see the tears in her eyes. "I wish it could have been me," Kiki admitted finally, shame heating her cheeks.

"I'm sorry about your parents, Kiki," he said gently, reaching out again and brushing his fingers over her cheek in a comforting gesture. "But you have us. You're not alone."

The words should have made her feel better, but they only served to underscore the burden of responsibility she carried on her shoulders. With a huff of frustration, she rolled away from Turi and stared at the dancing flames.

Kiki tossed and turned for what felt like hours, her mind racing with all the what-ifs she used to dwell on as a child. What if her parents were alive and looking for her? What if they'd never given up hope? What would it be like to finally be reunited with them after all this time?

The more she thought about it, the more restless she became. Eventually, she gave up trying to sleep and rolled over, staring into the fire's dying embers. Turi was curled up in a ball nearby, his breathing even and steady.

Aurelia and Luna weren't asleep and were talking with their heads pressed close. Kiki shifted her head to hear them better, wondering what the smuggler was telling her friend now.

Luna played with the edge of her white apron. "Have you ever talked to a Healer before about restoring your eyesight?" she asked, her voice timid.

Aurelia smiled softly and reached up, brushing a strand of brown hair from Luna's face and tucking it behind her ear. "I'm not blind, Lulu," Aurelia said, a hint of mischief in her tone. "I just don't see the same way you do anymore."

"But if you could? Get your old sight back; would you be willing to try?" Luna asked as she continued to pick at the frayed edges of her uniform.

Aurelia paused as if in thought before speaking. "No. I wouldn't want to give up the sight I have now. Without it, I'd never be able to see the rips in the Cicatrix. I'd be stuck in here like everyone else and couldn't leave when my people need me to."

"What's it like?" Luna asked.

"It's like seeing the world through a prism. Everything is distorted and broken up, some things shine brightly, and others have this kind of darkness swirling around them," Aurelia said, waving her hands in the air as if she were touching those sparks of color. "Most people have some degree of darkness along their edges. But not you?"

"Me?"

Aurelia leaned forward and slid her finger across Luna's cheek. "No. Your aura is like a flower in full bloom. You're all petals and soft silk. Dusting your stem, you have specks of gold here and there. You have a wave of light that vibrates around you, pushing at the darkness of others. Sending it skittering away. You're like a flame in the darkness and breathtaking in every way."

Luna's breath whooshed from her lips, and she averted her gaze, a pink blush coloring her cheeks. "You barely know me," she whispered.

Aurelia reached out and wrapped her hands over Luna's. "I don't have to know everything about you to know that I want to bask in your glow for as long as you let me." She brought Luna's hand to her lips and brushed a kiss across her knuckles.

Kiki rolled her eyes and turned her back to them. Aurelia was certainly smooth talking and had managed to ingrain herself into Kiki's group in record time. Kiki still didn't trust the smuggler but decided that it would be best for her to keep her suspicions to herself.

From outside the border of the runes protecting their camp, Kiki heard a low rumble and the crunch of fresh leaves beneath clawed feet. Her breath stilled as she reached for her machete and curled her fingers tightly around the hilt. The sound of retreating footsteps against icy earth reached her ears, but she didn't put the blade down. She'd be getting no sleep this night.

CHAPTER TWENTY-TWO

HURTS LIKE HELL

YARI

Yari woke hours later but found the fire still roaring. Someone must have come into the room, added more logs, and stoked the flames. Probably Sergio. He seemed to be the one assigned to tend to Yari's every need.

Her stomach grumbled, and though she was due to join Arlando for dinner soon, she crept over to the leftover food on the tray. She ate one each of the buns and turnovers before going to the mirror and fixing her hair. She smoothed the frizzy bits around her face with her hands and ran her fingers through the curls to remove the tangles. Satisfied with the result, Yari ventured out of the room and found herself in a long hall, rooms with doors identical to hers lining either side.

The walls were made of polished granite and were decorated with neutral tones of brown and green, adding warmth to the atmosphere. The stone floors were covered by soft rugs in shades of silver and gold, stretching for fifty feet in either direction.

There were no slits in the stone to let in natural light, but hundreds of candles lined the walls and tables, offering a warm flickering glow.

The scent of fresh spices and warm bread wafted under Yari's nose, leading her down the hall and down a winding staircase covered in velvet carpets until she reached the main landing.

Here, Yari got a better sense of the house and realized it wasn't just a grand manor but a castle.

Stained glass windows hung from the roof and glowed softly with light from the candles. The walls were made of white marble and chased with gold, reflecting dazzling patterns across the floor.

The main hall stretched for a hundred feet and was adorned by two enormous stone fireplaces at each end of the hall, each with a roaring fire in the hearth. Tapestries and rugs covered the walls, and the ceiling was painted with images and scenes depicting a history Yari had never learned.

In the middle of the room was a single table. Yari wandered over and found plates piled high with fresh tortillas, more buns with bright-colored frosting, and steaming piles of meat. Bowls of fresh fruits were artfully arranged on either end of the table, and white lilies stood as a centerpiece.

Yari's mouth watered at the sight of the food, and she was grateful when Arlando entered the room, a smile spreading on his face at the sight of her.

"How are you feeling?" he asked as he pulled a chair from the table and motioned for her to sit.

Speechless, Yari moved to the seat and settled in, allowing him to help her scoot closer to the table. Remembering that he'd asked her a question and not wanting to seem ungrateful or rude, Yari cleared her throat. "I'm feeling much better. Thank you, again, for everything you've done for me."

Arlando moved around the table and reached for a decanter of blood-red liquid, filling her glass. Yari frowned at the sight but picked up the glass examining the contents.

"It's called wine," he said, gesturing to the crystal glass before moving to the other side of the table and serving himself. "Do you not have such a thing in, what did you call it, Eastern Ozero?"

Yari had never been treated with such courtesy before. No one had ever pulled her chair out, let alone poured a drink for her. She tipped the glass to her lips and sipped. An explosion of sweetness swept across her tongue.

"If we do, I've never been offered such a luxury before," Yari responded, taking another long sip before setting the glass down. Heat ran along the back of her neck and a giggle built in her chest, reminding her of the first and last time she'd ever tried tequila. Funny enough,

Kiki still turned green at the mere mention of the amber alcohol.

Arlando chuckled and poured her a glass of cool water. "In that case, maybe you should stick to the water."

Kiki felt a flush heat her cheeks, and she turned her attention to her hands in her lap. "Dinner looks delicious; thank you for inviting me," Kiki said to fill the silence, anything so that she'd distract his attention from her.

"The honor is mine, Yari," he said, his voice husky. "I don't often have company, save for my aunt, who visits occasionally. She's ill tonight but will join us for breakfast tomorrow."

Sergio emerged from a back room dressed in a crisp livery. He moved around the table, piling Yari's plate with food before offering it to her. He did the same for Arlando before bowing and fading into the corner of the room.

Yari tried the steaming meat first and resisted the urge to groan. It was perfectly seasoned, and the fat hadn't been cut from it to be repurposed for other uses as it was in the Demon Corps dining hall. No corners were cut for this meal.

As they ate, Arlando asked her about her life in Eastern Ozero. Being trapped in the Cicatrix for most of his life, he hadn't known that the kingdom of Ozero had survived in any way.

"It's a shame the east and west don't pull together their resources," Arlando mussed as they started in on the desert.

Yari swallowed a mouthful of sweet rice pudding and dabbed the corners of her mouth, mirroring what she'd seen Arlando do earlier in the meal. A wave of shame washed over her that she'd never been taught table manners or any of the protocols associated with fine dining. There had never been a need. Only the Commanders had use for such skills when dining with the nobles of the Protectorate.

"The Protectorate is more worried about keeping the rich happy inside their walls. The Demon Corps and the poor are their last priority."

Arlando set his napkin aside. "I'm sorry that you had to live that way," he said, his lips drawn into a thin line. "But, you never have to go hungry again. Or shiver in the cold. You are welcome to stay here as long as you'd like."

Yari stared at him in shock before regaining her senses. "That's very kind of you, but I can't stay." She shifted in her seat and turned her gaze to her empty plate. "I'm grateful for everything you've done for me. And for saving me, of course. But I have to be getting back to my base camp. They likely think I'm dead, and my friends will be worried sick."

Arlando cleared his throat. "I see," he said as he chewed his bottom lip. "There's only one problem," he added as he played with the edges of his napkin. "You see, those of us who are trapped in the Cicatrix can't leave. But that applies to anyone who comes inside of it."

Yari heard the words, but some part of her failed to fully comprehend them. "I don't understand," she murmured.

Arlando's blue eyes looked sad as he stood up and walked over to her. Kneeling on one knee, he reached for her hand and took it between his warm palms. "You can't ever go home. You're trapped here, the same as me." He traced circles on the back of her hand. "I'm so very sorry, Yarixa."

Yari felt as if her whole world were crumbling around her. "I can never go back?" she asked, needing to say the words aloud. "But my friends. By now, they must think I'm dead," she shook her head. "Kiki, oh, Kiki," she gasped.

"She'll blame herself. She'll never forgive herself. I have to go back." Yari could only imagine how Kiki must be feeling. Such a thing would crush Kiki. Luna would mourn, too, of course. But Kiki took all failures personally, and she'd definitely see Yari's disappearance as a failure. She'd beat herself up for the rest of her life; Yari just knew it. She didn't want that for her friend. "I have to get back. I just have to," Yari choked.

She didn't realize she'd started crying until Arlando pressed his thumb to her cheek and swiped it away. His blue eyes swirled with regret and despair. He dropped to a knee before her and placed her hand in his, offering his presence as a source of comfort. "I'm ever so sorry, cariña. But there is just no way. If there were, I'd move a mountain to give it to you."

Yari's heart leaped in her chest at such a statement, but it was fleeting as the tidal wave of grief washed over her. She always knew that she was never meant for the Slayer life. She just thought she'd always have Kiki and Luna to help her through the hardest parts of that life. Now, she had no one.

CHAPTER TWENTY-THREE

CHAMPION

SOLANA

S olana shivered as a frigid wind swept through the lean-to shelter for the hundredth time. Bernat huddled across the meager fire from her, urging the dying embers with a twig snatched from the wind-swept ground.

She thought about their crossing through the Cicatrix. The heavy weight of dread and fear consumed her as she and Bernat fought for every step through the oppressive darkness until they finally made it to the other side.

Bernat touched her knee. "Are you all right?"

Honestly? No. Despite how much Solana fought against the shadows of her past, something about the Cicatrix had brought forth all of her worst fears. But she couldn't show weakness to Bernat. He was her subordinate. She had to put on a strong face, if not for him, then for herself. To convince herself that the past was just that--the past. She was no longer that little girl on the brink of death, shivering in the snow.

No. She was Solana Ramirez. The youngest Slayer to graduate through the Demon Corps training program. The youngest to rise through the ranks and earn the prestigious title of Commander.

Solana felt another wave of cold slither down her spine and resisted the urge to shiver. "I'm fine," she said, teeth chattering against her will.

"You sure?" Bernat asked, narrowing his azure eyes at her. "Because I'm not."

Solana averted her gaze so he wouldn't see the fears that undoubtedly swirled within. Drawing her cloak tighter around her shoulders, she said. "What did you see?"

Bernat shook his head, a rueful grin tugging at the corner of his full mouth. "Nah-uh. You first. Then me."

Solana clenched her jaw at the insubordination in his tone. When Solana was first rising in the ranks, she'd grown accustomed to receiving flack from others. She had been younger than the Slayers who fell under her command and had yet to see that she'd earned her rank. She had made quick work of setting the tone and made it impossible for anyone to question her leadership. Though many considered her cold, no one could fault her results.

Bernat tended to toe the line with her but was never disrespectful. He'd been her aid for two years now, and she'd come to depend on his level head. What warmth she lacked in dealing with her subordinates, he more than made up for it with his easy smiles and ability to build rapport with others.

Despite how much she respected him, she couldn't let him speak to her with such a lack of decorum. She pulled herself up straighter and pressed her shoulders back. "I'm your superior officer. I expect you to answer me when I ask you a question."

"The moment I followed you into this hellhole was the moment we deserted the Corps." Solana opened her mouth to object, but Bernat didn't let her interrupt. "Like it or not, we're on a suicide mission. Either we find our people, bring them home and hope to receive a pardon from the Corps, which is unlikely. Or, we fail and die. In any case, we're not in the Demon Corps anymore. And I don't answer to you."

Disappointment curled around her throat, choking her. "Why did you come with me then?"

There was a long pause, and for a moment, Solana thought Bernat wasn't going to answer her. But then he sighed and ran a hand through his hair. "I followed you because I didn't want you to be alone. And because I'd rather die next to you than live the rest of my life not knowing if you're alive."

Her head snapped up, and she met his gaze. Something tightened in her chest at the sincerity she saw there. "You're an idiot," she muttered.

Bernat barked a laugh, the sound swallowed by the darkness surrounding their small campsite. "Yeah, I am." He paused, and then his face softened. "But I'd do it again in a heartbeat."

Longing welled in her heart at the honesty sparking in his stunning gaze. She wanted to lean forward, press her hand to his cheek, and rub her fingers along his mouth. But she hastily brushed those thoughts away.

She was likely infusing his words with more meaning than he intended. Bernat was loyal. He didn't mean anything more.

"You didn't answer my question earlier," Bernat whispered as he rubbed his palms over the small fire. "What did you see during the crossing?"

Solana turned her face away and stared out at the star-filled sky. "I saw myself in the snow. Freezing to death." She heaved a deep breath and exhaled slowly through her nose before continuing. "Before the Demon Corps took me in, I was a street rat. I had scraped together a pitiful life for myself, but every year I managed to survive. I'd sell anything I could get my hands on. Candles that still had some wick left.

Flowers in the springtime. Bits of coal that still had some life in them." She could feel Bernat's eyes on her, but she refused to meet his gaze. "During the winter of my tenth year, the crops had poor yield. Everyone was scrounging what they could and barely getting by. Spare coins didn't exist anymore." The memories of those days bubbled to the surface, threatening to drown her in a sea of grief and despair. She curled her fingers into a fist until her nails pressed so hard into her palms that she drew blood. "A man approached me one night. Asked if I wanted work. I was young. I didn't know what kind of work he was offering."

Bernat's breath hissed through his teeth.

Her chest tightened, and she swallowed the lump in her throat. "After he was done with me. He tossed me into an alley. It was so cold that night," she said as tears welled in her eyes. She brushed them away before Bernat could notice. She refused to be seen as weak, not even in front of Bernat. "If it hadn't been for a Commander passing through my town to get to her post, I would have died that night."

"Sol," Bernat whispered, his voice tight with despair.

Gathering the courage, she turned her face towards him, the heat from the flames warming her cheek. "After I healed, I made myself a promise. That I'd never be that cold again. The Commander who saved me, she had a heated tent. I enlisted in the Corps right away and haven't looked back. Until today. When we crossed the Cicatrix."

Bernat opened and closed his mouth like he wanted to say something but couldn't find the words. That was fine with Solana. She was done talking anyway.

Bernat reached out and placed his hand over hers, the heat of his skin seeping into hers. "Sol, so long as I live, you never have to face anything alone. You know that, right?"

Solana shifted uncomfortably. This was crossing a line. A line she swore she'd never cross. "I'm your commanding officer-" she whispered, feeling what little restraint she had left beginning to fray.

Bernat shook his head, his lips spreading into a grin, revealing his dazzling smile. "You're not my superior officer anymore, Sol." Her body went rigid at his use of the nickname he'd given her. Bernat leaned forward, propping his elbows on his knees. "But I'll always obey your commands," he said, his voice turning husky.

A shiver of pleasure ran up Solana's neck at the look in his eyes. How easy it would be to close the distance between them. To curl into his warmth and never be cold again. Her gaze drifted to the single bedroll they'd brought with them. But that thought sent fear lancing through her heart.

She couldn't do this. To do so would be to take advantage of her station. Her rank. She stood up in a rush and moved to leave their shelter. "I'll take first watch," she said and stepped out into the night.

"That's it," Bernat said firmly as he rose to his feet. "You're just going to walk away?" he accused as he joined her in the inky black darkness.

Solana cut her gaze away, staring out at the forest beyond instead. "Did you want to take the first watch instead?"

Bernat scoffed and turned her by the shoulders to face him. He towered above her by over a foot, and the heat radiating from his body made her want to lean closer. His eyes searched hers in disbelief. "You can be cold with everyone else, but not me."

Solana tried to wriggle from his grip, but he held onto her with strong hands. "I don't know what you're talking about."

He narrowed his eyes at her before speaking. "For two years, I have watched as you built a wall to insulate yourself from others. I've seen your ruthless pragmatism. The ice that runs in your veins when faced with impossible decisions. Your people are loyal to you not because they adore you but because they trust you. Trust that you take care of them and throw yourself into danger before sending them. You've kept everyone at arm's length. Everyone but me." His pupils were blown wide, and his thumbs had started to caress her shoulders. "I've seen the parts of you that you keep from everyone else. For two years, I've wanted nothing more than to pull you into my arms and carry the burden with you. For two years, I've dreamt of nothing else but you. And, finally, after two years, now that nothing is standing between us, I tell you how I feel, and you just walk away?"

He was so close, and Solana wanted nothing more than to give in to the desire blossoming in her chest. But she was afraid of what admitting her own feelings would do. How it would change their relationship.

She tried to pull herself from his grasp again. "You shouldn't say things like that to me," she muttered.

Bernat pulled her into his chest, then wrapped an arm around her waist as he brought the other to her face. The heat from his palm seeped into her skin, and she couldn't resist the urge to lean into that warmth.

Bernat's breath hitched. "Tell me you feel nothing for me. Tell me, and I'll never bring it up again. I'll follow you to the ends of this world, but I won't ever repeat my feelings that your find so disgusting."

Solana closed her eyes and let herself melt into his embrace. "I can't," she whispered.

Bernat tilted her chin up, forcing her to meet his gaze. "Why? There is no one else here to judge you. To question you. Why can't you be honest with me?"

Solana shivered in the cold and from the tidal wave of emotions battling within her. She turned her face away so Bernat couldn't see just how close she was to caving in.

After a few moments, Bernat sighed and stepped away. "I'll take the first watch. You should get some sleep." He pushed the cloak into her hands.

It smelled like him and was still warm from being wrapped around his body. "I can't accept this," she said, holding it back to him.

Bernat stretched his arms over his head and pushed the cloak back towards her. "I don't need it. I run hot anyway. This feels like heaven to me."

Solana opened her mouth to protest but thought better of it at the stern look in Bernat's eyes. Grateful, she drew his cloak around her, his scent wrapping around her like a lover's embrace. "Wake me in four hours," she said as she ducked back into the shelter.

A grunt was his only response. Solana curled up on the ground, using her pack as a pillow. The ground was hard, and the air was cold, but for the first time in a long time, Solana felt safe. She drifted off to sleep, dreaming of a warm fire and strong arms wrapped around her.

Bernat watched Solana as she slept. She looked so peaceful, but he knew a storm was brewing inside her. He had seen how her hands trembled when she spoke of her past. The way her eyes had hardened when she talked about the man who had abused her. Bernat's fists clenched in anger, but he forced himself to relax. There was nothing he could do about it now. All he could do was be there for her if she needed him.

The gentle rise and fall of her chest betrayed the deep sleep she was in. He allowed himself to appreciate her raw beauty before turning his attention back to keeping watch. It was going to be a long night.

Chapter Twenty-Four

FEAR ON FIRE

Solana

S olana opened her eyes, and her mouth stretched wide with a yawn; she could hear the faint chirping of birds as they celebrated the morning. Light streamed softly through the trees, illuminating everything with a grey light. She stretched her arms towards the sky and arched her back, inhaling deeply and exhaling contentedly.

She hadn't slept this well in years. The pressures of being a Commander weighed heavily on her shoulders ever since she'd been promoted. The lives of every Slayer and trainee rested in her palms, and that was a responsibility she didn't take lightly.

Just then, she realized that she shouldn't feel so well rested at all. Bernat was meant to wake her so she could take up her shift on watch.

Early morning sunlight streamed through the opening in the shelter, casting long shadows across her face. With a curse on her tongue, she bolted to a seat and ripped Bernat's cloak from her shoulders. Damn him for letting her sleep through the night! How dare he presume she was weak and needed him to treat her like a child.

She crawled from the lean-to, angry words ready to sail from her lips when she found Bernat hunched over with his arms wrapped around his middle. A groan escaped his lips, and he dropped to one knee.

Forgetting to be upset with him, she rushed to his side. She did a quick scan of their surroundings but found no imminent threat. "What's wrong?" she asked, hating the note of fear she heard in her own voice.

Bernat moaned again, his face twisted in pain. "I don't know," he said through clenched teeth.

"I don't feel right," he added as his shoulders shook.

Suddenly, his body convulsed, and he vomited onto the ground. Solana didn't flinch at the sight, having seen and smelled worse while guarding the Wall.

"It's okay, I'm here," she said, rubbing his back as he continued to empty the contents of his stomach. His body radiated heat into her palm, indicating he had a fever.

He dry heaved for a few moments before collapsing onto his side, trembling all over. "What's happening?" he asked, his voice barely above a whisper.

"I don't know," Solana said, her mind racing as she tried to think of what could be causing this. She racked her brain for any possible illnesses or toxins that could cause such violent symptoms but came up blank. "Just rest, Bernat," she said helplessly as she watched him curl into himself in an attempt to stop the shaking.

His face was flushed red and shiny with a thin coating of sweat. Solana laid her palm on his forehead. His skin was so hot to the touch that she yanked her hand back in shock.

Just then, Bernat's body began to twist and contort before Solana's eyes. He arched his back and groaned in pain as his body lengthened and widened with muscle. The golden brown skin of his neck erupted with black fur, and silver hairs sprouted all along his limbs. As his limbs lengthened, his fingers separated and lengthened into large, sharp claws. His ears shifted and rounded out as his nose lengthened into a snout. Sharp teeth sprouted from his mouth, and he gave a loud growl as he transformed into a massive bear.

The bear moved toward her, and she pulled a tlazon from the sheaths strapped across her chest. The metallic shlikt-shlikt-shlikt of the small lance scraping against the leather scabbard echoed in the quiet of the morning like the warning call of a bird of prey. She leveled it at him and loosened another, the long tip slicing through the air. The bear swatted the small lance with a giant paw and roared, his blue eyes flashing. He swiped for her, missing by a hair. The fur on his back stood up as he snarled.

Solana reached for her machete sheathed at her hip, only to find that it wasn't there. She'd removed it before going to sleep, and it was still in their shelter. The bear advanced, and Solana lunged toward the lean-to.

She scrambled towards the tent, arms pumping, the bear's steps pounding the ground behind her as she dove inside and grabbed her machete. She turned just in time to see the bear's massive body slam into the structure. The whole thing collapsed on top of her, pinning her underneath the weight of debris and lumber, making it hard to breathe as she tried to squirm free.

The bear began to tear at the pile of tarp and limbs surrounding her. She had to get out of here. She began to claw at the blankets and branches with all her might, trying to reach her machete. She needed to defend herself. Each swipe at the ground yielded nothing but more dirt under her fingernails.

The bear clawed at the tarp with its powerful front paws and dug its claws through the fabric. Finally, she felt her hand come into contact with a smooth, hard surface. Claws swiped at her shoulder, digging in as she bit down on a scream of pain. Her hand closed around the cold hilt of her machete, and she pulled it out of its sheath in one fluid motion. Grabbing another tlazon from her chest sheath, she drove the sharp edge into the bear's paw. The bear recoiled with a roar, and she felt the weight lift off of her.

Untangling the tarp from her body, she scrambled to her feet and searched for higher ground. The bear made a keening sound as it pulled the tlazon from its paw with its teeth before spitting it onto the ground. Not one to waste precious time, Solana dove for the trees. She could hear the bear crashing through the woods behind her, every step shaking the ground, but she didn't dare look back. She focused on putting one foot in front of the other as she sprinted towards a nearby tree with a wide trunk.

She pushed herself to run faster, but the bear's hot breath was on her neck, and she knew that she wasn't going to make it.

Just as the bear was about to overtake her, she dove to the side and came up swinging with a primal roar on her lips. The sound of her battle cry echoed through the woods as the machete sank into the bear's shoulder. The bear bellowed in pain as it reared up on its hindquarters, flinging Solana to the ground. The force of the blow knocked the wind from her lungs, and she scrambled backward on her hands and feet until she hit the trunk of a tree.

The bear thrashed about, the machete still embedded in its shoulder. After a few moments, the bear stopped trying to dislodge the machete and turned its attention to Solana. The bear was upon her now, its teeth bared and saliva dripping from its mouth.

Her heart hammered in her chest as she stared at the bear that was once Bernat. But instead of attacking her, the bear made a soft noise in the back of its throat and nuzzled his nose against her cheek before scooting back to sit on its haunches.

Solana let out the breath she was holding and quirked her head as she stared at the bear. He looked just like any other bear except for his eyes. They were human eyes, azure and filled with intelligence. Bernat's eyes. The bear blinked at her and opened his mouth in a wide yawn, revealing rows of white teeth and a pink tongue.

"Bernat?" she asked, her heart beating wildly with fear and confusion. "Is that really you?"

The bear made another softer sound, almost like a sigh, and nodded its head. Looking apologetic, if a bear was even capable of such a thing, it dropped its bushy head to the ground and inched toward her, nudging her foot with his nose.

Solana didn't understand what was happening and felt as if the ground had slipped out from under her as she just sat there, staring at Bernat, or rather bear-Bernat. After a moment of shock, she felt the confident and assured part of herself click back into place.

She had to fix this. Somehow. She didn't know how she'd turn him back into a human again, but she owed him her dedication to finding the solution. So, despite a tremor of fear vibrating in her chest, she held out her hand and ran her fingers through the bear's silky soft fur.

CHAPTER TWENTY-FIVE

WHEN IT'S ALL OVER

KIKI

T he rays of the growing morning crept over the horizon, chasing away the shadows and cloaking the campsite in grey pre-dawn light.

Kiki's eyes burned with fatigue, her body tense as a bowstring. She flicked her ears back and forth, listening for any sound that was out of place. She paced the perimeter of the campsite, not willing to take any chances. She didn't trust Aurelia and wasn't about to blindly accept the smuggler's word that the rune markings would protect them from roaming demons.

Turi shifted in his sleep. He'd shift into a bear any minute now and be lost to her until nightfall.

A pang of guilt sank its teeth into her heart, knowing full well that he wouldn't be in this position if he hadn't helped her in the first place. She quickly shoved the feeling to the back of her mind. It didn't serve her to dwell on past mistakes. All she could do now was move forward.

She rubbed her tired eyes with the back of her hand and stifled a yawn.

Suddenly, the woods fell eerily silent, and the air became brittle. Kiki's spine stiffened, her senses on high alert to the dread festering in her stomach. Then, a deafening roar shattered the calm, sending a shiver of fear through her heart.

Turi bolted upright, his head whipping around in search of the source. Luna huddled close to Aurelia, her hand curled into the silver-eyed girl's shirt.

Luna's eyes were wide and unblinking. "What is that?" Luna whispered.

"It sounds like another bear," Turi said, his head quirking to the side.

"Or a demon," Luna said, her voice trembling.

"We're safe inside the circle of runes; whatever it is, it can't hurt us," Aurelia replied, waving her hand dismissively in the air.

An ear-splitting yell echoed through the woods. A human yell.

Kiki's heart leaped into her throat at the distinctly high-pitched sound as if the source were feminine. "Did you hear that?" Kiki asked, whipping to face the others. "That was a person. They need help."

Kiki started toward the sound, but Turi wrapped his hand around her arm. "Wait, you don't know that. It could be a trick." Sweat beaded his brow, and the heat of his hand seeped through the fabric of her battle leathers, warming her skin.

"That could be Yari," Kiki hissed, yanking her arm from his grip. "Either come with me or get out of my way."

Turi recoiled at the sharpness of her words but stepped to the side.

Another blood-curdling scream pierced the silence, draining the color from Kiki's face. She sprinted headlong towards the sound.

Behind her, she thought she heard something. Turning around quickly, she saw Turi on the ground, writhing in pain, his face twisted in an expression of agony.

She hesitated for a moment, unsure if she should continue towards the woman screaming or help Turi. Though she'd only seen him shift once, the first time hadn't seemed painful for him.

Her stomach fluttered with unease as she turned her back on him and raced in the opposite direction. Her choice made her ill, but deep down, she knew it was the right one to make. Luna and Aurelia were already crouched by his side, tending to him. He was in better hands with the healer and his cousin than with her. She'd have nothing to offer him. But the screams, she could help with that.

She burst into a clearing and saw a black and silver bear rushing into the woods at the far side. She saw a small flash of red ahead of the bear's path and rushed forward. That person could still be Yari.

Hope fluttered in her chest as her feet pounded against the frozen ground. She raised her obsidian machete, ready to strike the creature across the neck when she recognized the person on the ground.

"Solana?" Kiki yelled, her arm faltering as she recognized Solana's fire-red hair, the curls escaping her usually perfect bun.

"Quirera?" Solana asked, her eyes meeting Kiki's in surprise.

At that exact moment, the bear whipped around to face Kiki. It roared at the sight of her machete, and Kiki quickly retreated a few steps as it reared onto its hind legs.

Kiki raised her machete again, prepared to defend herself, when Solana rushed to stand between them. "Stop!" she ordered, her voice as commanding as ever.

Before Kiki could ask if Solana had completely lost her mind, another roar tore through the air. Kiki whipped around to find Turi had shifted into his bear form and was racing headlong for the other bear.

Turi collided with the larger bear, his maws open in a vicious snarl as he tackled the creature to the ground.

"No!" Solana yelled as she dove for her own weapons scattered across the ground.

"What are you doing?" Kiki cried as Solana gripped her bow and was notching an arrow with trembling hands. She pushed Solana into a nearby tree, knocking the arrow from her fingers.

Solana drew her knee up and rammed it into Kiki's gut, causing Kiki to double over, gasping for air.

"You won't believe me, but that bear is Bernat," Solana said as she brought her elbows across Kiki's back.

A grunt escaped Kiki's lips, and she collapsed to the cold ground with a thud.

Solana retrieved her arrow and notched it in place.

"Stop," Kiki gasped, her voice coming out in a choked whisper. "You'll kill Turi."

Solana paused, the arrow pulled back and ready to loosen it. "What?" Solana snarled.

Just then, Luna and Aurelia caught up, their breaths heavy as they doubled over, resting their hands on their knees.

Panting, Luna said, "The other bear is Turi."

Solana looked between all three of them, her face lined with confusion. "Someone explain to me what is going on here," she demanded.

Kiki pushed herself to her feet, using a nearby tree for balance. "It's some kind of curse."

Aurelia stepped up then, her hands held in front of her in a gesture of peace. "If you just put the weapon down, we can all talk calmly."

Solana shifted her sights to Aurelia. "It's you," she sneered. "The smuggler from the dungeon. You threw acid on me."

Aurelia winced. "I don't suppose it's too late for an apology?"

Solana bared her teeth in a snarl as she drew the string back, pointing the arrow's tip at Aurelia. "Start talking, or I'll send this arrow straight through your heart."

CHAPTER TWENTY-SIX

START A WAR

ERASMO

The day was bright, and the sun burned with a fierce heat. Erasmo shielded his eyes from the sun's glare with his hand and felt the sting of the shift pushing against his flesh. He touched the carved wooden pendant hanging from his neck and breathed in the scent of sweet grass. As long as he kept it on, the totem would protect him from becoming the beast during the day.

He had ridden through the night until Ocaso's legs trembled and his muscles quaked.

He had left his stallion with a kind villager who offered his barn for a few coins in return.

He watched the Ocaso drowsily nibble on hay and thought how he must look to the old man as he passed a few pieces of gold into his papery hand. Sweat and grime covered his skin, and his boots and tunic were covered in foul-smelling mud.

He rubbed his horse's nose and said, "I'm sorry, boy. But I can't stop until I've found her. My mate. She's out there, and I can sense her every feeling. I'll be back. I promise."

Ocaso chuffed and butted Erasmo's arm with his muzzle before snuffling at the bag of oats.

After hours of walking, Erasmo rounded a bend in the road and stopped. He stretched his neck, rotated his shoulders, then paused and sniffed the air. A sudden rush of emotions filled him--excitement, adrenaline, trepidation--but he didn't know why. Erasmo closed his eyes, concentrated, and reached out to search for the woman who had been in his head his entire life.

He could feel her every emotion. Something was happening, and he was too far away to do anything about it.

A growl ripped from his lips, and he continued his trek toward her as if drawn by an invisible string.

She was close. So very close. But she wasn't alone.

Two more strings within grew taut and pulsed with heat. They tugged at Eramo's heart and compelled him to follow them as well.

He stopped dead in his tracks as he followed those two threads to their source and felt a stab of pain in his gut when he reached the end.

"No," he whispered with a pained gasp. "It can't be. They can't be here."

His heart hammered in his chest at the realization that all of the elements of the prophecy were finally coming together. His lost brothers were here. There was no denying the feeling in his heart leading him to them.

They'd crossed the darkness, and the curse had taken them. He could feel their shift as if it were his own, and he clamped his mouth shut, letting the scream of pain die in his throat.

Everything he'd been avoiding his whole life was coming together into one awful cluster, and if he didn't hurry, the prophecy would come true.

Erasmo crested the top of a hill when he felt his mate's terror like a physical blow. It brought him to his knees, and he inhaled sharply through his nostrils. He felt the shadows shifting beneath his skin, itching to be released. The fear from his mate calling them forth. But he couldn't release them.

Each shift stole more and more of his humanity. Led him into the dark swirling abyss, and if he kept pushing it, he'd never again climb back out.

Gritting his teeth and pushing to his feet, he pushed onward. He had to find his mate and warn her about the prophecy before it was too late.

He finally reached the edge of his territory and stopped, looking out over the vast expanse before him. He could see for miles in every direction, but there was no sign of movement. No sign of life.

But she was here. Erasmo could still sense her. He turned to head down the ridge to continue on his way when he heard a branch snap.

Erasmo spun around, his hand going to the knife at his waist.

Standing before him were two figures, their faces hidden by hoods pulled low over their heads.

"Who are you?" Erasmo demanded. "What do you want?"

The figures said nothing, only stepped forward menacingly.

Erasmo could feel the shift inside of him stirring, the beast within him rising to the surface.

He fought against it with everything he had but could feel himself losing control. The beast within wanted out. It wanted blood. It hadn't feasted in days, and it was growing restless.

"I'll ask you again," he growled through gritted teeth. "Who are you. And what do you want with me?"

As if waiting for his challenge, one of the figures slowly drew back its hood.

Erasmo growled. It was Tomás. The smuggler.

"Did you really think you could get away with slaughtering my men?" Tomás asked, his face pulled in a sneer. "You messed with the wrong man, prince," he hissed.

The beast within rippled under Erasmo's skin, and he rolled his shoulders as the shadows he kept tightly tucked away leaked from his skin.

The air around his body shifted as the shadows curled around him, pooling at his feet and rolling over the ground. Erasmo fought the shadows, his chest heaving as he tried to reign them in. But it was no use. The beast was hungry. Starved. It wanted out, and it wanted out now.

On a pained exhale, Erasmo said, "That's where you're wrong, Tomás. I'm more than just a prince."

Tomás had the sense to take a step back as the shadows grew, and his eyes widened at the claws pushing from Erasmo's knuckles.

Erasmo rolled his neck, the pain in his muscles begging to be released. His lip curled at the corner of his mouth as the beast rose above the surface and spoke through his mouth. "You should know better than to go hunting monsters."

With a snarl, Erasmo launched himself at the nearest figure, his talons extended fully from his hands as he slashed down and ripped the man in half.

Tomás whistled, and a group of hooded men slunk from the nearby trees. They charged toward Erasmo with battle cries sailing from their lips.

In an instant, Erasmo was locked in a combat of talons against blades. He roared as the shadows rippled from his skin and lashed out at the nearest attackers, the darkness rushing into nostrils and eyes until the men dropped to the ground, dead.

Tomás yelled for his men to keep attacking, and suddenly, Erasmo felt a sharp pain in his neck.

But it didn't slow him down for a second, and he continued his attack on the bandits before him, determined to take them down one by one and protect everything that mattered most to him.

But soon, his movements became sluggish. His next swipe with his claws missed, and he spiraled face-first into the dirt.

He felt his blood thicken, and Tomás came to stand over him. "Not so tough now, are you?" He held a dark between his fingers and smirked.

"Just a little dose of nightshade to keep you under until I can get you back to the boss."

Erasmo frowned at that. He didn't know Tomás to be one to work for anyone. As his eyes slowly drifted closed, he noticed a metal charm hanging from Tomás's belt, and a growl ripped from his throat.

A pewter rose glinted in the light as if mocking him.

The Rose of the North. The symbol of his brother. Arlando.

So his brother had finally made his move. So he wanted to start a war.

Erasmo fought against the sleep that tugged at his body, but the poison running through his veins was too much and before long, the darkness claimed him.

Chapter Twenty-Seven

SAVAGE

Kiki

K iki leaned against a tree and picked the dirt from under her nails with a knife. She stood within earshot as Aurelia explained the Ozero curse to Solana and the connection between Bernat and Turi. Once Aurelia's tale was done, Solana's breath whooshed from her lips as if she'd been punched before she sank to the ground and hung her head.

Kiki couldn't help but take a small measure of comfort that Solana's frozen exterior seemed to crack under the news. Kiki hadn't crumbled to the ground, after all.

Pushing off the tree, Kiki came to stand before the Commander. "We've answered your questions. Now, it's our turn." Solana's eyes narrowed at the harshness in Kiki's tone. "What are you doing here? Did you follow us?"

Solana got to her feet and met Kiki's hard gaze, standing inches from her face. "Watch your tone, Xochicale. I'm still your Commanding Officer, and you'll show me the proper respect due to my station."

Kiki scoffed in the Commander's face. "Look around you, *Commander*, "Kiki sneered, motioning to the forest around them. "We're not in the Demon Corps anymore. I don't answer to you anymore."

Solana raised an eyebrow, her gaze darkening. The air between them crackled with hostility as the two Slayers glared at each other, both holding their ground, unwilling to budge.

Before either of them could say another word, Aurelia rushed forward and placed a hand on each woman's shoulder in an attempt to separate them. "Come now," she said with a smile on her face. "We're all on the same side here. There's no need for all this macha energy.

Let's take it down a notch and discuss what we're going to do next."

Kiki pulled away from Aurelia with a scoff. No good could come from Aurelia talking sense. Solana nodded in agreement, not once taking her frozen gaze from Kiki.

The tension slowly dissipated as they turned their attention to Aurelia.

Aurelia rubbed her palms together as she looked between the two Slayers. "Good. This is good. See? We're making progress here."

"Get on with it, smuggler," Solana huffed.

Aurelia shook her head at the interjection and pointed an accusatory finger at both Kiki and Solana. "You two are more alike than you think."

Both Kiki and Solana threw the other matching sneers before turning their faces away.

"Now," Aurelia began. "We're going to have to work together if we hope to end this curse. So, until then, no more in-fighting. Agreed?" She looked between the two women expectantly.

Kiki peered at Solana through her peripherals and hated to admit that in one thing, Aurelia was right. She and Solana were both as stubborn as mules. If Kiki didn't offer a truce first, it would never happen.

Kiki turned and held out her hand to Solana. "Commander," she said the word like salt on her tongue.

At the use of her official title, Solana faced Kiki and eyed her outstretched hand as if it were a pile of tapir dung. Heaving a sigh, Solana jutted her hand out and gave Kiki's hand a brief shake before jerking it away.

"Now what?" Solana asked, her tone full of annoyance.

Aurelia hid a smirk behind her hand but quickly wiped it away. "Now we regroup and go find those bears."

Aurelia led the way with Luna by her side as they set out in search of Turi and Bernat.

Kiki dropped to the back to keep an eye out for any threats, but she wasn't the only one with the same idea. Next to her, Solana adjusted her pack on her shoulders, her head on a swivel as her gaze scanned the trees.

The tension between them was still thick in the air, and it set Kiki's nerves on edge. Every broken tree branch from a passing animal had Kiki drawing her machete, ready to fight.

"Will you stop that?" Solana huffed after Kiki had whirled around to face off against a very startled deer.

"Oh, I'm sorry. Am I bothering you?" Kiki asked, her voice dripping with sarcasm. "Maybe you don't mind being eaten by a demon, but I do."

"Fine, what do I know anyway," Solana quipped.

The reminder of Solana's superiority made Kiki clench her teeth together to keep from snapping back a response. Once she'd gotten herself under control, Kiki sighed heavily and turned to the Commander. "You never answered my question. What are you doing here?"

Kiki didn't put it past Solana to have traipsed through the Cicatrix with her signature arrogance for the sole purpose of dragging drag Kiki back to the Corps to face punishment.

Solana's jaw clenched, and her step faltered before she quickly recovered. "Do you remember the night of the breach? During the graduation carnival?"

"Obviously," Kiki sneered. "Yari was taken that night, and when I reported her disappearance to you, you refused to believe me. Instead, you threw it in my face that she was a piss-poor Slayer and wasn't set to graduate. You're the whole reason I'm here."

Solana cleared her throat and adjusted the high collar of her Slayer gear as if it was suddenly too tight. "I may have been too quick in passing judgment."

Kiki's mouth fell open. Was Solana Ramirez apologizing? Or as close to an apology as Kiki was ever going to get. Impossible!

"Oh, stop it," Solana grumbled. "After you, Healer Luna, and Officer Artchete deserted, there was a second breach. Several Yearlings, Attendants, and Slayers went missing. No bodies were found. Just gone."

A sense of victory washed over Kiki at knowing she'd been right. Though she'd known in her heart that Yari wasn't dead, hearing Solana's report only made Kiki more confident in her theory.

"What happened to the rest of your group? Or did the Corps send only you two?" Kiki asked.

Solana's throat bobbed as if she were choking on a lump of dry meat. "It's just Bernat and me."

Kiki quirked her head at the way the Commander was mincing words. "Did you ask for reinforcements, or did you really think just you and your second could storm in here and rescue the Slayers taken?" Solana remained silent, the air thickening around them with unsaid words. "Not even *you* are that arrogant, "Kiki mused as she ran through the limited facts Solana had divulged. "Wait," she barked. "Did you desert? The great Solana Ramirez, the prodigy of the Corps, deserted?"

Solana whipped around the face Kiki, her ice-blue eyes filled with a fire that Kiki had never seen before. "Those Slayers' lives are my responsibility. I owe it to them to do everything I can to bring them home safely. The Corps be damned for their short-sightedness. I wasn't about to let my people die without fighting for them first."

Kiki retreated a step back as shock rolled over her. "I didn't realize you cared so much," she said, a note of bitterness in her voice.

Solana clenched her hands into fists at her sides. "And *that*, Xochicale, has always been your greatest weakness, "the Commander sneered as she pushed past Kiki to follow after Aurelia and Luna.

"What's that supposed to mean?" Kiki barked back.

"Empathy," Solana growled. "You have none. You think only of yourself. You mask it behind the guise that you are looking out for your friends, but at the core of it, you're incredibly selfish. You give no consideration for how others feel and possess full conviction that the path you've decided is best. You never doubt yourself. It's what makes you a great Slayer, but it's also what makes you a shitty human."

Solana's words hit Kiki as if she'd been stabbed in the gut. Something about the accusation poked at a secret fear Kiki had buried within her heart long ago.

"Aurelia was right about one thing. We're more similar than either of us care to admit. Because if I lack empathy, then you're guilty of the same," Kiki hissed.

Solana shook her head, her eyes full of pity. "You don't know the first thing about me, Xochicale. The worst part is you likely never will. You're too in love with yourself to care for anyone else," Solana sneered. "Look at you.

There is something clearly wrong with Luna, but are you with her? Comforting her? Doing whatever you can to help her? No. You're not. You're back here fighting with me. And Turi? That boy has loved you for longer than you even know. Yet do you care? No. And now he's part of some curse that will eventually strip away his humanity, yet what are you doing about it? Nothing."

Kiki suddenly felt cold, as if the winter winds had seeped into the marrow of her very bones until they were frail and brittle, primed to shatter with the least amount of pressure.

Kiki clenched her jaw so hard that her teeth hurt. "I hate you," she hissed.

Solana snorted. "Grow up, Xochicale. Be better. If any of us are going to make it out of this mess alive, we're going to need you at your best."

Solana increased her pace, leaving Kiki alone at the back of the group, her heart heavy.

CHAPTER TWENTY-EIGHT

ALONE TOGETHER

YARIXA

Yari woke the following day and found herself back in her room. She vaguely remembered Arlando carrying her to her bed while she cried over the news that she was stuck in the Cicatrix.

Her heart was still heavy and full of grief as she rolled over on the feather-soft mattress. She burrowed deeper into the fur blankets and was about to pull the blanket over her head when she noticed a crimson rose sitting in a glass case on the bedside table.

A notecard with print scrawled across it lay on the table next to the flower. Yari it up and read it aloud. "I found this flower in the gardens while on my morning walk," Yari felt warmth run down the sides of her neck as she realized the note was from Arlando. "The sight of it so bright and full of life against the bitter cold reminded me of you. May it bring a smile to your face as it did mine." She set the note aside and glanced at the flower once more. The stem and bud spun suspended in the air, seeming to radiate with an inner glow.

Sure enough, the corners of Yari's mouth lifted as she imagined the handsome Arlando walking around the castle grounds, his face serene as he plucked the resilient rose.

A soft knock at the door pulled Yari from her daydream, and she called out, "Come in!"

Sergio cracked open the door and peered inside. When he saw that Yari was dressed, he pushed the door open and walked over to place a silver tray full of steaming buns and turnovers on the little table in front of the fire. "Master wishes you a good morning," he said as he set the tray beside a jar of honey. "He hopes you slept well and asks that I check if you have everything you need."

Yari's eyes flicked to the dwindling fire and the cold seeping through the stone. She knew she was a burden to Sergio and Arlando, but she didn't want to trouble them. She appreciated their kindness. "I'm fine, thank you," she replied, her voice soft. "You've both been so kind to me; I couldn't have asked for a more gracious host."

Sergio followed where her gaze had lingered. "I didn't realize the fires were dying," he said stiffly, and he began to silently move chunks of firewood from the pile to the fireplace. As the fire sparked and crackled, the room gradually warmed.

Yari stepped out of her plush bed and softly padded over to the tray of food. She resisted the urge to snatch everything off the tray, her instincts warring with her desire to give off an air of civility. As the fire roared to life, Yari sighed with relief. It was as if the fire were trying to erase the pain that had settled in her heart like ice.

After a few minutes, Sergio stood up and brushed soot from his hands before straightening his livery. "It's a little warmer," he remarked. "Master would like to pay a visit if the lady is willing," he added, a note of annoyance in his voice.

Through a mouthful of sweet bread, Yari responded, "Of course! I'll be glad to see him. He doesn't need to ask permission; this is his home, after all."

Sergio stood straighter as if her answer pleased him. He bowed again, turned on his heel, and left the room.

Once the footman had left, Yari couldn't help but feel a wave of guilt wash over her. She was an unwelcome guest, even if Arlando didn't make her feel that way. Arlando was of good enough breeding not to let his true feelings show. On the other hand, Sergio had no qualms about making her feel like the intruder she truly was.

She wouldn't become a burden to Arlando or Sergio. She'd have to make herself useful if she was truly stuck in the Cicatrix. Earn her stay here in the castle.

After she ate breakfast and washed her face in a basin of water, she dressed in a simple pair of black fleece-lined leggings and a gray fur-lined poncho. She wandered out of her room and to the main hall where she had dined with Arlando the night before, determination filling her to find a way to pay Arlando back for all of his kindness.

In the late morning light, the hall seemed colder than it had during dinner the night before, with its candles and hearth glowing. The structure was bare of any decoration. Not even a single picture hung on the walls for Yari to imagine the household's former glory.

She walked over to the solid oak table but didn't sit down. Her fingers traced the edges and the grooves of the wood surface. She wondered how many people had sat in this very room.

What happened to the people Arlando had cared about? Where were they now?

Yari imagined that Arlando had seen much grief in his life, and the dreary castle was proof of that.

"That is such a lovely view," a familiar voice said behind her.

Yari spun to find Arlando descending the grand staircase. He wore a bright blue tunic over white pants with a white fur cape draped across his shoulders. Rays of sunlight filtered through the stained glass windows, casting him in an ethereal glow that stole Yari's breath away. She couldn't help the heat that rose in her cheeks and quickly looked away, blushing.

When he stood an arm's length away, he reached out a tucked a strand of her loose brown hair behind her ear. "Beautiful," he said, almost breathless.

Yari looked down at the ground to hide her pleasure at his compliment. "You don't need to flatter me," she said softly. "You've done so much for me, saved my life, given me somewhere warm to sleep and clothes to wear. I can't ask for more."

"You could ask the world of me, and I'd do anything to give it to you," he hummed.

Yari bit her bottom lip as his words sent a rush of delicious heat through her core.

Arlando quirked his head to the side. "Has no one ever told you how stunning you are?"

Yari glanced up at him through her lashes and shook her head.

Arlando snorted softly, then reached out and brushed the back of his knuckles against her cheek. "Or how waves of gold spread around your face when the sun hits your hair, making you seem like an angel? Or how when you smile, your cheeks dimple?"

Yari could feel her eyes filling with tears as Arlando spoke with that earnest tone. No one had ever said such things to her. Least of all, a man like Arlando. Her breath caught in her throat as she stared at him, unable to speak.

He brushed his fingers along her cheek as he whispered to her, "You are everything I have ever wanted." She quivered as he caressed her skin, sending tingles of pleasure racing through her body and stirring feelings she'd never known. He pulled her closer and said, "Everything I ever dreamed of."

She looked up at him, unable to stop asking, "How can you say that? You've only just met me."

Arlando's eyes burned into hers and his lips curved into a soft smile sending a flame blazing through her heart. "I've waited a long time for you, Yarixa," he said, his voice husky. "Now that you're finally here, I won't let you go," he purred as he wrapped his arms around Yari, pulling her close. His touch sent tingles of pleasure racing through her body, stirring a longing deep in her heart. Yari let herself melt into his embrace, the rightness of it filling her with courage as she'd never had before. His words sent waves of excitement bursting through her veins. "Do you feel it too? That feeling like you're alive for the first time? Like you've been wandering around this life, but now it's like the sun has burst inside your heart, filling every dark crevice with joy?"

Yari nodded her head, her breaths coming in ragged gasps. She wanted to stay in Arlando's arms forever. He made her feel safe and cherished, as if she had come home.

Arlando grinned as he combed his fingers through her hair, sweeping it aside, then dipped his head down and pressed a feather-light kiss to her lips. His lips were soft against hers, and she melted into the warmth of his touch and the pure love that radiated from him.

As their kiss deepened, Yari was consumed by the feeling that she'd finally found what she'd been searching for her entire life. She'd been searching for him, and there was no place she'd rather be. For the first time in her life, she felt truly alive. She returned his kiss with equal passion as she pressed her body to his muscular chest.

He pulled away from her and stared into her eyes, as breathless as she was. "I promise I will explain everything to you," he whispered, inches from her face. "How I've been searching for you. How I'd given up all hope of ever finding you, but for now, can we just have this moment?"

Yari responded with a simple "yes." She liked the sound of that. She wanted to be with Arlando, where she felt cared for and safe. Where she could feel like her life had a purpose and that she wasn't just a meaningless, useless waste of space anymore.

He leaned in to kiss her again, and Yari opened her mouth to him, unable to resist the desire that pulsed between them. She wrapped her arms around his neck and leaned in to deepen the kiss. They broke apart after a few moments, and he grinned at her, mischief glinting in his eyes.

"Come with me," he said with a gleaming smile. "I have something I want to show you."

Yari let him pull her away from the great hall, and they walked down the stone corridor together, her heart full and beaming.

CHAPTER TWENTY-NINE

FAKE

YARIXA

Arlando led Yari through the grand halls of the castle. Great beams of oak and pine supported the vaulted ceilings and ran lengthwise down the length of the corridors, the most ornamentation she'd seen so far. They were intricately carved with scenes of battle and triumphs. The air was warm and smelled like wood smoke. Like the great hall, there was little decoration, and the walls were bare of portraits.

Yari assumed he had lost many loved ones to the darkness that consumed the land and didn't ask him about it. She knew well what it was like to have everything she loved stripped from her.

Arlando paused at a set of double oak doors banded with metal strips. His eyes gleamed with excitement. "Do you trust me?"

Yari nodded, a giddy feeling in her chest. This was the happiest she'd ever been.

Arlando moved behind her and placed his hands over her eyes. "No peeking," he whispered, sending a shiver down her spine.

Yari allowed him to lead her through the doors and trusted him every step.

"Now, open your eyes," he said, his tone full of reverence.

Yari slowly peeled open her eyes, and what she saw made her gasp. All around were bookcases full of leather-bound tomes. Shelves stretched from wall to wall, each crammed full of books and scrolls. Books were stacked on the floor, on top of chairs, and sprawled over desks all around. The library had three more mezzanine levels, all full of shelves bursting with leather tomes.

"Do you like it?" Arlando asked, a note of uncertainty dimming the spark in his eyes.

Yari turned to him, shocked beyond speech. Finally, she managed to find the words. "It's wonderful! I've never seen so many before!" she exclaimed.

He beamed as he took her hand and led her toward a shelf. "For years, I've been plagued with this feeling to add more to the collection." He gestured to a frame full of colorful spines.

Yari reached out and plucked a familiar title from the rest. "Romance books?" she asked, looking up at Arlando.

"I don't even read them; I'm more of a history reader. But I couldn't shake the sense that I had to bring these here. That it was vitally important. Now I know why," he said as she smiled and brushed the side of her face with his fingertips.

Yari bit her lip, lost in his gaze. She leaned forward to touch her lips to his when a soft knock at the entrance to the library interrupted the moment.

Arlando's piercing blue gaze flicked to the source, and he blew out a frustrated breath. "What now, Sergio?" he asked, his tone full of annoyance.

Sergio lurked in the shadows with a letter in his hands. "Urgent news, my lord."

Arlando turned back to Yari and pressed a kiss to the center of her forehead. "Stay as long as you want; it's yours."

Yari took a step back. "What?" she gasped. "I couldn't possibly-"

Arlando pressed his lips to hers to muffle her protests. "Everything in my lands is yours now. Including me," he said, his voice turning husky. "I'll return as soon as I'm able."

Yari frowned. "What's wrong? Is something happening?"

Arlando waved away her concerns. "Just some silly border disputes. The Eastern territory is always trying to stretch its wings. It's nothing for you to worry about," he said with an easy smile.

He kept his gaze on the paper as he and Sergio left the library. Yari did her best to read his expression, but he didn't give himself away. Still, she couldn't shake the feeling that more was going on, but he was too kind to burden her with it. Yari smiled at the thought that he cared for her. This library, full of books meant for her, was all the proof she needed. It felt right, her being here with him. She set aside her worries and turned to find a new book to read. There were so many. She didn't know where to start! What a great problem to have.

Yari turned the page in the book she was reading and shifted in her seat to get a better view of the text by the candlelight. Finishing the chapter, she closed the tome with a contented sigh and glanced out the window to see that the snowy landscape had been cast into dark shades of blue. The sun had long set, and now the winds were blowing snow flurries across the windowpane. She wondered what time it was. Her stomach growled, reminding her that many hours had passed since she'd last eaten.

She backtracked through the maze of corridors in search of her room. As she twisted down the hallway, she realized she was lost. She slowed her steps as she made her way back to the library to start over, then paused as a shadow darted down the hall ahead of her.

She called out, "Hello? Is anyone there?" She didn't get an answer but stepped on light feet to catch up.

She rounded the end of the corridor and came face to face with a woman with wild hair and a crazed look in her eyes. The stranger hissed at her, baring white teeth, and reached out as if to scratch Yari's eyes out. Without thinking, Yari cried and stumbled backward, frantically trying to escape the madwoman's clutches.

"Leave this place!" the woman snarled as she curled her hands into Yari's poncho, her grip tightening. "Death lurks here. Darkness breeds. Run for your life, child!" The woman released Yari and pushed her down the corridor. "Run!"

Yari's heart pounded in her chest, and she ran as fast as she could down the many winding hallways of the castle, desperate to get away from the deranged woman.

Finally out of breath, she collapsed against a wall in an empty hallway and tried desperately not to hyperventilate. She closed her eyes for a moment and took several deep breaths, trying to calm herself down before continuing on her way.

She wondered who that woman was and why she'd seemed so unhinged. Yari hadn't seen other people in the castle save for the servants. The woman seemed like she didn't belong there, and Yari decided that she should inform Arlando immediately.

Yari bit her lip in thought as she retreated a step back and crashed into a full and firm chest.

She whirled around to find Sergio standing right behind her. "What are you doing in the east wing?" he asked, his beady eyes narrowing as he looked her up and down.

Yari shrank back at his cold appraisal, then coughed to clear her throat. "I got lost," she said, barely an audible squeak. "I was looking for my way back. There was a woman—"

Sergio grabbed her arm in a vice grip, making the words in her mouth disappear. He pulled her towards the other wing. "Master would be furious if he knew you were down in the east wing."

Yari's mouth went dry. "I didn't mean anything by it," she said as tears slipped down her cheeks. Sergio's knuckles turned white as his grip on her arm increased. "You're hurting me. Let go!" She yanked her arm from his grasp and rubbed her hand over the red marks left by his fingers.

Sergio huffed as he pointed down the hall, scowling. "Your quarters are that way."

Yari frowned as she pushed past him and returned to her room. She didn't understand why Sergio seemed to hate her. She hadn't done anything to him. Or at least nothing that she could think of.

A sense of unease blossomed in her gut at meeting the deranged woman and Sergio's strange behavior. She resolved to keep Sergio's actions to herself. She didn't want the footman hating her more than he already did, and she was reluctant to cause further problems for Arlando.

Sighing, she settled onto the bed and pulled the covers over her chest. A sense of longing made her chest tight as she thought of Kiki and Luna. She wished she could go back to the way things were. To the safety of what she knew. But that was impossible, and that thought alone made her eyes well with tears.

CHAPTER THIRTY

PLAY WITH FIRE

KIKI

S weat trickled down Kiki's forehead, cutting rivulets through the grime on her face. The expansive forest was suffocating. Hours had passed since she last glimpsed the sun, and all she could smell was the rank decay of winter in the air, making breathing more difficult as she squeezed through the dense trees.

Kiki jogged to catch up with Luna and pulled her friend to a stop. "What's going on with you?" she asked. "You haven't been yourself lately."

"I'm fine," Luna whispered, her jaw tightening as she shook her head, but a glimmer of a tear betrayed her.

Softly, Kiki tried again. "You're not," she said, resting a hand on Luna's shoulder. "I'm worried about you."

Luna turned to face Kiki and sighed. "It's nothing," she muttered. "You wouldn't understand."

Kiki's eyes flashed, and her shoulders tensed. "No? I've seen you with blood up to your elbows as you pumped a Slayer's heart with your bare hands, keeping them an inch from death. You have nerves of steel. Nothing shakes you up. Whatever you saw was enough to rock you to your core."

Luna shifted from foot to foot as she pulled her shoulders up to her ears.

The sting of rejection burned through Kiki's veins. Luna had never shut her out before.

Kiki frowned. "You can either tell me, and we'll work it out together, or you can turn to some pretty stranger you've known for a few days and divulge all your secrets to her," Kiki snapped.

Luna glared at Kiki. "Leave Aurelia out of this."

Kiki scoffed. "So you're trusting the smuggler but not me?"

"At least she's been there for me," Luna mumbled.

Kiki stepped back as if Luna had slapped her. "Well, don't stop now," Kiki said, her voice flat and cold. "Go ahead and say what you really mean."

Luna bit her lip. "I didn't mean it like that," Luna whispered as she turned away from Kiki.

"Fine," Kiki scowled, her shoulders slumping forward. "Trust the random stranger you barely know rather than your best friend." She stomped towards the front of the hiking group where Turi and Bernat were waiting.

She sidled up to Turi and ran her fingers through the soft fur along his neck. "Ugh, why am I such an ass," she grumbled as she buried her face in his fur. She took his grunt to mean that he agreed with her. "I don't mean to be insensitive," Kiki whined. "I just don't know how to express myself sometimes." Turi snorted as if to say he knew that all too well.

Kiki didn't like the feelings of jealousy that stirred in her heart every time she saw Luna and Aurelia together with their heads bowed as they talked in whispers. Kiki didn't like feeling as if, one day, Luna would sweep her aside and discard her once Kiki no longer had a purpose.

It had always been her, Luna, and Yari against the world. No one else mattered. No one else was ever more important. They were sisters, if not by blood, then by the blood they had shed together.

She was so caught in her own thoughts that she didn't notice the sound of a blade sliding free from its sheath. The cold steel pressed against her throat before she even knew what was happening to her.

The next thing she knew, a group of men burst from the trees and attacked the rest of the group. Turi and Bernat reared up on their hind legs and growled, swiping their giant paws through a row of men lunging at them. But they were quickly hit in the chest by darts that made them teeter on the balls of their feet. Before they could regain their balance and attack, both bears were knocked to the ground by a second volley of darts.

Solana was a righteous fury as she fought to defend their group. Screams of pain surrounded her as she slashed her obsidian machete through a group of men trying to corral her. But even the fearless Commander couldn't fight back all of their attackers and was soon disarmed and pinned to the ground.

As Kiki was shoved to the ground by her attacker, she turned to find Aurelia defending Luna with bared teeth and a short sword in her hand. She pushed Luna behind her against a nearby tree, trying to keep the Healer away from the swarm of attackers. But another man snuck past her and grabbed Luna as he held a knife to her throat.

"Look what we have here," a cold voice said.

Aurelia immediately stopped fighting when she saw the knife to Luna's throat.

The man turned his gaze to each bear and snickered as he surveyed them. My, what a prize you've brought me indeed, "he said as if he were admiring a chest of gold.

Aurelia stepped forward, her sword still in hand, but the man pressed the blade against Luna's neck until a thin trickle of blood bloomed across the tender flesh. "Put your weapon down, Aurelia, or I will slit the pretty girl's throat."

Kiki jerked forward to defend her friend, but the man restraining her pressed his foot against her lower back. "I wouldn't if I were you, muñeca."

Kiki bared her teeth and locked gazes with Solana's piercing blue eyes. The Commander stood stiffly, with a knife to her throat and her arm twisted behind her back. Her eyes narrowed at Kiki, bearing a silent message. *Wait for the right moment. Watch, and then strike when it is advantageous.*

Kiki nodded slightly to signal that she understood the Commander's order. Kiki may be more stubborn than a mule, but she knew that Solana had the same goal as her. To keep everyone safe.

Aurelia dropped the short sword to the dirt and held her hands up. "I was just on my way to see you, Tomás."

A fire roared to life in Kiki's gut as the smuggler spoke to the man holding Luna as if she knew him.

Tomás snorted. "You're two months late on your payment."

An easy smile slipped across Aurelia's face. "I was a little tied up. You'll have your money, though."

Kiki scoffed. Of course, she was in debt to unsavory people like these men. Kiki expected no less of the smuggler.

"When?" Tomás spat.

Aurelia shifted from foot to foot. "I don't have your money right now, but if you just give me a bit more time, I'm sure my cousin will help me."

Tomás's eyes narrowed. "It's funny that you mention the Bastard," he said as he slid the flat side of the blade down Luna's cheek. "He paid me a visit recently. Said he was looking for you. Even paid off your debt to me."

Aurelia's throat bobbed as she swallowed a lump in her throat, her eyes glued to the knife hovering over Luna's face. "He did?"

Tomás's eyes glittered with malice as he bared his teeth. "He unleashed that psycho cousin of yours on six of my best men. Drained every drop from their bodies. Smiling like a lunatic."

Kiki's blood chilled as she imagined the scene and instantly regretted following Aurelia. If her cousins were capable of such violence, how did she ever expect them to help her?

Aurelia stepped forward, her hands in the air. "You have your money. What else do you want?"

Tomás's eyes glazed over as if he were reliving some horror in his mind's-eye. "I can't sleep. Their screams haunt my dreams. Their blood hangs in the air everywhere I go," he said, his voice hollow. He tightened his grip on Luna, causing her to yelp. "What I want is retribution, and I'm going to start with killing each one of you."

"That would be such a waste," Aurelia said in a rush, her gaze never leaving the blade. "Leave that one; she's useless. A trembling doe." She pointed to Kiki and Solana. "But them. They're feisty. Once you break them, you can use them in your ranks. Or whatever else you want to do with them."

Kiki growled at hearing Aurelia bargaining with her life as if she were cattle. Kiki couldn't hold her tongue any longer. "Whatever the scum owes you, we have nothing to do with it," she shouted.

Solana blew out an exasperated sigh, her gaze piercing Kiki with disapproval.

But Kiki couldn't just sit back and watch; she had to do something. "Please, whatever debt she owes you is between you. We don't know her. She's been our guide, nothing more. Take her with you and do with her as you wish. Just let the rest of my group go."

Tomás laughed, exposing his silver fillings and rotting teeth. "We'll take everything we want, I assure you." The rest of his group joined him as laughter rolled through their ranks. "Take every weapon you can find," he shouted. "Tie the bears up and bring them; the fur will make for some nice blankets. I have no need for women that don't know their place. Bind the snake with the other two and leave them for the beasts to feast on tonight."

Panic ripped through Kiki's heart at the thought of Turi being skinned alive. She roared as she twisted and kicked her captor in the knees. He went down with a groan of pain, but Luna's cries of pain made her freeze in place.

Tears streamed down Luna's face as Tomás slashed a long gash into her arm. Blood trickled down her smooth skin and splashed to the ground.

Someone kicked Kiki's knees out from behind her, and she careened to the ground. Her machete was quickly grabbed, and she was disarmed and tied with rope before being tossed at the base of a tree. The men promptly bound Solana and Aurelia before throwing them on top of her.

"Nice job, Xochicale. Now what?" Solana hissed as she wriggled off of Kiki and settled with her back against the tree trunk.

Kiki struggled against her bonds. "I didn't see you doing anything," she snapped.

"I was biding my time. Calculating our next move. I was coming up with a plan when you had to go and open your big mouth," the Commander growled as she fought to free her hands.

Aurelia sat on Kiki's other side with her head bowed and her hair a mangled mess around her face.

Kiki kicked the smuggler's foot. "If it weren't for this dirtbag, we wouldn't be in this situation to begin with," she sneered. "You know, I shouldn't be surprised you would barter my life away."

Aurelia didn't say a word to defend herself; she only scooted away from Kiki and her wrath.

Kiki growled in frustration and banged her head against the tree. "What are we going to do?" she asked no one in particular as she stomped the ground with her boot.

The bandits were sorting through the weapons they'd confiscated while the leader, Tomás, was sitting on a nearby tree stump holding Luna in his lap.

A group of men tied a rope around Turi's and Bernat's paws, their jeers filling the air.

Kiki hated the feeling of helplessness that washed over her as she watched her friends being bound and the look of fear on Luna's face as the leader of the bandits whispered into her ear.

She struggled against the bindings with renewed vigor, the skin chaffing and turning raw. She let out a roar of fury, which only made the bandits laugh with malice.

Suddenly, the ground beneath Kiki's palms shook, and the sound of hooves pounding against dirt filled her ears.

A group of soldiers clad in black armor and emerald capes stormed into the clearing. The bandits reared back at the intrusion, and Tomás began barking orders, his arm wrapped tightly around Luna's waist as he fought off the onslaught.

A man dressed in black pants and a fur-lined coat leaped off his horse, knelt before Aurelia, and began cutting the ropes that bound her feet.

"Marui!" Aurelia said to the man. "What are you doing here?"

The man, Mauri, growled in response. "Could ask you the same question, cousin." After freeing her feet, he moved to the rope behind her hands. "Have you seen Erasmo?" he asked gruffly.

Aurelia whipped her head to face Mauri. "Erasmo? No, why would I?"

Mauri ran a hand through his black hair and growled. "Never mind," he said as the rope slipped off Aurelia's wrists.

Anger filled Kiki's chest at seeing Aurelia freed. "Hey," she shouted. "That snake is the one that got us into this mess. Don't free her; free us!" Kiki shouted at the soldier.

His brown eyes flashed, and Kiki swore she saw red flash through his irises before it faded away. He swore under his breath at Aurelia before striding forward to free Kiki.

"Who the hell are you?" he asked, his calloused hands rough as he sawed at the rope binding Kiki's feet.

"My name is Kiki," she said, then jerked her chin toward the Commander at her side. "This is Solana. We're Slayers in the Demon Corps."

"The what?" Mauri smirked, his lip curling at the side.

"We're from the other side of the Cicatrix, from the base in Norcera," Kiki explained.

"The words coming out of your mouth are making no sense to me, doll," Mauri said before he turned to free Solana.

Kiki huffed in frustration. "Our friend was taken by a demon from our base. It brought her into the Cicatrix, and we tracked her here."

Mauri's eyebrows shot up. "So you're from the other side of the darkness."

Kiki threw her arms in the air, "Yes, that's what I've been saying!"

Mauri's eyes scanned the length of her, taking in her empty bandolier and weapon's belt. "You expect me to believe a tiny thing like you kills demons?"

Kiki balled her hands into fists and was about to show him that he'd regret calling her a 'tiny thing' when a scream cut through the clearing and pierced Kiki's heart. She whipped her head to the source to see Luna struggling against Tomás as he hauled her over his shoulder and disappeared through the trees, a squad of men guarding his back.

Mauri swiveled in time to catch sight of Tomás's retreating form, and his eyes locked on Luna. His skin seemed to pale, and his mouth dropped to form an 'O'. "Aw, shit," he muttered under his breath.

Kiki didn't have time to think about Mauri's strange reaction. She just acted. She grabbed the sword sheathed at Mauri's waist, dismissing his cries of protest, and rushed towards the heat of battle.

The bandits retreated into the thick woods and moved so fast that Kiki could no longer see Luna. Kiki plunged into the woods after them to rescue her friend, knowing she had no time to lose.

She saw a flash of light brown as Luna fought to free herself, and Kiki ran along a ridge, gaining on them from above. With a battle cry, she dropped down in front of Tomás and stabbed him in the leg. Luna tumbled from his shoulder and rolled across the ground.

"Run!" Kiki shouted to her. "Get back to the others!"

Luna didn't have to be told twice; she raced back the way they'd come. Kiki held her ground, keeping the bandits from chasing after her friend. They'd have to go through the Sicario if they wanted to get Luna back, and there was no way Kiki would let that happen. She bared her teeth in a feral snarl.

Tomás howled as one of his men wrapped his leg wound. "Take her down!" he screeched.

Kiki braced for a fight but didn't expect the dart that whizzed past her sword and sank into the flesh of her arm. With numb fingers, she plucked the dart from her arm and stared at the needlepoint, her vision blurring. Suddenly, her world tilted sideways, and her body crumbled to the ground, her knees striking the earth first, then her head. A tunnel of darkness narrowed her vision until all she saw was the smirk of victory on Tomás's face.

CHAPTER THIRTY-ONE

TOXIC

YARIXA

Night had fallen over the Winter Keep, and Yari ventured out of her room, hoping that Sergio was in some far-off part of the castle and that the deranged woman was long gone.

She quietly shut the door to her room when Arlando stepped into the hallway, closing the door to his own quarters. His eyes lit up upon seeing her. "I was just on my way to see you," he said, his smile wide and gleaming. "Did you find something you liked in the library?"

Yari glanced over his shoulder, wondering if Sergio lurked in the shadows. She considered telling Arlando what Sergio had done but thought better of it. She'd never win the footman's favor by ratting him out. Instead, she forced a smile to her lips and faced Arlando. "I did! I had gotten so caught up in the book that I didn't realize what time it was and that I should get cleaned up for dinner."

Pleased with the answer, Arlando drew her arm through the crook of his elbow and hummed. "That's the best feeling." They ambled down the hall towards the main room, and Yari winced as her arm rubbed against Arlando's in the same spot Sergio had grabbed her.

Arlando didn't fail to notice. "What's wrong?"

Yari tugged her poncho lower over her arm to hide the mark. "It's nothing," she lied as her face turned crimson.

Arlando drew his arm from hers and lifted the fur hem. His eyes turned to stone, and his face grew hard as he traced the red marks that lined her skin. "Who did this?" he asked.

Yari's mouth went dry as she searched her mind for a believable story.

Arlando asked again, the very air seeming to shift around him. "I'm only going to ask one more time," he growled, a muscle feathering in his jaw. "Who did this to you?"

Yari bit her lip. "Sergio," she whispered. "But I wasn't where I was supposed to be. I got lost and-"

Arlando's nostrils flared as she rambled on. "No one touches you," he snarled as he cupped the side of her face with his hand. He trailed his thumb in lazy circles over her bottom lip. "I will deal with Sergio," he added. "He will never lay eyes on you again."

Yari felt relief wash over her, and she pushed onto her tiptoes to plant a feather-light kiss on his lips. A wave of tingles ran down the length of her spine at the contact before she drew herself away.

Arlando's bright eyes were full of hunger as he swayed in place. "I'm not that hungry anymore," he said, his voice husky.

Yari wanted to agree with him, but her traitorous stomach gave her away with a loud gurgle. "My stomach seems to disagree," Yari said, sheepish.

Arlando chuckled and led her down the grand staircase.

The main hall was cast in the warm flickering light of candles and the roaring hearth. The table was set for three, and already, a woman was seated at the end. She was dressed in an elaborate blue gown with white embroidery and had a gray fur shawl draped over her bony shoulders. Her hair was pulled back into a bun, revealing streaks of gray through her hair.

Something about the woman seemed familiar, and Yari quirked her head, trying to place where she'd seen the woman before.

Arlando approached the table and motioned to Yari. "Tía Pilar, meet Yarixa; she's going to be staying with us."

Yari bowed her head, unsure what to do in the circumstances like this, and offered the woman a smile. "It's a pleasure to meet you, señora."

Pilar cast a dismissive glance down Yari's plain clothing and dragged her cup of wine to her lips without uttering so much as a greeting.

Yari felt Arlando stiffen at the slight and noticed a vein in his neck jump. Recovering, he turned to Yari and leaned to whisper in her ear. "Don't mind her; she hates everyone. Including herself," he said with a mischievous grin.

Yari resisted the urge to laugh and allowed Arlando to help her sit in the chair to his right. On the other end, Pilar continued to sip her wine, her raptor-like gaze not once leaving Arlando.

"So, how long do you plan to stay this time?" Pilar asked Arlando, her eyes narrowing as she spoke.

Arlando stilled at his place at the head of the table. "Now that I've found Yari, I won't be leaving any time soon," he said, pulling a linen napkin from the table and setting it in his lap.

Pilar's lips curled into a smirk. "So, you're the one?" she said, her tone dripping with insinuation.

Yari shrunk back at the woman's words, her face twisting in confusion. "I'm sorry?" Yari looked to Arlando for help with pleading eyes.

Arlando cleared his throat and leaned his elbows onto the table. "I'll remind you, Tía, that you are a guest in my castle," he said, his tone sepulchral and blue eyes clouding with ice.

Pilar swallowed a lump in her throat and averted her gaze, the silver charger in front of her suddenly very interesting.

Yari wrung the napkin in her lap and only stopped when Arlando reached out and placed his hands on top of hers.

"Maybe I should go," Yari whispered, feeling very much like an intruder.

Arlando's brows shot to his hairline. "Are you unhappy here?" he asked, his eyes filled with worry.

Yari shot a glance at Pilar before shaking her head. No, she was blissfully happy here. But the others who lived here weren't as welcoming as Arlando, and she didn't get a good feeling about them.

With a gentle squeeze of her hands, Arlando leaned in close and pressed a soft kiss to her forehead. "Then stay," he said with a smile. "You belong here with me. To hell with what anyone else thinks."

Sensing that Pilar was watching them intently, Yari nodded and pulled away, unsure of herself.

Dinner was served by a pair of servants Yari hadn't seen before. They were dressed in the same livery as Sergio and set out plates of steaming pork, rice, and beans. Stuffed peppers and meat-filled turnovers were added to the spread, and Yari wondered how just the three of them were expected to eat everything.

Yari was in the middle of enjoying a bit of tortilla stuffed with meat and covered in cheese when Pilar cleared her throat. "If the girl is to stay, perhaps she should know of the troubles the estate faces," she said. "It's your intention to marry the girl, isn't it? She should know what she's getting into."

Yari choked on a bite of food and stared at the old woman with wide eyes. Marriage? She admitted that things were moving quickly with Arlando. But marriage was another thing entirely.

Arlando stiffened but quickly recovered as he dabbed the corner of his mouth with his napkin. "I hadn't planned on burdening Yari with such things so early. We have plenty of time to get to know one another before we get into all that."

"What trouble does the estate face?" Yari asked quietly.

Arlando sighed and turned in his seat to face her. "I haven't been completely honest with you about who I am," he said as he averted his gaze. "I'm not just the Lord of this castle; I'm its Prince." Yari sucked in a breath of shock. "When the darkness took over the kingdom, both my parents died, leaving just my brother and me to rule the kingdom. As we got older, we grew apart, and my brother turned against me. You see, my brother and I are twins, but I'm the oldest by mere minutes. However, as the oldest, that left me as the heir to my father's throne. Erasmo didn't like that and plotted to overthrow me. He failed, but our division split the kingdom into many factions. Some are loyal to me, and others are loyal to my brother. To make matters worse, those hungry for power seized control over their own territories. So, you see, demons roaming Ozero is just one of the many problems we face here in the north."

Yari shifted in her seat, and her heart sank as she realized the magnitude of the situation. Arlando was not only a prince, but he was also fighting to bring together his shattered kingdom. And she had inadvertently become a part of that struggle.

"That's a lot to take in," she admitted. Arlando ran a hand through his silver hair and tossed a glare at his aunt. "I understand why you wanted to wait to tell me all of this, but I'm happy you did." She reached out and placed her hand over his. "Now, I can share this burden with you. What can I do to help?" she asked, determined to stand by him no matter what. She couldn't explain the feelings that swirled in her heart whenever she looked upon Arlando. All she knew was that it felt right to be here with him.

Arlando smiled and took her hand in his, rubbing the top of her knuckles with his thumb. "You've already done more than you know," he whispered. "You're everything I dreamed of and more."

Heat bloomed across Yari's nose at his compliment.

Arlando turned his gaze to his aunt, who had a look of disdain etched into her features. "You see, Tía. Your attempts to undermine me have failed. Yet again. Yari isn't some faint-hearted simpering fool that you can just manipulate against me."

Pilar stood up from the table, her chair screeching against the hardwood floors. "I never said she was a fool," she muttered. "But you're the fool if you think this plan of yours is going to work out." She snorted down her nose at both of them, then stormed out of the dining hall.

Unease festered in Yari's stomach at Pilar's behavior. Something was definitely familiar about the woman, but Yari couldn't put her thumb on it.

She quickly banished those thoughts when Arlando turned his blue eyes on her. Reaching out, he brushed a stray lock of hair behind her ear and grinned. "My aunt thinks she knows what's best for Ozero. But I think you're what's best for my kingdom," he said, his voice husky.

Yari's heart fluttered as she stared into his eyes. Without a word, Arlando leaned in and pressed his lips against hers in a searing kiss. Arlando wrapped an arm around her waist, pulling her close as he deepened the kiss. Fire raced through Yari's veins, igniting a passion that she never knew existed before this moment. The heat left her reeling, but before things could get too carried away, Arlando took her hand and led her out of the dining hall and up to her room.

As soon as they stepped inside, Arlando wrapped his arms around Yari's waist and pulled her close for another passionate kiss. His hands roamed hungrily over her body, leaving trails of fire wherever they touched.

Yari trembled in his embrace as every nerve in her body came alive under his fingers. She was lost in him, consumed by the fire burning between them. She could feel that their connection went so much deeper than just physical attraction or even love. It was fate that had brought them together, and nothing would tear them apart now.

A knock at the door made Arlando stiffen before he reluctantly pulled away. "Enter," he commanded, not once taking his eyes off Yarixa.

A servant cracked the door open and bowed before stepping over the threshold. "A letter, Sire."

Arlando pressed his forehead to Yari's and groaned. "I must deal with this. There is much unrest among the territories. My brother is causing a lot of trouble lately."

Yari nodded her understanding, but before Arlando left, he kissed her one last time.

"Good night, *mi amore*," he whispered against her skin before he slipped from her room and shut the door behind him, leaving Yari breathless with desire and longing for what was yet to come.

Yari spun in a circle and wrapped her arms around herself as she launched herself onto the giant bed. She buried her face in the fur blankets and grinned. She'd never felt like this before, and though everything was happening quickly, she didn't regret one moment she'd shared with the prince.

CHAPTER THIRTY-TWO

FAR FROM HOME

SOLANA

S olana barreled into the chaos of battle, searching for Xochicale and Luna. Leave it to Xochicale to run headfirst into trouble without a plan. She stumbled over a lifeless body and quickly recognized it as one of the bandits. She continued to jog forward, her breath creating a cloud of vapor in front of her face as she dodged around the main group of brawling men.

The soldiers bore the crest of a silver bear on their green tunics. They moved in organized groups, efficiently cutting through the bandits in synchronized movements. Solana couldn't help but admire their discipline and the way they continued to fight in coordination despite the havoc.

A wild mane of curly hair caught her attention, and she cut a path toward the figure.

"Luna," she called as she pulled the other girl to a stop. "Where's Xochicale?"

Luna pointed back the way she'd come. "She was right behind me," she said, her mouth opening and closing in confusion.

Solana hissed under her breath and was about to run after her charge but stopped when a hand landed on her shoulder.

Solana whirled around, a tlazon in her fist, but she dropped it the second she recognized the solemn face staring at her.

"Bernat?" she whispered, unbelieving as she scanned his familiar human features. Just moments ago, he'd been a bear. Solana shook her head. "How?" she asked, drawing near and placing her palms on his chest.

Bernat covered her hands with one of his and tapped a pendant hanging around his neck. "The soldiers are from La Aguilera, which is apparently my brother's territory. This allows me to shift into a human during the day. I don't really understand it all; that's all they told me."

Relief flooded Solana's chest, and she pointed in the direction Luna had come from. "Xochicale is still out there. I have to get her."

Luna stepped forward, determination filling her eyes with fire. "I'll come with you."

Bernat's lips thinned to a narrow line. "We don't know this territory, Sol. Nor the people who attacked us. I think we should go to La Aguilera, regroup and organize a search party. Kiki isn't the only one who has gone missing. Apparently, Erasmo, my younger brother, has also gone missing." Solana opened her mouth to protest, but Bernat cut her off. "We don't know the land, nor do we have the resources. This is the smarter play, and you know it."

Solana clenched her teeth, hating that Bernat was the one who had to tell her something so obvious. "You're right," she said as she realized her palms were still resting on his broad chest. She ripped herself away and took a step backward, a flush warming her cheeks. "Xochicale can take care of herself," she said to Luna, who was chewing at the inside of her cheek.

Bernat nodded and pointed back the way they came to indicate for the others to follow. They made their way back to the clearing, where La Aguilera soldiers were piling the bandits' bodies and collecting wood to burn them.

Aurelia stood by the tree they'd been tied to, her arms crossed over her chest as Mauri, the soldier who'd freed them, argued with her.

Solana noticed that Turi had also been given a unique pendant and resumed his human form. Seeing them, Turi rushed forward, his eyes wild. Solana knew well that he was looking for Xochicale. "Where's Kiki?" he asked.

Bernat answered for her and promised his brother they'd find Kiki as soon as they regrouped. Turi wasn't happy about it but accepted the facts as they stood. They were all tired and hungry. They didn't have a map of this land and knew nothing about the bandits. Their best option would be to learn more and then create a plan.

Mauri approached Bernat and tilted his head in a bow. "Cousin, we're ready to escort you back to La Aguilera."

Solana stepped forward with her hands on her hips. "While we're grateful for your interference, how do we know we can trust you? Who are you? How did you know where we were?"

Mauri his hand over his heart in a salute. "My name is Mauricio Ozetero, but you can call me Mauri. I'm the captain of Erasmo's home guard, and we were informed of your presence when you crossed into Aguilera territory. Our mages have spelled the boundaries to notify us of intruders."

Solana shot a glance at Aurelia over Mauri's shoulder. "You haven't answered whether or not we can trust you. Your own cousin was ready to sell us to those bandits. How do we know you're any different?"

Mauri glared at his cousin, who stuck her nose into the air in response. "My cousin will be dealt with, I assure you. The moment Erasmo hears of this, whenever we find him, that is, she will be punished. I promise you that."

Bernat placed a placating hand on Solana's arm. "Sol, it's okay. We're safe."

Solana tensed as the warmth of his hand seeped through her battle gear and sunk into her skin. She wanted him to move his hand away, but she also wanted him to keep it exactly where it was. She cursed her traitorous body for wanting to melt into his touch. "Fine. Take us to your base camp."

Mauri nodded and signaled to a pair of soldiers with horses. "These two lost their riders. The four of you can pair up and ride them back to the eyrie."

Blood was smeared across the sides of each horse, and Solana tried hard not to think about the loss of life. She sealed off that part of herself that felt heartsick at the thought and moved toward the white horse, placing a hand on the creature's muzzle.

Bernat joined her, the heat of him wrapping around her. "Which position would you prefer?" he asked, his eyes gleaming with mischief. "Front or back?"

Solana bit the inside of her cheek. "I'll ride with Luna," she said, looking for the Healer, but was sorely disappointed when she saw Turi already in the saddle of the brown horse and Luna climbing up behind him.

Solana caught Mauri's heated gaze trained on Luna and his white knuckles as he watched her wrap her arms around Turi's waist. He looked like a man possessed, and Solana resolved to watch the man carefully. Luna may not be under her command, but Solana would be damned if she let the man harm a hair on the Healer's head.

Bernat leaned his head forward. "Looks like you're stuck with me."

A shiver ran up her spine at his nearness. The proximity of his body made her skin tingle. He reached out and helped her into the saddle before following her. His muscled arms wrapped around her, steady and strong.

His body was flush against her spine. "Hmm, I could get used to this," he purred into the shell of her ear.

A pleasant shiver prickled the skin along the back of her neck. This man would be the death of her, Solana just knew. It took every ounce of resolve left in her to resist the urge to lean into him and simply enjoy the heat of his touch.

They rode through the woods for an hour until they reached a cliff that jutted out and dropped off into a ravine far below.

Mauri pulled up alongside them, a grin on his handsome face. "Welcome to La Aguilera, the ancestral home of the House Ozetero, residence to your brother, Prince Erasmo."

Behind her, Bernat exhaled in awe. A wooden bridge connected the cliff to a central mass of land that hosted a white stone castle. The castle's high stone walls reached the sky and merged with the slender spires, which protected a white monolith at the center.

The castle was lit up by torches and various colored lanterns, bathing the castle in warm reds, golds, and oranges. The castle was massive, like a sprawling mansion born from countless additions and renovations. A series of towers and balconies jutted from the stone walls. It should have been gaudy and ugly. It should have looked out of place on such a grand scale. Yet, it was beautiful.

Mauri led the group across the bridge, his shifting eyes resting on Luna any chance he had. The wooden planks of the bridge swayed slightly in the wind, the inky black waters below churning in the ravine.

They approached a torch-lit courtyard, where a group of curious onlookers had gathered. The air smelled of flowers and spices and happiness.

Mauri waved at the onlookers and motioned toward Bernat. "I give you the rightful King of Ozero!"

The crowd made 'oh' and 'ah' sounds as they threw their arms in the air with glee. A soft murmur hummed through the group until the voices rose into a chant. They cried 'long live the king', their faces filled with tears of joy, and music burst through the air in a chorus of drums and guitars.

Bernat got off the horse and began walking amongst the crowd. People approached him and told him their relation to him, mostly cousins but also faithful servants to the Ozetero house.

Solana swung her leg over and landed on the cobblestone floor. A group swarmed and praised her. For what? She had no clue. They began pushing bright flowers into her hands and hung crowns of petals on her head. Dancing started in the courtyard, and mugs of pulque were passed from fist to fist.

She looked for Bernat and found him smiling from ear to ear as he was embraced by his family. A pang of jealousy ripped through her chest, and Solana instantly wrangled it and stomped it out. It wasn't Bernat's fault that he had a family within the Cicatrix. He deserved this. Of all the people she knew, Bernat deserved happiness.

A question wormed its way into her mind at seeing him beaming with joy. The Cicatrix had ripped through Ozero fifteen years ago, which would mean that Bernat had been twelve at the time.

In all the years she'd known him, he'd never once mentioned being a prince of the lost kingdom. He must have known but had hidden it from her.

She couldn't help but wonder what else he'd hidden from her all these years.

As an uneasy feeling swirled in her stomach, Solana scanned the crowd, searching for Luna and Turi, and found them smiling as they gladly accepted drink and food. They both looked so happy that Solana decided against asking Turi about his past. He'd have been six when the Cicatrix spread, so he may not remember much anyway, and she was reluctant to cause him pain.

She caught a glimpse of Mauri hanging around the shadows, his gaze never leaving

Luna. He sipped at the mug of pulque in his hand and sucked on a lit cigarette, but his eyes betrayed the hunger within.

She was about to tell him to back off when a giant man threw his arm over Mauri's shoulder and pulled him away to drink with him.

Satisfied, Solana slipped away from the festivities and found a dark corner to hide in. She never liked parties much and preferred to be with small groups of people or alone.

Once out of plain view, she set the flowers aside and pulled the crowns of petals from her hair. She was plucking out several petals when a shadow blocked the light from the square.

"Are you hiding?" Bernat asked, his lips curving into a smile.

Solana plucked another petal from her hair and let it fall to her feet. "I don't care for parties. People get drunk and do stupid things. I'd rather not be a part of them."

Bernat set his mug of pulque down and sat on a stack of crates, the wood groaning beneath his weight. "Can I keep you company, then?"

Solana frowned and whirled on him. "Did you know about the curse? Before we came into the Cicatrix, did you know?"

Bernat's black brows drew together, and his lips thinned. "I wasn't sure."

Solana's breath hissed between her teeth. "Yet you came anyway?" She ran her hands through her hair and turned her back to him. "Were you ever going to tell me the truth?"

Bernat stood, and the heat from his chest warmed her back. "I didn't know what might happen when I crossed. I wasn't trying to hide anything from you."

Solana spun and stood toe-to-toe with him. He towered over her by more than a foot, but he took a step back at the look in her eyes. "I'm not talking about that. I'm asking if you were ever going to tell me you were a prince?" She bit her bottom lip and sneered. "Or should I call you the king?"

Bernat's eyes closed as he retreated back and sat back down on the wooden crates. "I didn't know, Sol."

Solana snorted in disbelief. "You would have been twelve when the Cicatrix spread. Plenty old enough to remember where you'd come from."

Bernat's eyes snapped open. "Yeah? And what good would that have done for me?" He shook his head and rested his elbows on his knees. "My entire life was ripped to shreds. I was abandoned. Left in an unfamiliar place with unfamiliar people. Anyone who might have cared for me was swallowed up by the darkness. We didn't even know that people had survived until a few days ago."

Solana's anger started to cool when she saw the pain in his eyes. She felt awful for making him revisit his past and knew well the trauma he'd endured, for she, too, had lived it.

Bernat dropped his head into his hands and took a deep breath, his giant shoulders rising and falling with each inhale. "I started to think I'd dreamt it all up. My life before the Cicatrix. I reasoned that it had all been a fantasy. Something an orphan crafted up in his mind to cope with being abandoned. For years, I told myself that none of this had been real, and I truly believed it until we crossed through the darkness."

"You didn't say anything because you still weren't sure," Solana finished for him. He lifted his head, and his dazzling blue eyes were rimmed with tears. He nodded, and that gesture alone made something inside Solana crack.

"I never meant to keep anything from you," he said, his voice full of regret.

"I understand," Solana said with a sigh. And she truly did. If he'd confessed any of this to her earlier, she might not have believed him. "What are we going to do?" she asked as she leaned against the wall and crossed her arms over her chest. "Xochicale is out there somewhere. You're cursed by some dark magic. And now your brother is missing, too. What's the plan here?"

"When you lay it all out like that, it seems like we're in over our heads," he said with a devastating grin.

"Now is not the time for jokes," Solana chided.

Bernat's brilliant blue eyes softened. "There is nothing we can do right now. It's dark. The demons will be roaming about at this hour. All we can do is rest and recover until the morning." Solana's nostrils flared at the suggestion to do nothing. "Dance with me," he said as he held his hand toward her. "There's no use in moping around."

Solana stared at his upturned palm. She wished she could just grab hold of it and never let go. But she couldn't. "Fraternization is against protocol. Go find someone else," she said, her voice cold as she pushed past him to find a new place to hide. Somewhere he wouldn't find her. Somewhere she could hide from even her own feelings.

Bernat caught her arm as she passed and pulled her into his chest. "Why do you keep pushing me away?" he asked, placing a gentle hand on her cheek. "I know you feel the same way. I can see it in your eyes. Every time you look at me. You want me as much as I want you."

Solana's heart raced in her chest; she feared Bernat might be able to hear. "I-" She started to speak, but no words would come out. She had a million excuses for why she shouldn't be with Bernat. But all of them crumbled into piles of ash as she stared into his eyes.

Being here with him felt right. Like the right key had finally found the lock on her heart.

Bernat trailed his thumb across her lips. "We're not in the Demon Corps anymore. Everything that kept us apart is gone. Tell me what you want. Even if that's to go away. To never bring this up again. I have to know. You have to say it, or else I'll keep torturing myself by chasing you."

Every last ounce of self-restraint seeped away at his words.

Bernat was everything she'd ever wanted. A protector. A friend. A confidant. He was all of those things to her and more.

Bernat pressed his forehead to hers, his breath warming her face. "Please, just tell me what you want."

Solana raised her hand and pressed it to his cheek. His breath hitched, and his eyes became hooded as he gazed into her eyes. "Why me?" she asked in a whisper.

Bernat closed his eyes and pressed his lips to her forehead. "It's always been you, Sol. I didn't know how I felt until two years ago when you were promoted to the rank of Commander, and I was assigned as your second. Before that, you were my comrade. I admired you and watched you grow from that stubborn sixteen-year-old into a woman that commanded respect and loyalty. From the beginning, I took it upon myself to have your back, to be your protector. I didn't realize how my feeling had grown until that night on Watch. When that demon nearly tore your throat out."

Solana winced as she, too, recalled that night. It wasn't one of her finer moments and had only happened because Bernat had been cornered. She'd thrown herself in front of him and taken the blow instead.

Bernat held her face in his hands and pressed his forehead to hers once more. "I was so scared. I thought I'd lose you. It was then that I realized I was more than just your protector. That I wanted to be more. That I wanted to be your lover."

Whatever walls Solana had left crumbled at his admission. Without warning, she pushed onto her tiptoes and pressed her lips to his.

Bernat's eyes widened in shock, but he quickly pulled her tighter against his body, his hard muscles flexing beneath her hands. His fingers trailed down her arms and curled around her waist so there was no space between them.

He pulled away, his breath heaving and his pupils blown wide. "Is this really happening?" he asked in disbelief.

A smile crept along the line of Solana's mouth, and she nodded.

Bernat smashed his mouth to hers once more, this time the kiss more demanding, and heat pooled in Solana's core as her body responded to his touch.

"You're my sun," he said breathlessly as he pressed his lips to her neck, a moan escaping her lips. "I love you," he murmured between feather-light kisses to her cheeks, her eyes, her nose, and finally, her lips. "Always," he added as he roped his hands around her thighs and lifted her, wrapping her legs around his waist. "My Sol," he whispered against her skin as his mouth explored hers.

And just like that, Solana's world shifted on its axis.

CHAPTER THIRTY-THREE

CRAVING

YARIXA

Yari jolted awake to a wail of despair. She winced as the fear in her chest was pulled so tight it hurt. Another scream ripped the silence, and she clutched the blankets to her chest, her hands trembling.

What could be making such an awful sound? Was it the demons? Had they invaded the castle?

Yari ducked further under the covers, feeling very much like a coward but too afraid to go out and investigate. Wasn't this why she would never graduate from the Demon Corps? Because she was so spineless?

Ice-cold irritation erupted from her stomach, tightening her muscles and causing her to throw the blanket off herself with a violent yank. She may be a coward, but if someone needed her help, she would give it.

The ice-cold floor bit at her feet as she sprung from the bed. The bedroom door was waiting for her, dark and foreboding. Goosebumps rose from her skin, sending chills down her exposed back.

She tiptoed to her door and glanced outside. Every candle in the hall had been extinguished, sending swaths of shadow slithering across the floor like malevolent serpents. Her breath hitched in her throat, and she moved to close the door and bolt it shut, but a choked moan coming from Arlando's room drove a dagger of dread into her heart.

Without thinking of her own welfare, Yari rushed to Arlando's door and tried to open it, but it was stuck. She kicked it in without hesitation, ready to kill whatever was on the other side. She found Arlando screaming and curled into a ball on his bed, trapped in some dark abyss of his mind.

Yari sprung across the room, flying at Arlando before she knew what she was doing. Her hand collided with his shoulder, and he recoiled before grabbing her by the arm and flinging her beneath him onto the bed. She gasped, frozen in place. The cruel metal of a dagger glinted in the moonlight. One wrong move and it would sink into her soft neck.

Arlando loomed over her, his bare chest heaving, his azure eyes blown wide and unfocused.

"Arlando!" Yari exclaimed, placing her hands over his to stop the dagger from pressing closer. "It's me, Yari!"

The fog lifted, and Arlando's eyes focused on Yari's face and the thin line of blood dripping down her neck. "Yari?" he asked, sounding scared and confused.

"It's me," Yari said calmly. She released her hands from his, showing him how much she trusted him.

As if realizing what he'd done, Arlando scurried off of Yari, tossing the blade to the floor as he did. He kneeled at the edge of the bed, his head bowed to his chest, his hands clenched into fists at his side.

The faint light that filtered into the room bathed him in silver light, and for a moment, Arlando looked like a tortured angel. His chiseled chest rose and fell in heavy breaths, and his muscled legs were splayed out, revealing that he wasn't fully clothed.

A blush spread across Yari's nose as she took in his full majesty.

"I'm sorry, Yari," he said, his voice deep, gravelly. "I didn't--"

"Shh," Yari said as she rose to her knees and placed a finger on his lips to stop his words. She took his tortured face between her palms and smoothed the furrows along his brow. "I heard you screaming in your sleep. I didn't know how to help."

Arlando squeezed his eyes shut and turned his face into her hand, pressing his lips to her palm. "I'm sorry you had to see me like that."

"I have nightmares, too," Yari said quietly. "I know what it's like."

Arlando's breath slowly evened out, and Yari became very aware that he was naked and she was kneeling before him. In his room. In his bed.

"I should go," Yari said, shifting to get off the bed.

Arlando extended his hand and grasped her elbow tight. "Please, stay," he begged. "I don't want to be alone."

Yari's heart broke at the way his voice wavered on the last word. She knew that feeling all too well. How many nights had she woken from a nightmare and crawled into Kiki's bed just so she wouldn't have to face the darkness alone? "Okay," she said, her voice quivering.

Arlando inched a little closer and pressed his hand to her cheek. "What did I do to deserve you?" he whispered, his eyes taking in every inch of her face as if he could memorize it.

"No," she said, her voice cracking. "I don't deserve you." She cast her eyes away, not wanting to see the moment he realized it too. Yari had always been the weak one. The one everyone else had to look out for. She was nothing. A burden. How could Arlando see her any differently?

Arlando's brows furrowed. "Never say that," he growled.

Yari froze. She couldn't move a muscle; she was frozen in fear... fear that he would pull away, fear that he wouldn't. Then, as if he had read her mind, Arlando cupped her face and kissed her.

A sigh of relief escaped her lips, and she melted into him, her arm sliding around his waist, her palm pressing to his bare back. Her heart swelled with love and the pain that had cocooned her heart for the past few years seemed to be pushed aside by his simple touch.

She parted her lips and deepened the kiss, letting all her pent-up fear and feelings of inadequacy go. She poured her every yearning and want into the kiss, showing him just how much she wanted him.

Arlando pulled away, his eyes full of hunger, and grasped the hem of her night dress, pulling it up over her head. Yari sucked in a breath of shock as the cool air kissed her bare skin and her heart pounded in her chest as she realized what was about to happen.

Arlando's hands slid down her back and gripped her bottom, pulling her against his chest as he gently guided her onto her back so his weight rested over her.

Yari's heart pounded against her chest, and she marveled at how right it felt.

He started by pressing a soft kiss to her lips as if he was uncertain, but Yari parted her lips and let him in.

Arlando's kiss deepened, and Yari's head swam with an overload of sensation; she clutched at the blankets and Arlando's arms in a desperate attempt to ground herself.

She could feel hot lips on her neck, teeth nipping at her earlobe, hands exploring, pressing, teasing. One hand slipped up her side, leaving a trail of fire in its wake. Her body was alive as she had never felt before. A fire started low in Yari's belly and traveled through her veins, setting her skin aflame.

Arlando's hand slid below the hem of her nightdress and tugged it up around her waist. He reached between her thighs, grazing the sensitive flesh, and Yari's breath hitched in her throat at the unexpected contact.

Arlando's calloused fingers slid against the soft flesh, teasing, pinching, and Yari gasped when his thumb found her most sensitive spot and rubbed.

A jolt of pleasure shot through Yari, and her body contracted beneath him as she cried out.

Arlando's breath quickened, and he buried his face in her neck, kissing her shoulder as she shook beneath him.

Unable to think, Yari gripped his shoulders and pulled him down for another kiss. She pulled his face closer, deepening the kiss, letting all her love for him pour into him. Or maybe it was the other way around; she wasn't sure anymore.

Arlando broke away, his lips leaving a hot trail up Yari's neck. "Do you want this?" he asked, his voice deep, gravelly.

"Yes," Yari answered without hesitation. As much as she was scared, she wanted to be with him. Completely. Fully.

Arlando paused and stared at her, the moonlight casting his face in shadow. And then he smiled a full-lipped, beautiful, heart-stopping smile. He kissed her again, sweetly, lovingly.

And Yari's heart soared as she realized just how much he loved her.

Arlando's lips captured hers, and he pressed his body to hers. Her nipples hardened with the roughness of calloused hands as he cupped her breasts. The scent of him filled her nose, and she breathed him in. He tugged on the loose neckline of her dress, pulling it down enough to expose one of her breasts. Yari gasped when he freed it, and he lowered his head, taking her nipple into his mouth and sucked, nipping at it, making her squirm with pleasure.

It was almost too much to handle, and Yari grasped at his sides, digging her nails into him. But Arlando didn't pull away. He just kept going, sucking, licking, and nipping at the tender flesh before he moved to the other breast.

He removed his hand from between her legs and slid it along her stomach, trailing up until he cupped her face. The heat from him, the scent of him, drove Yari crazy, and she kissed him back with everything she had.

Arlando reached down and slid his hand up her leg slowly. His hand moved over the sensitive flesh, sliding, exploring, teasing.

Yari's eyes fluttered closed, and she moaned as he moved higher and higher, igniting the fire inside her once again.

Arlando's lips moved to her neck, and he nipped and kissed a trail upward, nuzzling her ear. "Mate," he whispered and nipped at her earlobe, sending a rush of pleasure through her body.

Arlando lifted her legs until they were spread wide, and he gazed at her center with a look of desire. He lowered himself and wrapped her legs around his waist as he positioned himself at her entrance. He pushed his hips forward, sliding inside her, slowly filling her, not once taking his eyes away from hers.

Yari gasped with pain as he entered her, and she took a deep breath as the unexpected pain gave way to warmth and pleasure as he moved inside her. She breathed out hard, her skin flush and tingling as he continued to fill her slowly, pushing against her walls. She reached for his arms to hold on as he leaned over her, his breath hot on her neck.

The muscles in her legs tensed, and she dug her fingernails into his flesh, the feelings stirring inside her intense and the overwhelming urge for more filling her to the brim.

She moaned as he withdrew, but before she could protest, he thrust back into her, stretching her until a moan escaped her lips.

She dug her nails into his shoulders, and soon they were both driving toward a peek that shimmered on the horizon, coaxing the fire that had started low in her belly until it was a burning inferno.

Arlando pushed her hair away from her face and kissed her again, his tongue exploring her mouth. Yari moaned against his lips, and Arlando groaned in response. She wrapped her arms around him and wrapped her legs around his waist.

Arlando pushed deep inside Yari, over and over again, until her thighs were slick with sweat. He slid his hands along her hips, pressing his long fingers into the soft flesh at the side of her waist. He pounded into her as she tried to catch her breath and called out his name as he thrust into her faster and faster, each time bringing her closer to that edge. She clung to him, digging her heels into him as she let the waves of pleasure crash over her.

Arlando sped up and found Yari's lips with his. His tongue explored her mouth, savoring her taste. He kissed and thrust deep inside of her, drawing her into a world of pleasure. Yari moaned as his tongue tasted hers, and he thrust inside of her again and again.

Arlando groaned and shuddered as he exploded into her, their bodies lost in ecstasy.

Arlando collapsed onto her, his weight crushing her into the bed.

Yari wrapped her arms around his shoulders and ran her hands up his back, feeling the slick sweat. Her heart was pounding, and her breathing was ragged. She pressed soft kisses to his cheek and neck, loving the feel of his heated body on top of her.

She had wanted this for so long but actually experiencing it was so much better than she had ever imagined. No longer was she afraid, unsure of where she belonged. She had found her place, the place that she belonged.

And all she wanted to do was stay right here, pressed against Arlando, forever.

As they lay in the afterglow of their lovemaking, Arlando wrapped his arms around Yari and pulled her against his chest until she was curled up in his arms, her head tucked under his chin, his heartbeat thudding in her ear.

"Are you okay?" he whispered, pressing a kiss to the top of her head.

Yari relaxed into his hold and sighed, her heart full and soaring. "I've never been better."

Arlando hummed in agreement and nuzzled his face against her neck. He held her tight for the rest of the night, their hearts beating in tandem, their secret fears held at bay, if only for the night.

CHAPTER THIRTY-FOUR

VENDETTA

ERASMO

E rasmo awoke with a start, his heart pounding in his chest. Memories of being ambushed by Tomás and his gang flooded his mind.

He looked around himself to see that he'd been tied to a tree. Thick rope wrapped around his chest and behind his back, binding his arms together. He tried to move his hands, but they wouldn't budge. His feet were also bound together, so he could not run away. He cursed and struggled against his bonds, but it was no use.

He tried to call forth his shadows, but the poison in his veins made his blood sluggish. It had been a long time since he last put so much effort into bringing up the beast; normally, it would respond at a thought.

The beast flicked its rounded ears and stretched out its claws but fell back into slumber before it had even risen from its den.

Erasmo cursed it for being so lazy at a time like this! It was almost like the beast was punishing him for keeping the darkness at bay.

A ruckus at the edge of camp drew Erasmo's attention. A group of men was dragging something into the camp, shouting and kicking. They kicked the shrieking thing, and Erasmo caught sight of a woman.

She wore a black outfit made from supple leather that clung to her hourglass figure. A pair of boots with black steeled toes ended just below her knees. Her face was marred with cuts and welts. Her black chin-length hair was matted against her head, and her black eyes narrowed as she spat at her captors.

Something within him clicked into place as her eyes scanned the camp and stopped on him.

He inhaled sharply through his nose, and he could feel the beast within open a single eye in interest.

It was her. She was here.

His mate.

Tomás gripped the woman by her hair and yanked her to her feet. Her mouth wrenched open, but she didn't cry out as if refusing to give the bandit satisfaction.

Tomás brought his mouth to her ear and whispered something. Whatever it was took the fight out of her limbs, and her head bowed to her chest in defeat.

Seeing the way Tomás held her and brought his mouth to her ear made Erasmo's mouth fill with the bitter taste of rage, and his eyes saw red. A primal urge to claim her as his mate, to protect her, to make her his own overcame him. She was his. And he'd rip the throat out of any man who dared to touch her.

A growl escaped his lips, and Tomás's eyes drifted over. At seeing Erasmo, the bandit smirked. "You're awake! Do you like my prize?" he asked as he grabbed Erasmo's mate by the neck and swung her around to face him.

The woman's eyes met Erasmo's, and her mouth dropped into an 'O' before her brows knitted together in a confused frown.

"What are you going to do with her?" Erasmo asked, his teeth clenched so hard that his jaw hurt. If only he could get the beast to wake fully. He'd rid himself of these ropes and rip Tomás's throat out with his fangs.

Tomás pushed his mate to the ground, and she landed on her knees with a sharp crack. "I haven't decided yet," the bandit said, his eyes wandering over the woman's form on full display in the skin-tight leathers.

Erasmo's blood boiled. He'd make Tomás suffer. He'd pay for this. As his eyes looked around the camp at the dozens of bandits gathered around, he resolved that they would all die at his hands. Slowly. Agonizingly.

His mate scowled at Tomás, and Erasmo's heart filled with pride at seeing the fight hadn't left her after all.

Tomás kicked her face-first into the ground with his boot and ground his heel into her back. "Tie the bitch up, and someone clean her face. I don't want her looking like a street urchin when I take her."

A laugh rolled through the camp, and Erasmo tightened his fists until his nails punctured skin and blood pooled in his palms.

Tomás would certainly suffer. As soon as Erasmo was free, he'd make sure of it.

His mate was dragged away to the other side of camp, and Erasmo struggled against his bonds to see her, but she was taken from view, which only served to enrage Erasmo further.

Tomás walked up to him and placed his boot on Erasmo's leg. He held a dart in his hand and examined the point with reverence. "Funny how such a tiny thing can take down the Bastard of the East," he mused.

Erasmo snarled, baring his teeth, and pulled against the rope around his waist. "Your minutes are numbered, Tomás. I swear, if you lay a finger on her, your death will be most agonizing."

Tomás scoffed. "Why do you care? She's just a woman."

Erasmo yanked at his bonds even harder, that the rope around his waist started to fray.

Tomás's eyes missed nothing, and he jabbed his heel into Erasmo's chest. "Oh no, you don't, princey. I'm under strict orders to deliver you safe and sound. I won't be failing the boss again." He raised the dart and pricked Erasmo in the neck.

That same sluggishness returned, and Erasmo cursed at Tomás before he slipped from consciousness.

CHAPTER THIRTY-FIVE

MONSTER

KIKI

Kiki waited patiently for night to fall. Her hands were bound behind her back, and her ankles were tied together. Still, she was determined to escape the bandits, and the cover of darkness would be her only ally.

The bandit camp was composed of a ramshackle collection of tents and lean-tos. A meager fire in a dirt circle prevented the cold from penetrating the camp. Smoke lazed into the air and crawled toward the forest canopy. The remaining bandits circled the fire and warmed their hands over it. Tomás tossed her an angry glare and bit into a loaf of bread before angling his back to her.

Good, the more he underestimated her, the better. When the bandits were all asleep, Kiki made her move. Her heart beat in her ears as she made her way closer to the group, inching forward on her side like a worm. She could see the glint of a knife in one of the bandit's hands, and she knew that was her only chance.

She angled her mouth toward the blade and gently slipped the knife from the bandit's fingers, taking the hilt into her mouth. She wriggled back to where they'd left her and dropped the blade on the ground. She angled her hands to grab the knife and quickly got to work to free herself. The sharp blade bit her skin, and she stifled a cry of pain.

Once her hands were free, she quickly wrapped the cut on her wrist in strips of cloth torn from her battle leathers. She quickly worked the rope around her ankles and scanned the camp for the armaments they'd stolen.

She knew full well that she should just leave, but she couldn't bring herself to leave her weapons behind. Demons likely roamed these woods, and she'd be a fool to wander around defenseless. Moving as quietly as she could, she made her way towards the edge of camp where the bandits had piled all the weapons they'd stolen.

She stopped short when she spotted the man she'd seen earlier when she was dragged into camp. His head rested against his chest, and his eyes were closed. She considered freeing him but paused when she was a few feet away.

She didn't know this man or what he was capable of. Just because he was also a captive didn't mean that he was a victim.

By the looks of him alone, his powerful build, and barrel chest, Kiki surmised that he was a warrior and could take care of himself.

She crept past and found the crates of weapons. She quietly tucked the few tlazons she found into the bandolier across her chest and found a machete. The claws Turi had designed glinted in the moonlight, and she quickly added them to her arsenal.

Just as she was about to make her escape, a shrill keen echoed through the trees.

Kiki's heart stopped.

She knew that sound.

Demons.

The bandits jolted awake, and Kiki stilled like a deer caught in an archer's crosshairs. Tomás scrambled to his feet and drew his cutlass, scanning the darkness for the source of the sound.

"What was that?" one of the bandits cried out in a shaky voice.

"I don't know," Tomás said, his voice tight. "But whatever it is, it's coming this way."

Kiki backed away, blood pounding in her head.

There was a loud boom as something crashed through the trees toward the camp. The bandits leaped to their feet, scrambling for their weapons. Kiki quickly ducked behind a tent as a group of demons descended on the camp.

The demons were skeletal creatures, their flesh rotting off their bones. Their eyes burned with an otherworldly hunger, and they snapped at the bandits, taking them down. The bandits fought back, but they were outnumbered and outmatched. Kiki knew she had to do something, or else she'd end up on the business end of a set of talons.

She leaped out from her hiding spot and charged at the nearest demon, blade raised. The demon hissed and swiped at her with its claws, but she dodged out of the way. She brought her machete down on its back and felt the satisfying crunch of metal against bone. The demon screeched and flailed as it tried to reach her, but she was already moving on to the next.

Kiki fought as she'd never fought before. The machete became an extension of her arm, and she moved with deadly grace, taking down demon after demon. Demons fell left and right, but two more took their place for each one that fell. The bandits fought back with renewed vigor, but Kiki knew they didn't stand a chance against the demons alone.

An earth-rumbling roar pierced the air, and Kiki's blade stilled as she turned to face the source.

There, standing in the shadow of the trees, was a massive demon bear. Its fur was matted and bloodstained, and its eyes burned with furious fire. It roared again, challenging the demons. The demons hesitated for a moment before turning their attention to the bear, who let out another terrible roar as they charged toward it. Kiki watched in awe as the bear fought off wave after wave of demons, its claws slashing through them like they were nothing but wisps of smoke.

The bear was a force to be reckoned with, and Kiki could see the fear in the bandits' eyes as they realized they would be next. The bear swiped at a few of them, sending them flying through the air. The rest turned and ran in the opposite direction, leaving their weapons behind.

Kiki didn't know what to do. She was debating whether or not she should make a break for it when the bear finally noticed her. It stopped in its tracks and stared at her, blood dripping from its claws. Kiki's heart raced as she slowly backed away from the bear, her mind racing for a way to escape.

The bear stepped closer to her and sniffed the air. It seemed to be sizing her up, trying to decide if she was a friend or foe. Kiki decided that she wouldn't stick around to see what it decided. She turned and ran into the darkness, not looking back. She didn't get far before the bear was on her heels. She could hear its heavy paws pounding the ground behind her.

Kiki pushed herself to run faster, but she was already exhausted from fighting, and the bear was gaining on her. She could feel its hot breath on her skin, and she knew it was only a matter of time before it caught up to her.

The sound of rushing water reached her ears, and she dove headfirst toward the sound. Perhaps the bear couldn't swim. She doubted it, but she'd rather take her chances in the rushing rapids than let herself get eaten alive.

A river came into view, and Kiki's feet slipped on gravel as she launched herself into the water.

Her skin stung like a thousand needles were piercing her as the shock of the ice-cold water washed over her. She let out a strangled cry and spared a glance back. The bear was on the side of the river, head swiveling back and forth.

Kiki had a split second where she thought she'd escaped the bear when it jumped into the water, a spray of ice water splashing in her direction.

She cursed under her breath and kicked her feet with all she had to get to the other side. The water pushed against her, and she pumped her arms and legs. She reached the riverbank and dragged herself from the frigid waters.

Shivers immediately wracked her body as she urged her legs to run. The cold breeze whipped past her, chilling her bones and slowing her blood.

Kiki's limbs were growing numb, and she tripped over a fallen tree limb just as the bear crashed into her. Her head hit the frozen ground hard, sending a flare of pain through her body.

Black smoke enveloped the bear; before she knew what was happening, a thick corded forearm pressed her into the ground with deadly force.

A man wearing a black fur cape loomed over her, his azure eyes piercing as he held her captive.

His chest heaved as he stared at her, his eyes drinking in every detail of her face as if he were a man dying of thirst, and she was the first water he'd seen in days.

His eyes roved down the curve of her neck when his eyes suddenly rounded. His nostrils flared and his shoulders shook as he raised a trembling hand toward her throat.

Kiki struggled against his hold, but he towered over her, and his thick corded muscles were rippling beneath his skin, pressing her firmly into the dirt.

He reached up and yanked the bear tooth from around her neck. "Where did you get this?" he demanded, fury oozing through his pores.

Kiki grit her teeth. "Why do you care? It's a stupid tooth!" she growled as she struggled against his firm hold. She pushed at his forearm, but he possessed unnatural strength.

"Where is he?" he growled, eyes scanning the trees.

She shook her head, trying to buy some time. "I don't know what you're talking about," she insisted, her voice trembling slightly. "Let go of me!"

The man's grip tightened on her arm, and she winced in pain. "Don't lie to me," he hissed. "I can smell the curse on you."

Kiki instantly stopped fighting him. "The curse? As in the Ozero curse? What do you know about it?"

The man narrowed his eyes, and his grip on her tightened. "I am the curse," he growled.

"And I can tell you've been with my brother. Tell me where he is if you value your life."

Kiki's nostrils flared. "I don't know who you're talking about. But I have been traveling with two men affected by the Ozero curse."

The man's eyes widened a fraction as he scanned her face, no doubt searching for untruthfulness. "Two men?" he repeated skeptically.

"Yes!" she insisted. "We crossed through the Cicatrix, and as soon as we were through, both men in my group suddenly shifted into bears. A smuggler is traveling with us, and she explained the curse and convinced us that we had to get to someplace called La Aguilera to ask for help from her cousin," Kiki's words tumbled from her mouth in a tidal wave. "But we should have never trusted the smuggler because she led us into a trap."

The man considered her for a moment before finally releasing her from his grip. "You know Aurelia?"

Kiki's jaw fell slack. "You know her too?"

The man hesitated for a moment before lifting his weight off of her and getting to his feet. Taking a step back, he said, "Unfortunately, I do. My name is Erasmo. Aurelia is my cousin."

Kiki stared at the man with new eyes. His hair was black with a single silver streak that fell over his brow. He had the same azure eyes as Turi and Bernat.

She scrambled to her feet and wrapped her arms around herself as a brisk breeze swept through the trees.

Kiki mentally kicked herself for not seeing the resemblance earlier. But there was something distinctly different about Erasmo that neither Turi nor Bernat possessed.

Darkness seemed to cling to Erasmo like it was his lover. Shifting swirls of smoke radiated from him and pooled at his feet. An air of menace and violence hugged his muscular body as if it were a separate life force.

There was something else too. Something that Kiki couldn't shake.

When he settled his dazzling gaze on her, Kiki felt a sharp pull in her core, drawing her toward him. Her skin heated and her cheeks flushed as he continued to stare.

Erasmo broke eye contact and ran a hand through his tousled black hair. "Sorry about, well, you know," he said, motioning to her and the ground.

"If you're going to apologize for acting like a beast, at least do it right," Kiki scowled. Erasmo shot her a feral growl, but Kiki didn't back down. "You could start with apologizing for chasing me down like a rabbit, throwing me into the ground, practically strangling me, and then interrogating me as if I were some spy."

Erasmo's lips tilted upwards slightly before he resumed scowling. "Is that all?"

Kiki huffed and wished the anger burning within her were enough to warm the rest of her body. Another shiver scuttled down her spine and her teeth chattered together.

Erasmo's eyes trailed down her body and he removed the cloak from his shoulders and handed it to her.

Kiki swatted his offering away. "I don't want anything from you. You almost killed me."

Erasmo's eyes smoldered, and his jaw tightened before he said, "You *will* die if you don't take my cloak."

Kiki refused to meet his stare as she reached out and snatched the fur cloak from his fingers. His skin brushed hers for a second and she felt a sharp crackled of energy ripple up her skin at the contact.

Erasmo's pupils grew large until his eyes were more black than blue. Clearly, he'd felt the same current as she had. His fists clenched and unclenched at his side and he shook his head as if clearing it.

Kiki slung the cloak over her shoulders and was immediately assaulted with his scent. He smelled like frost and midnight.

"Thank you," Kiki murmured as she tucked her nose into the furs.

Erasmo only grunted his response, but she swore she saw a satisfied smirk flit across his full lips. "We need to take shelter for the night. You won't get far before the frost kills you." He turned on his heels without another word, his long legs carrying him quickly through the trees.

"Hey, isn't La Aguilera East? Why are we heading North?"

Erasmo didn't bother to look back at her. He continued on as if she weren't even there. "The nearest shelter is North of here."

Kiki assumed a jog to catch up to him and glanced behind her toward the East and hoped her friends were doing alright. She didn't have much choice but to follow the cursed prince.

They continued through the forest, picking their way around fallen logs and over trickling brooks.

Eventually, they came to a small hut in the middle of the woods. It was made of rough stones surrounded by a patchwork fence.

Erasmo turned to Kiki with a twinkle in his eye. "This is where we'll be staying tonight," he said.

Erasmo opened the gate and gestured for Kiki to go inside. She glanced at him before pushing past him into the dimly lit interior.

It was nothing more than a ramshackle cabin with a rickety wooden door and faded paint peeling off its walls. But it was shelter from the cold, which was all that mattered to Kiki right now. The hut was rustic and had sparse furnishings, with a large bed in one corner and a cold fireplace in the other. Kiki raised an eyebrow. One bed?

Kiki stared at him incredulously. "There's only one bed here."

Erasmo shrugged and began lighting candles. "And?" he teased.

"I'm not sharing a bed with you," she spat. "I barely know you."

"Well, I'm not sleeping on the floor," he said flatly. He reached for the edge of his shirt and pulled it over his head before tossing it into a corner.

Kiki felt her face grow hot as she averted her eyes from his chiseled, tattooed chest. Ink swirled across his abdomen and wrapped around his back. He pulled the fur blanket down and settled beneath them.

"Can't you light a fire or something?" Kiki whined, her knees knocking together from the cold.

Erasmo propped his head on his hand as he stared down at her. His hair was a tousled mess, and the muscles in his chest rippled as he moved. "No," he said, his tone flat. "The light will attract the demons."

Kiki scowled, rubbing her hands over her arms to generate some warmth. "Awesome," Kiki deadpanned. "I've always wanted to freeze to death," she hissed, venom dripping off every word.

Erasmo rolled his eyes. "For a warrior, you act like you've never had to survive in the wilderness. Take off your clothes and hang them over that stool over there."

Kiki whipped her head to face him. "What did you just say to me?"

Erasmo looked at her, his face completely serious. "Take them off and sleep next to me. You'll be warmer."

Kiki felt her heart hammering in her chest at the thought. "Absolutely not," she cried.

Erasmo plopped back down. "Your loss," he muttered before rolling over, his back to her.

"Just stay like that," Kiki hissed as she began to roll her leathers off her shoulders. "Don't even think about sneaking a peak either, because I'll now, and I promise it'll be the last thing you ever see."

Erasmo chuckled, his muscled rippling along his back as he did. "At least I'd die a happy man," he said, still laughing.

A strange exhilaration pricked at her skin at his words, but Kiki stomped the feeling down.

She quickly shed her leathers, draping them over the stool as Erasmo had suggested, and quickly climbed beneath the fur blankets piled on the bed.

The warmth immediately enveloped her from Erasmo's nearness, and she could feel his looming presence, the darkness shifting along his skin.

Despite the layers of blankets, Kiki shivered uncontrollably.

"Stop wiggling," Erasmo groaned as he rolled over, his front facing her.

"I can't help it," Kiki hissed.

Erasmo's breaths became heavy as he watched her with those piercing eyes. His voice was hoarse as he said, "Come closer."

Survival won out over Kiki's pride, and she inched forward, feeling the heat radiating from Erasmo's body.

"Closer," he said so softly that Kiki almost didn't hear him. Her heart hammered against her chest as she inched even closer, his gaze never leaving hers.

When their knees touched, Erasmo closed his eyes and breathed in heavily as if he were in pain. "Roll over," he said, his voice husky and strained.

Kiki rolled over and felt his warm arm wrap over her waist like steel bands. He shifted so that her soft curves molded against his body.

A groan slipped from his lips as Kiki exhaled a breath of relief. His body heat enveloped her, chasing the cold away.

"Better?" he asked gruffly, his voice a rasp in the darkness.

Kiki swallowed hard at feeling his hardness along her back, and she bit her bottom lip as heat of a different kind pooled between her thighs. All she managed to say was, "Yes," in a hushed whisper.

"Sleep," he muttered gruffly, his voice thick and husky.

Kiki didn't think she would be able to sleep for a second with Erasmo wrapped around her and the feelings swirling in her stomach at his touch.

That same tug lurched in her chest, and a sense of rightness settled over her nerves. It was enough to allow sleep to descend upon her tired body and claim her.

CHAPTER THIRTY-SIX

ENEMY

ERASMO

E rasmo sat up against the tree, his back pressing against the rough bark of the tree he was still tied to. He shook his head, trying to rid himself of the drowsy fog that still gripped his consciousness. The night sky was starless, and the air tasted of mildew and rot. A thick fog blanketed the ground, pressing in from all around.

The terrified cries of men filled the air, and the menacing howls of something chasing them. The smell of copper wafted under his nose, and his heart leaped into his throat at recognizing the smell of blood.

A shriek pierced the air, and Erasmo looked around frantically for his mate.

Please let her be okay, *he begged.*

He immediately rubbed his wrists against the tree, hoping to fray the rope enough to pull himself free.

A demon with six eyes skittered past him and sank its mantis-like arms into a fleeing bandit. Hot blood sprayed across Erasmo's face as the demon feasted on the corpse.

All around, the camp was littered with lifeless bodies, their blood staining the ground.

The ropes at his wrists frayed when a figure clad in black leather slid into view and cut down a demon with a black machete. The demon burst into a cloud of smoke, and the figure moved to face the next demon rushing forward.

Erasmo's breath caught in his throat as he realized his mate was fighting back against the demons. She was a hurricane as she slashed at the demons, beheading them and carving through their bodies like they were little more than soft cheese.

Seeing her fighting for her life ignited something within him, and the sleeping beast inside reared its head from its slumber. The full force of the shift overwhelmed him, and he felt his claws and fangs lengthen. His muscles rippled and bulged as he shredded the ropes holding him prisoner.

He let out a bestial roar as he sprinted toward the onslaught of demons, murder in his eyes, blinding him to everything except his need to crush the life out of the men who had dared take his mate and the demons who threatened her.

In a frenzy of blood and violence, Erasmo massacred the bandits. His claws raked across throats, and his teeth tore through tendons and bone. All he could see was the fury of battle, and all he could hear were screams. He didn't know if the creatures in front of him were humans or not, but he didn't care, either.

He found Tomás running from the bloodshed and snarled at his retreating form. A demon launched itself at him, and he swiped his claws down, cutting them into ribbons. When he looked back to the last where he'd seen Tomás last, but the bandit was long gone.

A snarl rippled from his jaws.

Tomás, you snake. Your days are numbered. There is nowhere you can go that I won't find you.

He turned his attention back to the demons and fought until all that remained was a bloodstained, churned-up field of death. The beast finally sated, he raced back toward the place where he had last seen his mate.

The sudden silence was unsettling. Erasmo stood on all fours in his bear form, panting heavily. He looked around at the carnage of shredded bodies and limbs, searching for her, when he caught a blur of black.

There she was. Staring at him with her dark gaze. Her machete dripped with black demon blood, and her chest heaved as she regained her breath.

Her scent wafted down toward him, and the beast within sniffed the air, relishing the smell of apples and cinnamon.

Mine, *the beast growled.* Mate, *he added, his voice almost ravenous.*

His mate took a step back, and Erasmo pleaded with her not to run.

Don't do it. Don't run from me. He'll chase you. And I don't know if he'll stop.

His fear came to life when his mate turned tail and ran headlong into the woods.

The beast within roared with glee at the chase, and Erasmo could do nothing to stop from launching after her. He chased her through the tangled trees and dove into the freezing river after her.

She pulled her tired limbs from the water and ran up the riverbank, only to trip over an upturned root.

His body collided with hers and his paws pushed her into the ground. Her dark eyes staring up at him broke him from his trance. The beast within calmed upon seeing her and retreated into the deep recesses of Erasmo's mind. In control once more, he shifted back into his human form.

His mate's body shivered from swimming through the river while he was completely dry, the curse returning him to his last state.

It was her eyes that called him home. Seeing her looking up at him, her mouth slightly open, her perfect full lips wet, and her cheeks blooming with color.

It was her. It had always been her. And now she was here with him.

Erasmo inhaled deeply, the scent of apples and cinnamon filling his nostrils. Kiki's breathing had deepened, and her tense muscles had gone slack when she'd fallen asleep.

Nothing had ever felt so right as holding her in his arms. He finally understood what he'd been missing his whole life. He'd been missing her.

His mate.

He pressed his lips to the crown of her head and released a breath through his nose.

Now that he had found her, he would do anything to protect her. Not that she needed his protection. She was a warrior. He'd seen the proof of it at the bandit's camp. She was fierce and full of fire. A fire that he never wanted to see die out.

The thought of someone hurting her made a growl rumble in his chest, and he had to shove the feeling down.

There was only one person responsible for this night. His twin. Arlando. His own brother.

Seeing his brother's crest, a silver rose dangling from Tomás's waist flashed before his eyes again, and this time, a growl did escape his lips.

Arlando had been behind everything. And Erasmo would see that his brother paid for this treachery.

Because if there was one thing Erasmo was sure of, it was this... no one touched his mate without losing their life.

The beast within rumbled his approval.

I'm coming for you, brother. You'll die by my fangs or my sword, but you will fall at my feet.

The End...for now.

If you'd like to continue on the adventure with Kiki and the Cursed Princes of Ozero, make sure to subscribe to Nicolette's newsletter to stay up-to-date on the latest Ozero Curse book news and get early sneak peeks!

https://nicoletteelzie.com/newsletter/

A CURSE OF TOOTH AND CLAW PLAYLIST

Each chapter title of *A Curse of Tooth and Claw* corresponds to a song. I am deeply inspired by music and have several playlists over 8 hours long for the books that I write. Sometimes I have multiple playlists. One for each character! Most of these songs come from my "Villain" playlist, so that gives you an idea of the vibe I was working with while writing.

I hope you enjoy these songs as much as I do. You can listen to the whole playlist on Spotify by searching for A Curse of Tooth and Claw in the app.

"Welcome to the Show" by VOSTOK
"Trouble" by Valeria Broussard
"I Disagree" by Poppy
"Happy Together" by Filter

"Glitter & Gold" by Barns Courtney

"DARKSIDE" by Neoni

"Playground" by Bea Miller

"Twisted" by MISSIO

"Doom Days" by Bastille

"The Mighty Fall" by Fall Out Boy/Big Sean

"Heathens" by twenty one pilots

"Sarcasm" by Get Scared

"Unsteady" by X Ambassadors

"Unconsolable" by X Ambassadors

"Demons" by Imagine Dragons

"The Violence" by Asking Alexandria

"Reaper" by Silverberg feat. Jordan Frye

"Dead Man Walking" by Chuxx Morris

"The Other Side" by Ruelle

"Irresistible" by Fall Out Boy

"Madness" by Ruelle

"Hurts Like Hell" by Fleurie

"Champion" by Neoni & burnboy

"Fear on Fire" by Ruelle

"When It's All Over" by RAIGN

"Start a War" by Klergy & Valerie Broussard

"Savage" by Bahari

"Alone Together" by Fall Out Boy

"Fake" by The Tech Thieves

"Play with Fire" by Sam Tinnesz

"Toxic" by 2WEI
"Far From Home" by Sam Tinnesz
"Cravin'" by Stileto & Kendyle Paige
"Vendetta" by UNSECRET
"Monster" by Willyecho
"Enemy" by Imagine Dragons, JID & League of Legends

Listen on Spotify

ACKNOWLEDGMENTS

I'll keep this short and sweet because otherwise, I'll cry. I'm the type who cries at Hallmark commercials. Go figure, since there's nothing fluffy about my books.

First, thanks to my husband and two children for supporting this author's journey. *A Curse of Tooth and Claw* isn't the first book I've written, but it's the first dark fantasy romance I've put into the world. Thanks, y'all, for the extra hugs when I started to doubt myself, my writing, and, let's be fair, my entire existence sometimes.

Thanks go to my ride-or-dies Yanelle and Nicole. You read every draft, snippet, and morsel of work I churn out. I can't thank you enough for always providing feedback, the late-night text messages/calls, and being my cheer squad.

Finally, I'd like to thank you, the reader. Thank you for taking a chance on an indie author like myself. It means more than you can imagine that you picked up my book out of the thousands available. You have my heartfelt gratitude. I'll ask one more thing of you. Please leave a review. Every review helps, no matter how short. A few sentences do wonders for getting the word out there.

I hope to see you online or on social media. I'm very active online and love hearing from readers!

ABOUT THE AUTHOR

Nicolette is an international-selling author known for her grimdark poetry book Babydoll. Her stories range from folklore to dark fantasy, but the root of all her novels is fierce love. When she's not writing, you can find her curled up with a good book, spending time with her family, or exploring the National Capital.

If you love Nicolette's work, please consider joining her newsletter and leaving a review.

Nicolette's Newsletter

https://nicoletteelzie.com/newsletter/

Follow Nicolette on TikTok

https://www.tiktok.com/@authornicoletteelzie

Follow Nicolette on Instagram

https://www.instagram.com/nicolette.elzie/

Follow Nicolette on Facebook

https://www.facebook.com/nicoletteelziewrites

Visit Nicolette on the Web

https://nicoletteelzie.com